Takeover

Liz Martinson

With thanks

Liz Martinson

TAKEOVER

Beautiful Jude Drayton, acting CEO for Aurora Technology, turns the ailing computer firm into a resounding success and is shocked when she's sacked by the new owner, who has reservations about the firm.

Richard Blake's memories of the company aren't happy ones, and he's arrived full of contempt for Jude, because he believes she's been his father's mistress, and he intends to close Aurora down.

But everything about Jude, and the company, makes him question his decisions, and his hate gradually turns into admiration and love.

However, someone is working behind the scenes, setting Jude up for a catastrophic fall from grace.

Will her hidden enemy succeed, or will Jude and Richard find a way through the lies to reach their happy ever after?

"I loved it. Romances aren't my usual read, but this was fun and thoroughly enjoyable." (Valerie Dickenson, author)

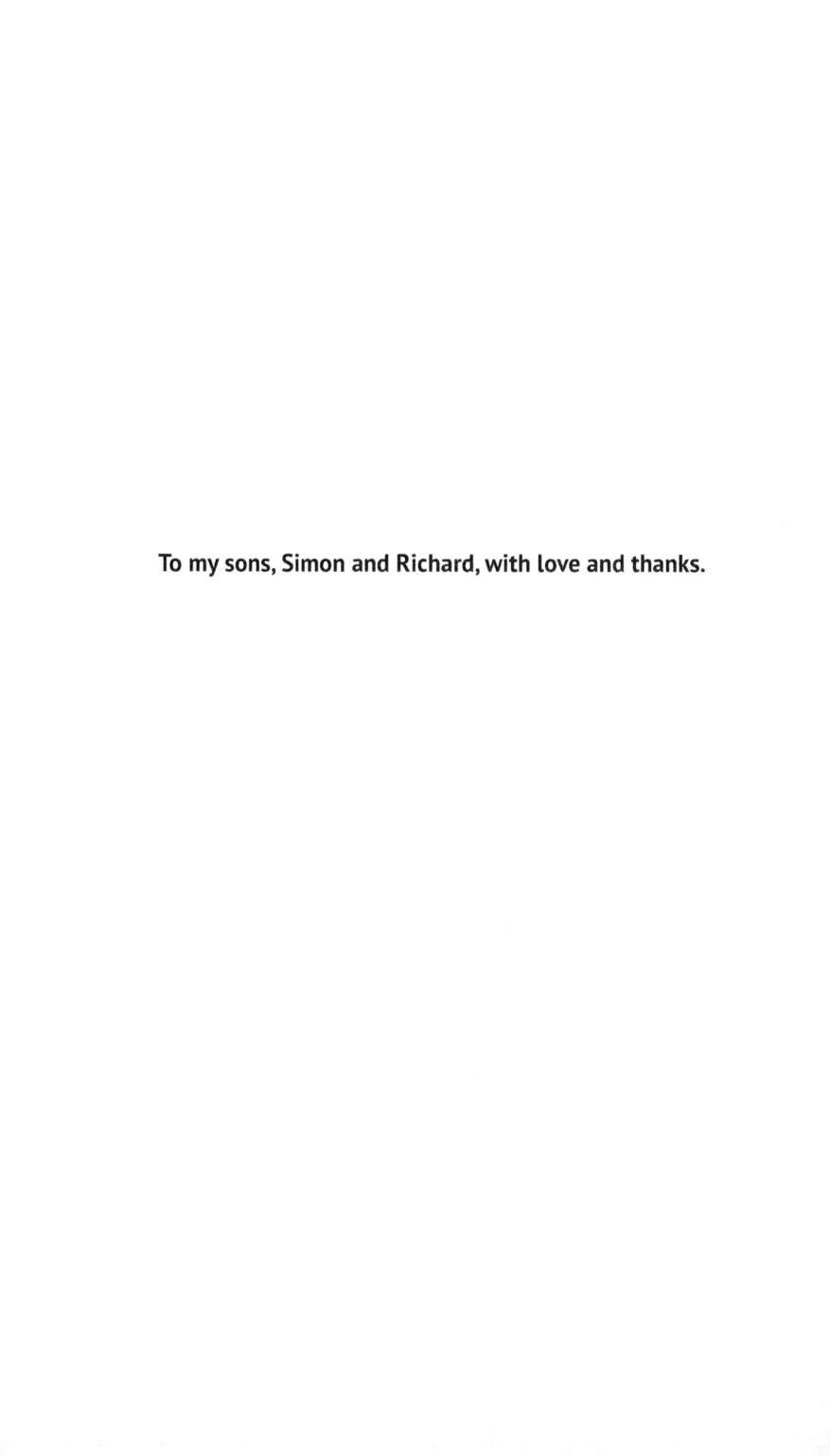

To my sons, Simon and Richard, with love and thanks.

Copyright © 2019 by Liz Martinson

All rights reserved.

No part of this publication may be reproduced, distributed, or transmitted in any form or by any means, including photocopying, recording, or other electronic or mechanical methods, without the prior written permission of the publisher, except as permitted by U.S. copyright law. For permission requests, contact Liz Martinson at lizmartinson3@gmail.com

The story, all names, characters, and incidents portrayed in this production are fictitious. No identification with actual persons (living or deceased), places, buildings, and products is intended or should be inferred.

Book Cover by Dave Slaney

2nd edition 2023

ACKNOWLEDGEMENTS

My very sincere thanks to everyone who has read and commented, suggested edits and were amazingly useful and helpful throughout the writing and subsequent revision of this book.

Any remaining errors are entirely my responsibility.

Katherine E Hunt, Simon Freytag, Rowena Hamilton, Jane Clack, Neelie Wicks, Kelly-Ann Woodford, Rachel Davis, Cynthia Davis, Pam Golden, Anne Riddle, Katy Martinek, Pam Wall and Louise Faulds all deserve a mention for help given in getting the first edition out.

Valerie Dickenson, Christine Hancock and Lynn Berry have also made valuable contributions to the revised edition.

Cover design: Dave Slaney

About the Author

About the author

Liz Martinson is the award-winning author of four novels, all of which have a romantic theme, but which also contain many of life's issues woven through the hero and heroine's story.

Some of Liz's books have received awards – Ullandale has received a Chill With A Book Premier Readers Award, and Counterpoint and Takeover a Chill With A Book Readers Award.

Liz has recently signed a contract for three novellas, to be published in the summer of 2023, by Romance Cafe Publishing, and she is also revising a historical novel which, she admits, is a new venture.

She uses research and her own experiences in travel, the countryside, hill-walking and kayaking to fuel her writing.

In her spare time, Liz enjoys a wide range of activities, which include cycling, reading and taking photographs, as well as cooking and music.

She hopes you enjoy reading her books, and if you feel you can leave a comment and rating, that would be great. Feedback is always valuable.

Her website is
https://lizmartinson.wixsite.com/author
You can contact her at
lizmartinson3@gmail.com.
Find her on Facebook, as well
https://www.facebook.com/lizmartinson3

She's always happy to respond to queries and answer messages.

Contents

1	1
2	17
3	32
4	42
5	51
6	63
7	72
8	86
9	100
10	108
11	113
12	122
13	132
14	140

15	154
16	162
17	166
18	178
19	187
20	191
21	197
22	206
23	211
24	216
25	227
26	232
27	242

1

Saturday was sunny, with small clouds making dappled shadows on the ground. Birdsong filled the air and the branches of the trees were clad with soft, fresh leaves. Around the edges of the town, the hills stood out clear and green. It was a day for picnics, for boating, or for going on long walks, but Jude saw none of it.

In a thoroughly black mood, she turned her car off the road and through the main gates of Aurora Technology. The security man looked up, lifting his hand in acknowledgement when he saw who it was. The carpark was empty, but Jude didn't want the carpark. She wanted reception. She had things to collect from her office.

Well, strike that.

Her lips tightened as her brows descended into a frown.

Her *ex-office,* after that email last Tuesday, which had said Richard Blake, the new owner, was coming back, Jude Drayton was to leave her post as chief executive officer with immediate effect, and the entire future of Aurora Technology was under review. She hadn't had time to clear out her personal stuff since then.

There had been too much to do.

Swinging too fast round the corner of the building, she saw a van parked in a space reserved for visitors. It was close to the double glass doors that led into the reception area of Aurora, and the rear doors were open. Jude caught sight of a pair of legs clad in blue denim retreating into the building. This was Saturday. No-one should be delivering... or removing... anything from Aurora Technology.

Bringing her attention back to her driving, knowing she was going too fast, Jude stamped on her brakes, shut her eyes, and uttered a fervent prayer. With a sharp squeal of rubber on tarmac, the car came to a halt inches away from the front bumper of the van. Even more annoyed by this recent turn of events, she turned off the ignition and opened her door, whipping round to the back of the van with no consideration of potential danger.

She glanced inside. One computer, of their own make, sat on the van floor, together with two pictures she didn't recognise, and three small cardboard boxes, which were no doubt bits and pieces of both hardware and software. She noticed with a shock that the computer was the latest Aurora Mercury model. They were expensive and good, and not yet on sale on the open market. The firm had put a lot into the research and development of them. There was a great deal of excitement in the world of technology as it awaited the launch of this new model at the computer exhibition in just over three months' time. It would be worth a fortune in the wrong hands, so what the *hell*...?

Cold fury seethed through her at this blatant daytime thievery.

At that moment, she heard the swish of the glass doors and turned to confront the man now emerging from the reception area, his arms empty, a questioning look in his golden-brown eyes.

Jude took in his tall frame and effortless movements before peering round him at the carpeted area in front of the main desk. Several boxes lay on the floor. He must have seen her and hurried out with nothing incriminating in his possession.

She raised her eyes and hesitated, her heart giving an unexpected thump, her stomach lurching. What a waste someone like this should have criminal tendencies. Thick brown hair, with a slight wave, fell attractively over his forehead. Brown eyes watched her with wary steadiness. High cheekbones, a classical nose. Square chin and a beautiful mouth, framed with a subtly defining stubble. A good-looking face, made more so by the obvious gleam of intelligence in those golden-brown... or were they hazel... eyes. She could smell a faint aroma of sun-warmed cotton and citrus soap, with just a hint of maleness creeping through.

Jude snapped her mouth shut, aware she was at a disadvantage staring at him like this, but his appearance and the unsettling effect he was having on her rendered her speechless. Damn it. She was the CEO of this company and here he was, caught red-handed stealing stuff from the building on a Saturday morning when no-one was around, so he wasn't someone to be admired. It was his bad luck she'd come in today to clear out her office.

She was confronting a burglar, and had to do *something* about it, even though for a moment she considered just shrugging and walking away. Why should she care if someone looted the entire contents of the Aurora offices? After that instant dismissal by email, she owed the new boss no loyalty at all.

Yeah, well—she wasn't the sort to walk away, even if she was no longer in charge. Gathering her wits, Jude spoke with icy calm. 'What do you think you're doing?' She drew herself up to her full height of five feet eight inches, but still had to look up at him. He had to be at least six feet, maybe a couple of inches more.

She realised the man had, all this time, been observing her just as carefully as she'd been observing him. Now he folded his arms across his chest. The questioning look had faded from his face, and he appeared impatient, brows drawn slightly together, eyes cool, and his mouth a straight and unsmiling line, saying nothing.

'Why is there one of our company's computers in the back of your van? We aren't expecting any to go out on delivery anywhere. We don't even do business on Saturdays. Wherever you took it from, please put it back. Now.' She paused, feeling at a disadvantage in the face of his imperturbable silence. 'How did you get in, anyway? The security man should have stopped you.'

'He did,' the man replied. 'I have to confess I'm not taking anything, but bringing stuff back. You see—'

'Bringing that *back*?' Jude pointed at the Aurora Mercury computer in the van, a frown crossing her face. 'I wasn't aware it had ever *gone* anywhere.' She wouldn't let him know how important it was.

'Ah, well...' he paused, his face shuttered. 'No. I don't think anyone knew, for sure. You have a new CEO coming in and—'

'*Him*,' Jude said, her eyes narrowing as he reminded her why she was here this Saturday, why she'd driven too fast into the carpark and almost crashed into his van.

The man raised his eyebrows and settled a hip on the dusty floor of the van, stretching out his long, jean-clad legs to prop himself into position. 'Boss problems?' he enquired.

Jude observed him, remembering who she was and realising she shouldn't, perhaps, consider discussing the firm's policy decisions with a delivery driver, no matter how personable he appeared.

His eyebrows lifted again, and a smile lit his face. 'Cat got your tongue?' he asked. 'Or are you too scared to criticise? Are the employees gagged at this super corporation? Siberian salt mines for those who complain at Aurora?'

A reluctant smile trembled at the corners of her mouth, but she protested. 'It's not like that.'

'So why the "him" in such feeling tones? Why the sudden silence? It doesn't sound as if you and your boss get on any too well.'

'I don't know how we get on,' she admitted, frowning. 'I've never met him.'

The driver of the van let out a peal of mocking laughter, his head falling back to expose the strong, brown column of his throat.

Jude shivered as she watched him. Normally, she was far too busy to consider the personable junior executives around her, many of whom would have been more than willing to take the boss out to dinner. Far too busy, and not very interested. Ever since Julian... Jude cut her thoughts off. Since Julian, she reminded herself, she'd made her job her life, and she intended to keep it that way.

But this one, he was getting under her skin. She felt attracted to him. He was a looker, no doubt about that, and gave the impression he might have a lively personality, too. What on earth was he doing as a delivery man?

'Penny for them?' He reached out a strong, long-fingered hand and touched her on the arm.

She saw interest in his eyes and realised he, too, was feeling attracted. There was something between them... a spark of interest on both sides.

'You're miles away. I said, a penny for them? Your thoughts?'

She shivered at his touch, confused by the sudden upsurge of feelings she'd long ago subdued. 'Mmm? Oh, sorry. It's a long story, Mr...'

He was silent for a few moments, rubbing his hand over his well-shaped mouth and chin. 'Adam will do,' he said at last. 'Why don't you tell me about it?'

His sympathy and concern seemed genuine. For a moment Jude was tempted to drop her hard, business-like exterior, her air of competence, and throw herself into his arms, bawling like a child for the loss of all her dreams and her hard-won achievements. She longed for the comfort of a strong embrace, and this man appeared very able to provide it. He also seemed a willing listener.

Jude continued to gaze at him, appreciating his lean length propped on the edge of the van floor, his faded denim jeans, and the casual shirt with rolled back sleeves displaying tanned forearms scattered with golden hairs. A heavy gold wristwatch emphasised his tan, and she noticed in passing he wore no ring. Thirty-four? Thirty-five?

'Will I do?' he asked softly.

'I'm sorry,' Jude said, trying to pull herself together, ignoring his last, far too personal, question. 'And thank you for your offer, but no, I can't discuss it with you. It wouldn't be ethical. I'm here because I've got work to do. I haven't time for the luxury of a chat.'

'Work? On a Saturday? A ferocious boss indeed if he can make you work on a Saturday when you haven't even met him.' He was laughing at her again, his face transformed from its earlier severity, lines radiating out from the corner of his eyes, an attractive crease in one cheek.

'You don't understand,' she began, then halted. What was the use? What was the point of explaining anything? It would only expose her raw hurt to his eyes and although he would no doubt drive off in a few moments and she would never see him again, Jude would forever consider it a weakness if she gave way and poured out her troubles, however attractive she found him. She had to face it on her own. Her world had ended. She was here today to put the nails in her own coffin and she found herself close to tears now it was about to happen. Aware of Adam's scrutiny, she turned away, blinking to hold back those tears.

'Hey,' he said, his voice turning gentle. There was the sound of movement as he stood and came round to face her. 'I'm sorry. I didn't mean to upset you. I'm not in the habit of upsetting people.' Adam smiled, his finger touching her gently under her chin so she had to raise her head and look at him.

His brown eyes fixed on her face and she found her troubles receding under the intensity of his interested gaze and was aware, again, of her reaction to him. Strange things were happening inside. A quick frown crossed her face. She really could do without lusting after the delivery man this morning. There were enough complications in her life without ending up in another damned entanglement. Jerking her head sideways, Jude glowered down at the gravelled drive.

'Hey,' Adam repeated, his hand now gentle on her shoulder, refusing to be brushed off. 'Why don't you do what you've come for, and I'll finish this…' he indicated the things still inside his van with a quick inclination of his head, 'then how about we go for a drink? I think you need one.'

Wiping the back of her hand across her eyes, Jude sniffed. Damn the man. Why did he have to be so kind?

'I need help anyway,' Adam continued, his voice still beguiling. 'I don't know which is the boss-man's office. Perhaps you could show me?'

'Oh, yes,' Jude said, her lips tightening. 'I can show you all right.'

'There you go again,' he said, leaning into the body of the van and pulling the Aurora Mercury towards him. 'There's a problem. Every time I mention the boss-man, you curl up like a sour lemon. Why are you here anyway?'

'I told you,' Jude held open the glass doors for him as he edged through into the cool, lofty reception area, the computer cradled in his arms. 'I have some work to do.'

'And I said, on a Saturday? Is the firm that inefficient it needs its personal assistants to catch up at the weekend?' His tone was mocking again, his eyes watchful.

Jude bit her lip and turned away from his scrutiny. 'I'll show you up to the CEO's office,' she said, not caring to correct his assumption she was a PA. 'We may as well take the lift. If we prop open the doors, you'll be able to load all this stuff in and take it up in one go.'

'Good thinking. I'll just clear the rest of it from the van.'

Despite her misery, Jude, holding open the glass doors, continued to enjoy watching his effortless movements as he emptied the van, before helping him put the computer and boxes in the lift.

In silence, she punched the button for the third floor and the lift swept upwards in a smooth surge.

'Interesting building,' Adam commented.

'It's an old mill. Bought by the previous owner to assemble televisions before being converted to make computers.' Jude replied.

Arriving, Adam placed a box against the open doors of the lift again and picked up the Mercury computer. 'Lead on,' he suggested to Jude.

She collected the two pictures and walked down a blue-carpeted corridor to the office she'd been told to leave empty by this coming Monday morning. There wasn't much to do, but she would make sure she removed every sign of her tenancy from the CEO's room. She had some personal possessions to clear out of the desk drawers and her laptop to pack away. A couple of shelves needed checking in case she had forgotten anything else belonging to her and not Aurora Technology. Mr Richard Blake would have no chance to suggest she was trying to avoid vacating the room in time for his arrival.

'I'll let you carry the rest of the stuff in,' she said in a flat voice. 'I've got things to do, to clear the room in time for Mr Blake's arrival on Monday. He—'

'You!' exclaimed Adam. 'Why you? I understood Miss Drayton was the acting CEO. Why can't she clear her own possessions out? Why does she need her PA to do it?' He sounded contemptuous as he strode across the outer room and into her old office, placing the computer gently on the desk before moving to glance out of the windows.

'What do you know about all this?' she asked, her voice sounding puzzled.

There was a slight pause. 'I was to find Miss Drayton's office. I understand it's a different room from the one old Mr Blake used.' Adam turned to face her, his voice devoid of all expression. 'I assume you've brought me to the right room?'

Jude nodded. Now was as good a moment as any to explain she was, in fact, Miss Drayton and not the PA he'd twice assumed she was, but then she hesitated. What did it matter to him that Richard Blake, apparently his boss, had thrown her out of her job?

'If this is Drayton's room, then I ask again, why has she sent a PA in on a Saturday to clear it out? Why didn't she sort it out herself yesterday?'

Surprise flitted over Jude's face as she heard the venom in his voice. Why did *he* feel such animosity towards her, when he didn't know her, wasn't connected to her, and would probably never meet her in any kind of professional capacity? There was a puzzle here.

'I don't see it's any of your business,' Jude replied through stiff lips, 'but if you must persist with your questions, Mr Blake allowed little time. His email came through on Tuesday morning. The directors had to be informed about what was happening. Mr Blake had demanded the entire factory should also be told about his imminent arrival, so...

Drayton, as you call her...' her tone dripped acid, 'had to let everyone know what was going on. She also had to cancel meetings scheduled for the next couple of weeks with customers, which needed doing personally. She didn't want to cause any offence or lose any orders which would be detrimental to the firm. Documents needed to be checked and filed online, and the whole lot brought up to date so she could hand everything over in good order. Overall, it's hardly surprising personal things had to wait, don't you think?'

And let's not forget Ian Grey, her second-in-command. Ian Grey, watching every move, sitting through both meetings, rubbing his hands together with a small smile of satisfaction every time she made a phone call to explain what was happening. Oh, no, let's not forget him and the extra pleasure he would've received, watching her remove her bits and pieces from this office. *That*, if the truth was known, was the main reason she was here this morning.

Adam had leaned back against the wall by the tall windows as she was talking, watching her through narrowed eyes, arms folded and long legs crossed at the ankle. 'Well, well, well. Loyalty, I see. That's nice to know. A spitting kitten defending her mistress. Mmm. Don't let me stop you, then. You finish your chores, I'll finish mine, then we'll go out for that drink, and you can tell me more about what goes on here. I can at least understand now why the boss-man annoys you so much. He's kicked out your employer.' He straightened and pushed away from the wall. 'Well, I'm not surprised. From what I've heard, Drayton is an opportunist who slid in through the back door and deserves everything that's coming.' His voice was icy and his lip curled in disdain as he strode from the room, leaving Jude gasping with shock at the strength of his dislike. Based, she supposed, solely on that of his boss, Richard Blake.

Ian had told her a bit about Richard Blake. When he'd been a young man working in the factory, his father had repeatedly humiliated him, although no-one could ever understand the motives of the senior Mr Blake. Some said he'd decided Richard wasn't his son, but he'd been the one known for a string of affairs, not his wife. That said, maybe the poor lady had found comfort elsewhere. Whatever the reason, old Mr Blake had treated Richard badly, refused to consider any of the reforms he'd suggested and eventually, Richard had enough and left for America, where he started the now international firm, Blake Laptops.

That was, what, six years ago? Yet nothing explained Richard Blake's apparent animosity to herself, which must be deep-rooted indeed, judging by her unceremonious eviction from her job. Further evidence of his dislike was coming from this Adam, who must work for him in some sort of capacity—maybe as his PA?

She shook her head and shrugged, before turning to her desk and pulling open the drawer.

As Adam came and went, placing the bits and pieces from the van around the room, she riffled through the contents, removing papers and her tablet. The other drawers held a few more papers belonging to her. It took her about twenty minutes to clear them, check the shelves for books, and pack up her laptop.

Moving over to the tall windows, she stared down at the formal gardens and the sweep of gravel, the view blurring as her eyes filled with tears. Damn this Adam man, with his prying questions and his parroted dislike of her, garnered from his boss. And damn the fact he was attractive, and she acknowledged some sort of spark between them.

She'd wanted to come here to lick her wounds in private and say goodbye to what had been her first major post. Contrary to what

Richard Blake and his odd-job man thought about her slipping in via the back door—and what on earth did he mean by that, anyway?—all the online technical journals had carried the job advert and she'd got the job fair and square. Jude had been working for TechDrive, a big multinational computer firm, and had held a top position on the management team there. She'd been going round with Julian Langley, who worked in the same department. She'd been in *love* with Julian Langley, more fool her.

Because Julian had used her. He'd talked to her at length about her plans for the department, then taken them over her head to their boss. As a result, he'd got the promotion she'd been hoping for. It wouldn't have mattered to her in the slightest if he'd got it on merit, but when she found *her* ideas and *her* plans being implemented, she realised how he'd done it. She'd been taken for a ride and it hurt. It hurt badly.

Jude could no longer trust him, and loving him was an impossibility. Nor did she want to work at TechDrive any longer. He'd undermined her professional skills. She wanted to move, to start afresh and prove herself. She wanted to try her ideas out, make her own decisions, and take responsibility for the consequences.

Taking charge of a small computer company on the verge of sinking without trace had proved just the challenge she needed. She'd fought old Mr Blake every inch of the way to introduce the changes which had taken the company from the bottom to the top. She'd succeeded in her reforms, where Richard Blake had failed, for two reasons. Mr Blake was too ill to fight anymore, and the directors had seen which way the company was going. To save their jobs, they took the risks and defied Blake senior, which they hadn't wanted to do when young Richard Blake had challenged the system, three years before her arrival.

For the second time, Jude rubbed the back of her hand over her eyes. Now she would pay the price. Ian was no doubt right. He'd suggested Richard Blake had asked her to leave her job because she'd done what he'd wanted to do. Seemed very petty-minded to her. She'd modernised and saved the factory, so he ought to be pleased. But... it also seemed, if Adam was to be believed, Richard Blake was certain the only way she could have done it was by inveigling herself with his father and gaining the old man's trust.

Huh. If only he knew.

The door behind her opened.

'All finished,' Adam said. 'How about you?'

Jude straightened, keeping her back turned. 'Yes,' she admitted, her voice subdued. She gathered herself together and turned to the desk, picking up her laptop, tablet and document case full of papers, juggling some books, which she tried to tuck under her arm. A wave of regret and sadness swept through her as she took a final look around the room from which she'd dragged Aurora into the twenty-first century, an achievement she was proud of, whatever Adam was saying. Richard Blake had got it wrong. Got her wrong. But it didn't look as if she'd be able to explain herself, and on Monday, she fully expected to be given a severance package.

'Here, let me take those.'

Before she could protest, he'd taken the books from her and now held open the door. Back downstairs, Adam led the way out into the sunshine. The smell of warm grass rose to meet them as they went outside, and somewhere a blackbird was singing. Jude glanced around, wondering where her next job would be. She'd loved it here.

'Car?'

'Oh... round the front of your van.' Jude led the way to the hatchback and put her things on the car roof, fishing in her pocket for the key. Opening the back, she piled her things into the boot. Adam brushed against her to add the books to the heap. She straightened, still feeling dazed, as he pulled the hatch down.

'I've changed my mind about the drink.' Adam was gazing over her head to the distant hills, sunlit and inviting in the warm, early summer air.

So had Jude.

Attractive he might be, but what he'd said upstairs had upset her, even though she realised he was only basing his opinions on those of Richard Blake. Okay, so his loyalty was to his boss and to be fair, he didn't realise who she was, but still... surely, he should have the strength of character to wait, and make his own judgements?

'That's okay,' Jude moved round to the driver's door, her voice flat.

Adam followed. 'Hey. Hang on.'

Her skin tingled as he touched her arm, and her stomach somersaulted. Damn it! Why, today of all days, did she have to meet someone she fancied? Especially as Adam was connected to Richard Blake.

'I said I'd changed my mind about the drink, but you didn't give me much chance to finish. It's too pleasant a day to be indoors. Could you leave your car here? There's somewhere I'd like to go... and I'd like you to come with me. I'd like to show you one of my favourite places.' He smiled down at her, and she could see a question in his eyes.

'Oh. I see. Thanks. Thank you, but no, if you don't mind. I'd rather not.'

'Oh, but that would be a shame.' Adam stepped closer. 'I think it's somewhere which might do you some good. You seem so down. I suppose I can't offer any references, so you'd be taking a risk, but it's a public place and there's bound to be others around.' His voice was soft and persuasive. 'I like you, and I like your loyalty to your boss, even if it's misplaced. No, wait.' He raised his hand and laid his finger in a fleeting, featherlight touch on her lips, as they opened to give a heated reply to his barbed comment. 'Please? I honestly think—well, I hope—you'll like this place, and it's the perfect day for it. And maybe you can tell me a bit about the company, too.'

The last comment annoyed her and rather took the pleasantness from his pleading. 'Why do you want information?'

'Useful for Mr Blake, don't you think?'

'And you expect me to play spy in the camp? Don't make me laugh.'

This was easier. Jude could cope better with arguments than attraction.

'If Ms Drayton's lost her job, perhaps it means yours has gone as well? I could put in a good word for you... if you help me?'

Jude stared, lip curling as she raised an eyebrow, replying through gritted teeth. 'You have an odd idea of loyalty if you think I'll give you the low-down on anyone here, or tell you what's going on. Let Mr Blake find out for himself because he won't find out from me.'

She turned once more to the car door. Despite his soft cajoling and saying he liked her, he was quite open about wanting information, and was prepared to use her to get it. Julian had duped her in the same way, and she wouldn't fall for it twice.

'Please—wait. I'm sorry. Really sorry. Don't go.' He went silent for a moment, chewing on his bottom lip. 'Look, forget what I said about telling me stuff. But still come with me? Please?'

Adam appeared penitent. She turned to face him, curious. He stared back, his eyes clear and direct, and she thought she detected a hint of pleading in their depths.

'Please?' he repeated, holding out his hands to her. 'I want to go myself and it'll be more fun with someone.'

Oh, why not? She liked him, despite some things he'd been saying, and what else was there to do but go back home and sit contemplating her bleak future? Why not go with him and try to forget, if only for a few hours?

'You won't try to get information out of me?' She looked at him with narrowed eyes.

'No trying to get information out of you,' he answered, grinning and laying his hand across his chest. 'Cross my heart and hope to die. Will that do?'

She hesitated for another moment before pocketing her car key. 'Okay, then. I'll come.'

She followed him back to the van.

'Hey,' he said, opening the passenger door for her. 'I don't know your name. Tell me your name?'

She remembered what he'd said when she had wanted to know who he was. 'Anna,' she said now. 'Anna will do.' She didn't know if he knew Miss Drayton's first name, but why risk spoiling this now by saying Jude? A day of escape lay ahead. Her middle name was fine.

2

Richard Adam Blake slammed the back doors of the van and climbed into the driver's seat. He sat for a moment looking at Anna, then shook his head, a slight smile on his lips, and turned the key in the ignition. 'Okay, let's go,' he said.

Not what he'd expected of the morning, meeting the lovely Anna. There were hidden depths to her, and he hoped, over time, to discover more about her. Ever since she'd shot round the side of his van, fury on her face, icy command in her voice, he'd been impressed. And not just with her courage, either, but also with her determined defence of her boss. She was easy on the eyes... very easy. That gorgeous tangle of tawny blonde hair, her full mouth and steady dark-grey gaze all attracted him.

Alongside everyone else in his company, Richard had spent the last six years working flat-out in America to ensure that Blake Laptops would be a success. Dating had taken very much second place and anyway, after the example his father had set, he was wary.

Wary of relationships, of whether he even had it in him to be faithful, as his father had most definitely not, and insecure, as well, for he'd had no role model while growing up. Just his father's contempt for his mother, suspicion of Richard, and a string of publicly flaunted mistresses.

He knew what caused his father's suspicion and there was a deep yearning inside him for it to be true—that he wasn't his father's son. The relief to know he wasn't related to such an obnoxious man would be great, and recently, he'd considered getting a DNA test done, keeping his father's toothbrush and hairbrush back when the house was recently gutted and re-decorated. It couldn't be a worse position than he was in now, for to all intents and purposes he was a Blake. If he found out he wasn't, well, the will had specifically named him as the heir to Aurora and his own relief would be considerable.

He drove carefully out of the carpark and turned towards the market town on the edge of the Yorkshire Dales. It would be busy in town. It always was on a Saturday, with the tourists wandering across the road, the coaches jostling for spaces, the market filling the cobbles. Looking at it as he edged slowly up the road, he'd never worked out whether he loved it or hated it, and still had the same problem.

He glanced at his silent companion, whose head was turned slightly to her left as she gazed out of the side window. Cynically, Richard was more than prepared for this awareness of Anna to fall flat. It was a stupid risk anyway, taking an interest in Ms Drayton's PA, of all people. If Anna knew who he was, she'd tilt that rather elegant nose of hers towards the sky and rapidly walk off.

Ms Drayton... his mind drifted. His father was someone who'd thought a woman's place was on his bed with her legs parted, so Richard had found it astounding he would take someone capable of running a business to his bed, never mind letting her become the CEO. It was the major stumbling block Richard had with the reports he'd been receiving from the board, by snail-mail, of all things. Reports which had started about nine months before his father's death. So far, he'd received five in total.

But... snail-mail, coming from a top-notch European computer company? He gave an inward snort of disbelief.

No recognisable name or signature, either—another thing which had caused him to hesitate. But, as far as he recalled from before he'd left, the headed paper was right, and the scrawl at the end typical of someone running through a pile of documents at the day's end and signing them off. Except... no-one did that any more, either.

However, despite his disquiet, he'd read them. They were general in content, giving updates of decisions and share prices, all of which were good, so someone was looking after his assets. It was only when they moved on to mentioning Ms Drayton the tome changed slightly. Each report suggested she'd no abilities at all. She'd been put in charge as a front, for the money, and was spying for old Mr Blake. It was the second-in-command who'd been the major force behind the company's success.

He'd sat in the dusk of his San Francisco house, brooding, wondering what was going on. Much made sense—the first parts of each one especially—but somehow, he felt uneasy because of the oddities. While his father was alive, he'd been unable to do anything, but as soon as the company was officially in his hands, he'd sent an email removing Ms Drayton from her post.

Now he was actually here, on the brink of deciding the fate of Aurora Computers and finding out the truth about Ms Drayton. Monday would soon be upon him, and on Monday, he might sort this mess out.

Ah, hell! Forget work, damn it. Today was for unexpected enjoyment. Something had kindled here, and for now he wanted to go with it. He thought she was interested too, although he sensed she was fighting it.

He concentrated on his driving, his eyes on the snarl of traffic and people ahead, all the time aware of Anna sitting next to him, silent and composed, her face now looking straight ahead as they navigated the tourist-filled high street.

They stopped in the supermarket's carpark which stood at the opposite side of town from the mill.

'Shan't be long. We'll need a picnic of sorts.' Richard smiled and jogged towards the entrance, leaving her in the van, wondering if she'd still be there when he came back.

Once inside, he grabbed some ready-made sandwiches, some fruit and chocolate, and a couple of bottles of water. Whizzing through the self-service checkout, he was soon back with a couple of carrier bags, which he deposited on the floor behind his seat, letting out a quiet breath of relief as he saw Anna still there.

'That should do us,' he said, smiling at her again, disappointed when she didn't return it, but simply nodded her head. She looked tired, he thought. Tired and dispirited. Had he even seen her smile yet?

Richard climbed into the driver's seat again. He wanted to touch her arm. It looked warm. Silky. Soft. He imagined his fingers lying on her soft skin and enjoyed the light perfume of lavender seeping into the van interior, maybe coming from her hair.

Sighing, he shook his head. Enough. He'd only just met her, for goodness sake. Not a time for fantasies, especially in such a precarious situation.

'Okay? Sit back and relax, enjoy the scenery. It'll take us about thirty to forty minutes to get there.' He swung the van out into the traffic, feeling an unfamiliar lightness and excitement.

After a few miles, Richard risked another quick sideways glance, and saw Anna still gazing out of the window at the rising hills, the stone walls, the lambs who ran and leapt on stiff legs, rejoicing in the sun and the green grass. Now he sensed she was genuinely curious and enjoying what she saw. He went back to concentrating on driving along the narrow roads and negotiating the blind bends.

'Lovely area, isn't it?' he remarked neutrally.

After a few beats, she responded. 'Yes. I don't think I've ever been up here. I don't get out as much as I'd like, but what I've seen of the country round here is very beautiful.'

Changing gear to climb a steep road which led to the higher, rougher countryside above the sheep fields, Richard smiled again. He was smiling a lot today. 'I'm glad you came. I've always loved this area, especially where we're going. It's not a secret though. Enough people find their way to it and I wouldn't advise ever going on a bank holiday.'

'I'm curious now,' Jude admitted. 'How far?'

'Oh, not far by road. We're just about there. But then, you'll have to walk. Do you enjoy walking?'

'Yes, I do.'

'My sort of girl.'

At last, Richard pulled off the road onto a smooth grass verge. The engine died. He opened his door, and the only sound to be heard was the sigh of the wind and the faint song of larks high in the sky as, with throats quivering, they marked out their territory.

'This is where we walk,' he said, jumping out of the van and reaching behind his seat to retrieve the carrier bags. 'There's an easier route, but parking's difficult and if there's going to be people around, that's the way they'll go. Mmm, pity I don't have a rucksack, but hey, spontaneous plans have to make do with whatever's available.'

The warm air smelled of grass and secret flowers hidden in the rough pasture. It was just about perfect, as far as he was concerned. Watching her as she looked round, he saw her shoulders relax and a smile spread over her face. That was better—she looked lovely when she smiled and he was glad something he'd done had caused it. Up until now, it seemed her day hadn't been going at all well.

'We head off over there,' Richard said, pointing with a raised arm across the road to the slope rising above them.

There was a path of smooth grass leading through the heather. Walking in single file, they climbed steadily. Richard knew he was setting a fair pace, but Anna seemed able to keep up. Every now and again, he stopped to look at the view and let her catch her breath. They'd reached the stage where a few exchanged comments about the weather and what they could see were acceptable. Otherwise Richard said little, and he thought Anna didn't mind being left in peace either, as she seemed happy to absorb the peacefulness of their surroundings.

The terrain changed. Heather gave way to the pale green turf. The millstone rocks gave way to smooth, grey limestone and in front of them lay a shadowed, narrow gorge, flanked by low white cliffs that stretched off on each side into the far distance. Entering the gorge, they climbed, stepping from boulder to boulder, scrambling up the occasional shelf of rock too high for a step. Neither had breath left to talk now. The gorge was chilly after the warmth of the sun, but the coolness was welcome to counteract the heat of their exertion. A last spurt, a climb over a fallen tree, and they emerged onto a plateau of short, sheep-cropped turf. The path continued, level now, and for a while, followed a dry stream bed. Even Richard was glad of the chance to catch his breath on the level section.

'There. Look.' He stopped and gestured in front of them. The stream bed was no longer empty, but ran with clear water, spilling and tumbling over stones and pebbles.

He saw the smile of delight which crossed Jude's face, her previous unhappiness apparently still banished.

'Why's there a stream here, but not one further down?'

'This is limestone,' Richard explained. 'Look, see where it seems to just disappear among the stones? It's called a sink. It'll be dropping into a cave or passage somewhere below us.'

'Where does it come out?'

'Over there somewhere,' Richard pointed off to their left, back towards the gorge. 'It resurges at the base of the limestone.'

'Fascinating.'

'It is, isn't it? Have you ever been down a cave? There are plenty in this area.'

'I'm aware. But no, it's not my scene. I don't enjoy being in confined spaces. I went down one of the show caves and wasn't at all happy when we had to bend almost double to go through a passage with a low ceiling. It was okay in the main chamber at the end, and I didn't even mind when they turned off the lights, but I was panicky in the low bits.'

He grinned. 'I've done a lot of caving,' he admitted. 'I could take you down somewhere. Are you sure you wouldn't like to try?'

'*No.*' Jude spoke with feeling. 'I much prefer being up here, outside with the sky above my head. No, thank you. I'll pass.'

Richard shrugged, one side of his mouth lifting in amused acknowledgement, and set off once more along the path. 'We don't stop here,' he said over his shoulder. 'It's a bit further yet. Are you okay?'

'Fine, thanks.'

They continued along the side of the stream, following its curve round the base of a hill. Richard, in front, stopped, stepping to one side to give Jude an unimpeded view ahead.

A white curtain of water swept down in front of them, to fall into a deep pool before it made its escape over a lip of boulders which formed a natural dam at the base of the fall. Where the water hit the pool, the bubbles frothed and dipped, silver in the deep, clear water. Soft moss coated the rocks, and the sun slanted over everything, creating an occasional rainbow as it caught the spray in its beams. A few orchids grew on the far side of the pool, their deep pink a sharp contrast to the greens, peppermint and whites of grass and water. Flat, dry rocks and soft turf bordered the waterfall and pool.

'Ohhh,' Jude breathed, her delight obvious. She moved forwards and sank to her knees on the grass next to the pool, staring at the heavy fall of water, mesmerised by the movement and the noise.

Richard sat down beside her, dropping the carrier bags before lying back on the grass, one arm flung over his eyes to keep the sun off his face, leaving Jude to gaze at the waterfall.

'Like it?' His voice was lazy.

'It's...' she hesitated. 'I don't think I can find the words to describe what it means to me. I love water and here... this... it's as near perfection as I think it's possible to get on this planet.'

'Uh-huh. I'm glad.' He'd been sure she'd like this place and was pleased to be right. It was a place he'd loved for years, and it seemed important that someone he felt an attraction to would also love the tranquillity and beauty of it, even if this never developed.

A few more moments of companionable silence passed between them. Through the crook of his arm he saw Jude turn her head, looking down at him as he sprawled on the grass.

'What made you come here today?' Her face was curious.

He pulled his arm further to one side and squinted up at her with one eye. 'It's one of my favourite places. I haven't been for a long time, and I'd planned to come soon. It just seemed a better idea than sitting in a stuffy pub. We can do that another time, when it's raining. I thought you might like it... or should I say, I *hoped* you might like it?'

'Thanks,' Jude said. 'The walk, this...' she gestured at their surroundings, 'both have helped. Sorry if I came across as uptight earlier. I feel better now.' She paused. 'But... how did you know about it? Here, I mean?'

He evaded answering her question. 'Ready for some food?

'Yes.' Her voice sounded surprised. 'Yes, I believe I am.'

'Why the surprise?'

'Oh,' she responded, waving her hand in dismissal of his question. 'Just not had much of an appetite recently. Too much turmoil at work.'

Richard sat up and pulled the carriers towards him and laid the contents out on the flattened bags. Jude selected a chicken and salad sandwich, and after carefully disentangling it from the packaging, took a healthy bite, chewing with satisfaction.

'You must come from round here,' Jude persisted, putting her sandwich down. She unscrewed the cap of a bottle and drank.

Richard watched her swallow, and it made him aware of his body as he responded to the movement of her tipped back head and throat. What would it be like to scatter kisses down her neck? Butterfly kisses, then further... his eyes drifted to the swell of her breasts before he determinedly brought his eyes back to her face.

Too soon.

What had she just said? Oh, damn, another question about where he came from.

'Mmm.' He wished she would drop this line of questioning. He didn't want to share his personal life with her yet. He wanted to enjoy the day and leave everything else for the future.

'Did you go away when Richard Blake left home, then? I mean, if you work for him...?' Jude sounded awkward.

'We agreed,' he looked at her, traces of a smile on his face, his voice gentle, 'not to talk about Aurora?'

'Oh. I... I said *I* wouldn't talk about anyone-'

'And neither will I,' Richard interrupted. 'Richard Blake is off-limits just as Ms Drayton and Aurora Technology are off-limits, okay?'

Jude nodded with reluctance. 'But... what about you? Can I ask about you?'

'Up to a point,' he conceded warily. 'Yes, I used to live near here and yes, I went off with Richard when he left. Does that answer your question?'

'It's six years since you went away, then?'

'Yes.' His terse responses finally silenced Jude. Richard was sorry, but he'd no intention of being more forthcoming with information about himself, despite seeing she was dying to ask him more questions. Maybe what work he did for Richard Blake. She must realise by now he was more than a delivery driver.

Castigating himself for the impulse which had led to his invitation, Richard realised it was more than likely they would meet up, and meet up soon, in an official capacity. And then what? Especially as she worked for Jude Drayton. Things wouldn't be easy. This hadn't been one of his most sensible moves. And now she was looking miserable again.

Reaching out, he touched her hand, and she raised her eyes. 'I've lost you again.'

'Yes... I mean... oh, damn.' She jumped to her feet, and he saw the sudden sheen of tears in her eyes before she turned and walked further toward the pool. She wrapped her arms round her body as she stood motionless, staring into the bubbling depths of the water.

'Hey, hey.' Richard moved up behind her, speaking softly. He placed his hand on her shoulder. 'Come on. Cheer up, okay? That was the point of coming here, to cheer you up.' Turning her round to face him, he looked at her in concern. 'You sure have troubles, lady.' His thumb came up to catch and wipe away a solitary tear that escaped from her brimming eyes, even has his mind was shouting at him to back off.

'I'm sorry.' Jude rubbed her eyes with her fingers and sniffed. 'Just a potential problem... nothing, really.'

'Nothing? Huh. Look, if it would help, tell me, okay?'

'Can't. We have a ban, remember?'

Richard pulled her down to sit next to him on a smooth boulder close to the waterfall. Cool spray fell, a few drops misting their hair. He kept hold of her hand after they sat.

'Yeah, a ban,' he said, his breath escaping in a sigh. 'Which tells me yet again your troubles relate to work. Look, I've said, don't worry. I can probably help you.'

'Only if I spilled the dirt.' Her voice was sharp.

'Oh, that.' Shrugging, Richard dismissed his former suggestion. 'I shouldn't have said that and I'm sorry. I'll help you, whatever.' Gazing at her, he saw doubt on her face. 'But look, let's change the subject if you don't want to talk about it. I don't like you being miserable. You wanted to know something about me. Well, I'd like to know something about you, too. Where are you from? Somewhere round here?'

Although if she had been, surely he would have bumped into her before leaving?

There was a brief pause as he watched a variety of expressions flit over her mobile face.

'I grew up in the Midlands, south of Birmingham. I only came up here when I... I got my new job.'

'What made you change jobs? What were you doing before you came up here?'

'I was working in...' How much would Richard know about Miss Drayton's résumé? Better be cautious. 'It was a computer firm, but bigger than Aurora.'

Richard looked surprised. 'What made you leave them and come to a small firm up north?'

'Because I... needed a move.'

'Why? Surely the openings in a bigger firm are better? And the money would be better, too.'

'Mmm.' Jude wished he'd drop the subject.

'It doesn't seem a good career move to me,' he persisted.

'Look, I don't want to talk about it.'

He looked at her and capitulated. 'Okay.'

They sat in silence once more. It seemed all attempts at a conversation reached a dead-end. Slipping his arm round her shoulders, he pulled her closer, aware she was trying to resist.

'Relax, okay? Relax, Anna,' Richard murmured, releasing the pressure a bit. He didn't want to push anything. After a few moments she relaxed and leaned against his side. It was a very pleasant sensation.

'Anna... is that short for Annabel?'

'Just Anna.'

'Anna...' his voice softened as he turned her so she was half-facing him.

'No.'

Her protest was half-hearted, and Richard wasn't taking much notice of her. His eyes wandered over her face, lingering on her lips, as his hands slid up to her shoulders before cupping her jaw and drawing her face towards his.

'No.'

'Really, no?' he murmured softly, drawing back. 'I'd very much like to kiss you.'

He saw her eyes darken and couldn't fail to notice the sudden response of her nipples as her breathing quickened and she ran her tongue over her lower lip. This was a woman who wanted his kiss but was also reluctant. He wouldn't force things, though. That wasn't his style.

'Anna?' he asked again. 'Really, no?'

This time, Richard saw her eyes close as she swayed towards him, and he allowed his lips to touch hers, feather light and tender, their pressure gently deepening. His hands lifted to move through her thick, tawny hair before sliding down her back and gathering her close. At last, her mouth opened under his and the kiss became equal on both sides.

Seconds, minutes, went by. Richard didn't know how long they stayed in the embrace but only knew, when Jude drew back, that he was reeling from the feelings inside him. Like the water in the pool next to them—joyous bubbles of excitement and lust, interest and admiration. Whoa—what was going on here? He needed to cool this, he really did.

'Look,' Jude said, and he could see her face was worried. 'Understand I didn't want that to happen, okay?'

He shot her a look of disbelief, as he drew back. 'What? The day? The kiss? I gave you plenty of chances to stop me. I think you were enjoying yourself as much as I was.'

'Maybe,' she said, her voice cool, 'but it shouldn't have happened. I'd... I'd rather you forgot about it, please.'

'Forgot about it? I'd rather not. I like you and I don't think I'm way off base if I say I think you like me, too?'

'No.' Her voice was flat, her eyes narrowed.

Shock flared across his face. 'I'm sorry. It seems I totally misread the situation.'

With those clipped words, Richard rose to his feet, adjusted his jeans, and strode along the path which led up the side of the waterfall. Hauling himself up the steep incline helped him shake off his hurt and, he had to admit, his anger. He stood at the top, breathing hard, his mind a maelstrom of mixed feelings. Anna had wanted him to kiss her, he was certain of that. So why the sudden recoil? It was confusing, having her encouraging him one moment, pushing him away the next. Turning, he strode away along the narrow path leading to the moors, resorting as always to his favourite occupation when he needed to think things over, be it personal or business.

It was some twenty minutes later Richard, now calm and determined to tread gently with Anna, returned to the pool to find her lying asleep on the soft grass. Damn, he hadn't meant to upset her, but he was still sure she'd enjoyed kissing him as much as he'd enjoyed kissing her. He hadn't worked out what her problem was, but he was determined to hang around, find out and sort it if he could.

Bending down, he gently shook her awake. 'Hey, I'm sorry.'

Jude sat up, her eyes blinking in the sunshine, looking confused. Then her face cleared, and she gave a small smile. 'Oh. Yes. So'm I.'

'Let's see what happens, okay? I'd like to know you better.'

Surprise crossed his face as he saw her flinch. 'What?'

'It's not a good idea. It really isn't. This... it won't work. You'll see. You'll understand.'

He stared at her and shook his head. What did she mean? 'Sorry, Anna, sweetheart. Can't agree. I think it could work very well. I like you and I know you like me whatever you're trying to say.'

Richard touched her cheek lightly and, bending, he dropped a gentle kiss on her forehead, before pulling her to her feet, the soft lavender perfume of her shampoo causing his nostrils to flare in appreciation.

Jude helped him pack up the remains of their picnic and they set off to walk back down the hill to the van. Richard looked at her questioningly as he caught hold of her hand in his. She allowed her fingers to rest within his warm clasp and they walked on, talking now about books, music, and other general, simple things.

Once back at Aurora Technology he tentatively kissed her a second time. Her tense body, at first stiff within his arms, yielded as it had before as she returned the gentle kiss.

Releasing her, Richard laughed in relief. 'You see?' he murmured, shaking his head at her. 'You see? Anna, where do you live? What's your number? I want to see you again.'

'Work,' she said, pushing against his chest. 'I'll see you at work. Let me go.'

Astonished by this second abrupt rejection, Richard watched as Jude slipped out of his arms and ran across to her own car, not looking back as she climbed in and drove away.

3

Monday came. Jude's stomach churned continuously, making her feel sick. She knew she couldn't win. Richard Blake had dismissed her from her position as CEO because he'd linked her to his father, with whom he apparently had issues. Why he'd done so wasn't clear, but no doubt she'd find out sooner or later. Jude thought it was sad she'd become the central object in someone else's feud, and as a result, was going to lose her job. Already suspended, she fully expected to be dismissed this morning, probably with severance pay to compensate for the rest of her contract.

She had to face Adam this morning, as well. She was dreading the dismay she would see in his eyes when they met. Except... maybe he'd stand by his own judgement of her from Saturday and refute Richard Blake's opinion? Unlikely, in view of the fact he'd left with Richard Blake six years ago and had only known *her* for less than six hours. Oh, she shouldn't have given in to her impulse on Saturday, she really shouldn't. For her, attraction was generally fleeting these days and if she'd said no and gone home, no harm would have been done. As it was, she'd allowed herself to like him and, even worse, allowed him to kiss her. After Julian, she'd sworn she'd never mix work and a love interest, so what the hell had she been thinking on Saturday?

Aurora Technology was only a short drive from the Victorian terrace where she lived on the outskirts of Crossfield. This morning, the drive seemed even shorter. Jude was oblivious to the cool morning air, which gave promise of warmth to come, and the glorious freshness of the surrounding hills and fields. She swung her car in through the gates, smiling mechanically at the security man, her clammy hands trembling on the wheel, nausea continuing to sweep through her.

Slowing to enter her usual parking space by the main staff entrance, Jude received the first concrete intimation of the differences there would be in her life. There was a sleek BMW 4x4 in the place where she normally parked her modest Focus. The rest of the managerial staff took all the other spaces, so she drove into the main carpark and added her car to the rows of others already there.

It was a long walk back to the entrance.

'Hi, Jude.' Annabel, blonde and lively, was the receptionist of Aurora Technology. This morning, she was quieter than usual, her face solemn.

'Hi.' Jude rested her laptop case on the polished wooden surface of Annabel's desk. 'I presume Mr Blake has arrived, then? There's a swish BMW in my usual spot.'

'Yes, he's arrived. And he's left a message you've got to see him as soon as you come in. Sorry.'

A chill swept through her. 'Just what I need,' she mumbled under her breath, looking down at her white-knuckled hands gripping the laptop case. Deep inside, she felt hurt and bewildered. As well, she knew, somewhere, sometime, she'd encounter Adam and then what? What would he think? What would he do? What would he *say*? Jude shut her eyes in dismay at the thought.

Raising her hand in salute to Annabel, she walked to the lift, wishing she was anywhere but here.

In trepidation, Jude opened the door of the outer office. Helen was sitting behind her desk as normal. The churning in her stomach lessened a little. Having decided Adam must be Richard Blake's PA, she'd expected him to be in here instead. It was a relief not to run up against him immediately.

'Morning, Helen.'

Helen was also looking unhappy.

'Goodness, what's wrong with everyone this morning?' Jude injected a false brightness into her voice, belying her inner tension. 'He can't be that bad?'

'Well, no,' Helen admitted, 'but no-one's too happy about his vendetta against you, which is puzzling, to say the least.'

'It's hardly a problem, is it?' Sighing, she put her laptop down on the floor and rested one hip on Helen's desk. 'I shan't be here long enough for it to matter. Where's Ian this morning? I'm surprised he's not camping outside the door, ready to tell Richard Blake all his woes.'

'He tried, but Mr Blake wasn't having any. Told him to go away, and that he wasn't doing anything until he'd seen you. Then he went in there and said no calls, no interruptions. You were the only one to see him, and that, as soon as you arrived. Chin up, Jude. He can only sack you.'

'He's done that already.' Jude slipped off the desk and stood up. 'Well, no point in prolonging the agony. Let him know I'm here, will you?'

With a silent look of sympathy, Helen leaned forwards and pressed the intercom button on her desk. 'Mr Blake?'

'Has Ms Drayton arrived?' A crisp, somewhat distorted voice issued from the speaker. 'Send her in, please.'

Helen shrugged and indicated the door with a tilt of her head, sympathy detectable in her eyes. 'You heard,' she murmured. 'In.'

Jude pressed her lips together to still their sudden trembling and went through into what, until Friday, had been her office.

Richard Blake was standing over by the windows, hands in his pockets, shoulders hunched, staring out across the grass and gravelled forecourt. Jude stopped dead, her breath hissing from her body as she absorbed the shock.

Gone were the faded jeans and casual shirt, but there was no disguising those shoulders, the height, the head of thick brown hair, the muscular, lithe grace of his body, now clad in an impeccable, expertly tailored, dark-grey suit.

Adam.

Adam was Richard Blake?

What the hell was going on?

He spoke coldly, without turning around. 'Thank you for coming to see me, Ms Drayton. I shouldn't take up too much of your time.'

'I hardly had any choice,' Jude said, her voice dry as the shock washed through her, leaving her body icy-cold and shaking with dismay.

The man at the window froze. Then, slowly, he withdrew his hands from his pockets and turned.

'*You?*' In his eyes she saw equal shock, and, as she'd feared, disappointment and a flash of anger, before his expression became masked. Only his clenched fists betrayed his agitation.

'Quite,' Jude responded, recovering some of her equilibrium. '*You?*' She held her body tight against its continued trembling, hoping the pounding of her heart wouldn't be audible in the silent room.

'What the hell are you doing here? I asked to see Ms Drayton, not her PA. Ms Drayton... she must be older, surely? Much older?' There was a note of panic in his voice.

A multitude of feelings swept across his face, which Jude tried to read. Anger. Horror. Dismay. It seemed he did indeed hate the idea of Jude, but the fact she'd been Anna the day before yesterday also meant something. Not much, but something.

However, Jude doubted it would do her much good. 'Sorry to disappoint in the matter of age, but I'm not Ms Drayton's PA. I'm Jude Drayton herself.'

'Then on Saturday, you deliberately misled me?'

'I think, on Saturday, I was not the only one to be misleading... *Adam*?'

She saw his face colour as he accepted the truth of her acerbic comment. 'Adam is my middle name.'

'Well, well, well, what a coincidence... Anna is *my* middle name too.' She walked over to a chair and sat down, her cool tone belying her inner turmoil. 'We'd agreed not to discuss Aurora Technology on Saturday. I was happy to escape for a day, as I think you were too. Equally guilty, perhaps?'

How appalling to discover that the lovely Adam, to whom she'd felt an instant attraction, was the same person as her apparent enemy, Richard Blake. She'd wondered if she would see Adam again and how he'd react. Well, now she had her answer, and she knew his reaction would be even worse than she'd imagined because of her perceived deceit. It was bad enough when she'd decided Adam was Richard Blake's personal assistant. Catastrophic that it turned out he was Richard Blake himself. She glanced across at him, shocked by the contempt and self-loathing she saw on his face. *Why* did he hate her so much? It couldn't just be linked to improving the factory, surely?

'Well, Mr Blake...' her voice cracked as she struggled to maintain her composure, 'perhaps you could let me know what you want me to do? I presume, as you've relieved me of my duties, you'd prefer me to leave? I'm sure we could reach some agreement about salary instead of notice, and then I can go as soon as possible?'

'Hold it.' Richard Blake sat down behind the desk and raised his hand, his eyes glacial, his face rigid. 'I don't want you to leave. Far from it. You're to stay on.'

Her eyes flared open. That was the last thing she'd expected. Stay on? How? In what capacity? She stared at him. He studiously avoided her gaze, seemingly captivated by his laptop screen. Her eyes dropped to his hands. They were clasped together, the knuckles white.

Had he changed his mind because of Saturday?

'Stay *on*? In what capacity?'

'Hmm... I don't know yet. One thing I suppose you could do is to sort out the staff when I—'

'Close the place down? Oh, sorry, no, not close it. Let me get it right. You're going to *re-organise* it as an adjunct of your American company. What do you think the people made redundant will do for employment if you do that?' Jude, at last, allowed her anger to burn.

'Just a moment—' Richard's brown eyes narrowed in annoyance at her interruption.

His annoyance meant nothing to her, but her workforce did. She knew them. Knew the ones coming up to retirement, the ones who'd just got married or had a baby, the ones buying their first house, and interrupted him again. 'No, Mr Blake, I won't wait any longer to say what I want to say. Frankly, I don't think much of your plans as we've understood them. Or, come to that, *you*.' Inside, her heart slowly disintegrated, and she cursed herself for a fool. 'On Saturday, you deliberately misled me and tried to elicit information about what was going on here. Prior to that, you'd sent an email which kicks me out of my job and says you aren't going to continue with this factory as it stands. That means I'm not the only person who'll lose out, but I'm fortunate. At my age, with a good reference, I'll be able to get another job, but a lot of these people won't.'

'A good reference?' Richard stood up and walked back over to the windows, turning his back, his tone cool. 'And tell me, Ms Drayton, just where will you get a good reference from?'

'Why, Aurora Technology, of course,' Jude asserted, before her voice died away and she looked at him with dawning horror. 'You wouldn't dare,' she breathed.

'Wouldn't dare what, Ms Drayton?' His voice cracked as he wheeled round to face her. 'According to you, I'm a monster. I'm going to shut down this factory, remember? I'm going to make all these good people redundant.' His arm swept in a wide gesture. 'So what...' he came forward and leaned with both hands flat on the desk, bending towards her. 'So *what*,' he repeated forcefully, 'makes you think I'll give you a reference?'

Jude stared into his angry eyes, remembering their tenderness on Saturday, the proximity of his body bringing back memories of his kiss as her anger slowly burned. How dare he threaten her like this? No-one did this to her these days—not after Julian! If he wouldn't offer a reference then she would find a job without one. She was well known in the computer manufacturing world and it would be a simple matter to ask round, but one thing she was sure of... she wouldn't let Mr Richard Blake know what she was doing.

She was glad of her anger. It stopped the memories of Saturday from overwhelming her and, she was sure, reducing her to tears.

Richard turned and sat down again. 'Now, having made that clear, you will listen to what I say and then get on with some work. Is that understood?'

Jude couldn't tear her gaze away from the man. This was insufferable. If Ian was right, nothing she did would suit him because Richard Blake equated her with his father, so didn't he just let her go?

If she walked out... now there was an idea. Her mind tried to process it all, but underlying everything was simply pain. An ache deep inside. Seeing Adam... Richard... again made her realise the effect he'd had on her on Saturday.

'I said,' Richard's voice was cold, his eyes unforgiving, 'is that understood?'

Jude wouldn't satisfy him by saying a simple yes. 'There's a problem with that. There's no longer any available office space, so there's nowhere I *can* get on with work. This,' she added, her voice bitter, '*was* my office, but...' she shrugged, hands spread wide.

Richard looked taken aback and Jude smothered a grim smile at his momentary confusion. She saw his glance as she dropped her head to hide the smile. When she looked up again, he was frowning, still looking annoyed. A silence fell as he tapped his fingers on the desk. When he next spoke, Jude reeled. This was turning into a farce, and she'd no idea what was going on in his head.

'Right,' said Richard. 'There's plenty of room in here. I'll have them bring in another desk. And that way,' he added, 'I can keep my eye on you and make sure I'm getting my money's worth.'

Work in here? With him? In the same room? Jude gazed at him in horror. This would be hard. Every time she looked at him, she wouldn't be able to prevent recalling the precious moments they'd shared, which made a bleak comparison to his harshness of today. Plus, every time she considered what he wanted to do with the factory, she wanted to chew him up into a million fragments and feed his remains to the fish. She shook her head in denial.

'Yes,' Richard Blake looked at her, his eyes flinty. 'A good idea. I'll organise it now.'

'Um, there might be another slight problem here.' Jude was clutching at any straw to prevent her from sharing an office with this man.

He gazed at her in cool enquiry.

'There aren't any spare desks.'

'That's no problem at all,' Richard said between gritted teeth, standing up and moving round the desk. 'If there are no spare desks in stores, I have a spare desk at home in the garage. We can drive over there in my car and bring it back in the van.'

'We can't just leave... you've only just *got* here... someone may want you...'

'We can. If I've only just got here, no-one will know yet, and anyway, you must have left the place on occasions? Who's that man... Ian Grey, isn't it... who's second-in-command and been trying to trip me up ever since I arrived?'

Jude stifled a slightly hysterical spurt of laughter. Well, if nothing else, it seemed he'd summed up Ian soon enough.

Unnoticing, Richard moved across the floor to the outer door as he continued to speak. 'He can run the place for half an hour, can't he?' Opening the door, he spoke to Helen in the outer office.

A silence fell. Richard leaned against the door frame, hands in his pockets, looking tense. Jude could hear Helen speaking on the phone. A couple of minutes later, she replaced the phone. 'Sorry, Mr Blake, but no. There are no spare desks in stores.'

'Good. Because in any case,' Richard spoke over his shoulder to Jude, his glance antagonistic, 'I want to take you out to the house, and now is as good a time as any. Come.'

Take her out to the *house*?

Why?

She'd never been there before, ever. Even at the funeral, she'd only attended the church and graveside ceremonies, excusing herself from going back to the house of someone who'd regarded her with bitter mistrust and who'd made her job as difficult as possible until he'd become too ill to interfere.

Jude still didn't believe he could be serious until she found herself hustled through the outer office and into the lift. As they passed, Richard spoke brusquely to Helen. 'Ms Drayton and I have some business to do. We'll be back later this morning. Any calls you can't deal with yourself, take their name and number, and I'll sort them out when I get back. Tell what's his name... Ian Grey... to do some work. He seemed keen enough this morning.'

Helen stared at them, her mouth open in surprise, murmuring an acknowledgement.

They travelled in silence in the lift, both standing stiffly, a wide space between them, not looking at each other. The doors opened and Richard marched through reception, Jude doing her best to match his angry stride. Opening the passenger door of the BMW for her, he waited until she'd fastened her seat belt before closing the door and walking round to slip into the driving seat.

Now what? What was so important he had to take her to the house? Jude couldn't imagine anything worse than what the morning had already thrown at her.

4

He drove fast but well to his house, aware all the time of the closeness of Jude's warm body and the smell of her shampoo. A pity he couldn't enjoy it, as he had on Saturday. He'd no idea what he was doing, anyway. When she'd arrived this morning, he'd fully intended to tell her to get out, with six months' salary instead of notice. So why the hell had he told her she was staying? Even worse, why was he determined to torture himself by having her in the same room? Yet something about her defiance on Saturday, and the subsequent day they'd shared, tugged at his heart and he still wanted to understand the real Jude. Was she his father's mistress, as he'd been informed, or was she innocent of the charges and maybe the victim of an ill-wisher? Perhaps he'd glean something by bringing her to the house? If she'd been his father's mistress, she'd be familiar with the place and maybe show some feelings?

They arrived at a four-square, gated Georgian house, set well back from the lane in a walled, lawned garden. Fields already thick with grass surrounded it, waiting for the farmers to harvest the silage crop. A short way further along the lane was a farm, and beyond that, a small village lay just over the next hill. It was quiet. As Richard stopped the car and swung open his door, all they could hear was the rustle of the grass as the wind stirred it, and the far-off sound of a tractor at work.

'Out,' Richard commanded. Now he could face her with the truth, here, where his father had reigned all-powerful. Face her with the truth, then forget all this stupidity about keeping her on. Better to cut all ties with her, as he'd done with his father six years previously, when he'd finally accepted he wouldn't change the man's rejection and dislike.

But... what of Anna, a small voice nagged in his head?

Simple. He had to forget her. She didn't exist. *She didn't exist.*

Jude glared at him as she complied with his curt demand.

Opening the front door, Richard led the way into a cool, spacious hallway.

'I've had the place completely re-done since my father died, as you've probably noticed,' Richard said, his shoulders tense as he opened the door on their right and led the way into a well-proportioned sitting-room. French windows led onto a patio overlooking the gardens at the back of the house, and he liked the lighter walls, the dull gold of the furniture and the few antiques he'd opted to keep from the multitude which had overcrowded the house before.

'It's lovely,' Jude couldn't help but comment on the attractiveness of the room, her head turning this way and that as she assimilated it, then continued, her voice cool. 'But I can't make comparisons with what it was like before, because I've never been here before.'

'You're trying to tell me that as my father's mistress, you've never been here before?' The intense contempt in his voice was shocking. 'Oh, come on. Who do you think you're trying to kid?'

He looked towards the window, and didn't see Jude's hand fly up. As he turned back to her with a sneer distorting his mouth, her hand connected to the side of his face with a most satisfactory crack, jolting his head sideways. His shock and surprise were obvious, as was the loathing and fury he saw etched on her face. That was a potent slap and made him hesitate about considering her guilty of his accusation.

'Don't you dare,' she said in a voice under tight control, 'don't you dare, *ever again*, imply that your father and I had a relationship. I have *never* come here, and I *never* met your father. I gather he was an unpleasant and difficult man. Well, like father, like son, it seems. If he was anything like you, I'm grateful we never did meet. How on earth could he have had a mistress anyway, in the state he was in? Don't be so stupid and never insult me like that again!' Jude turned her back on him and strode to the doorway. 'Find your own desk, Mr Blake. I don't want to remain in your company any longer if this is the type of thing you're going to accuse me of.'

He hesitated. Those were brave words with a definite ring of truth, and if he hadn't seen the reports with his own eyes, it might have convinced him of her innocence. Doubt filled him. Had he got it wrong? But...how?

Reaching the front door, Jude was struggling to open it. He strode after her and placed a hand on her shoulder, then turned her round to face him, surprised at her compliance. When she was facing him, he saw why. She was silently weeping, snot running from her nose, pawing at her eyes with her fingers, her chest heaving.

His heart crumbled. This was surely someone who was telling him the truth.

Or furious at the loss of her excellent position and pay, a snide little voice whispered.

Silently, he withdrew an old-fashioned pristine white handkerchief and tucked it into her hand. Jude scrubbed at her eyes, blew her nose and let her head drop. She looked exhausted.

'Ms Drayton...' Richard's voice was low. 'Ms Drayton... you'll stay here until we've loaded the desk into my van and you'll return with me to the factory. This is office time. I'm still paying you a small fortune to be at work. You'll do me the courtesy of earning your money—if you're capable of it.'

She finally raised her eyes to meet his. He saw the embers of anger flickering in their depths. 'I don't understand how you can suggest I had a relationship with your father,' she choked out. 'I can't imagine what made you even consider such a thing. *And take your hand off me!*'

Her final words were spoken with such venomous fury that, taken by surprise, his hand, still resting on her shoulder, dropped to his side.

'I considered it,' Richard replied, 'because I was told it was so.'

Jude went still, her eyes widening in shock. She shook her head from side to side, mutely denying it. It took her several attempts before she could speak.

'Would you like to explain?' She sounded dangerous. 'I mean, come on. His mistress? It's laughable.'

'Someone sent me quarterly reports from the company. They told me you'd got the job on my father's say-so, because you'd spent a lot of time out here with him. In a relationship. As for his age and the state he was in after his stroke, I agree there would've been no physical side to a relationship, but I gather he was still lucid, even though his speech and movement were impaired. Lucid enough to be flattered and coerced and do what you wanted him to do, perhaps?'

Jude looked at him, her horror and disgust showing in her wide eyes and contorted mouth. 'And you believed that? With no further proof or even asking me politely?'

Doubts swirled in his mind before he unwillingly cast *Anna* aside and focused again on his dislike of Jude Drayton. 'If I asked you,

you'd only deny it. Bringing you here might have surprised you into exclaiming how much the place has changed.'

'I can't comment. I told you, I've never been here before.'

'And tell me why I shouldn't believe these reports? You've achieved everything for Aurora I wanted to do, but could never get past the board because of dad's disapproval and his constant refusal to consider my ideas. My father was an intractable, an *inflexible*, man. There was no way he would ever change his mind, even when he was on his last legs. Especially if he was on his last legs, from sheer spite. Unless you *were* coercing him. Then he might have allowed change... or at least, blindly signed any papers you might have stuck under his nose.'

'Your father, from the time I started work here until the day he died, only spoke to Andrew French who, as you know, was the finance director. I never met him, I never knew him before I came up here from the Midlands, and I *never came here*. He fought everything I proposed. Everything.' Her eyes narrowed as she stabbed her finger at Richard.

Richard gave an inward huff. That sounded more likely, if he was honest. And yet...

'Someone sent reports to me,' he replied stubbornly. 'The first told me about the initial reform you pushed through. Updating the software. Such a damned obvious thing to do, but my father had always refused. He said there was nothing wrong with what we were using. Said people were being too clever and any new technology would fail. So how come you got this past him?'

'Because I persuaded Andrew French there'd be no factory left in six months' time if we didn't update our products,' Jude snarled. 'And pointed out the sale figures, which were plummeting. This was, what, three years after you'd left? By then, the place was in a very serious state. You were forward-looking in what you wanted to do, but didn't achieve it. By the time I came along, Aurora Technology was in serious trouble. Who wrote these reports, anyway? The email address would tell us if they were genuinely from the company and the person responsible for sending them.'

Richard stared at her, a cold pit opening inside. 'I don't know. They came by post on company-headed paper, purporting to be from the Board of Directors. I assumed they were official. They seemed to be genuine enough, to me.'

'Snail-mail? You have to be joking? *Snail-mail*, in this day and age? We never send paper out. Ever. Did you not think to check with the company about this, after receiving the first one? Did it never occur to you they might be malicious?'

Richard stepped back, colour rising in his face. Hell—she had a point. Why had he so blithely accepted the reports as genuine? The very fact they'd not come by email should've at least made him query their origin.

'No, I didn't check with the company, and okay, yes, it's strange they came by post. But I know I never effected those changes, and I know my father's character and that he had mistresses throughout my entire life, so yeah, you know what? I was inclined to believe them.'

'But *anonymous*?'

'Not entirely anonymous. From the Board of Directors on headed notepaper, with a list of the directors' names and a scrawled signature.'

'A readable signature?'

'No.'

Jude shook her head and leaned back against the door. 'So I'm condemned because of these stupid reports?'

Richard's face went blank, and he dropped his head, stabbing his toe against the tiled floor. 'I hated my father. I hated him for the humiliations he put my mother through with his affairs. I hated him for what he put me through at the factory. I hated him for forcing me into exile. I hated watching the factory go down. I even hate what you've achieved. So yes, I've been more than happy to read what the reports have said about you over the past several months.'

'You wanted to believe them,' Jude said quietly. 'Someone knows your history and fed you exactly what you wanted to hear. How often did they come?'

Richard frowned. 'Quarterly.'

He turned away and walked back into the sitting-room, his shoulders hunched, his mind swirling with conflicting thoughts. His father wouldn't have allowed change lightly—and if she was a cunning bitch, she might have sucked up to him, deluded him and persuaded him to back her. Yet... wouldn't there have been gossip? He was still in touch with a couple of people here, and one of them in particular would surely have told him, unless it'd been kept very quiet? But he had to remember his father's communication skills were impaired, and he'd always been a secretive bastard, and Jude herself wouldn't have let on. She could have slipped up to the house in the evenings... but what about the nursing staff? Maybe they just assumed she was a relative or something to do with the factory, and taken it for granted she'd visit? It could all have been possible.

But just as Jude had said a few moments ago, Richard wanted to believe them, despite the oddity of them coming by post and not having a readable signature. Oh, *fuck*! This was crazy. If she was only a figurehead, who on earth was stupid enough to allow their work to be passed off as hers? If she'd really effected the improvements, surely this meant the reports were a lie, and she was genuinely good? Brilliant, in fact? He could surely get over his pique that someone else had succeeded where he'd failed?

He turned to see Jude had followed, and had dropped into a chair, her head in her hands. Richard already hated his father, so he was quite ready to believe the worst of her. The poison was too deep for him to shrug it off immediately, but he had to admit his doubts were being bolstered by her heated denials and the time they'd shared on Saturday.

Which brought him back to who'd sent them? Who hated her so much? How come they pandered so cleverly to his past history with his father, and even with the factory? Playing on it, feeding it... he shook his head.

This was getting him nowhere.

'Ask.' Jude suddenly spat out. 'Ask Richard French how I got the job. Ask him if I ever met your father. Ask if it was ever easy to implement the changes. Ask why the changes were allowed. And, even more importantly, ask why there's a healthy factory ready for you to take over, which you apparently intend to ruin out of spite for your father.' Jude stood up. 'I'm going back to the factory to collect my car. Then I'm going home. I don't think I can take any more today.'

'Wait.' Richard sprang forwards and blocked her way to the door, all the doubt and confusion still swirling in his mind, but knowing he mustn't... he *couldn't*... let her go. Somehow, they had to work through this. If she'd never been his father's mistress, then he... Goodness knows, surely someone would know if she had, and would tell him? 'You can't... you can't walk anywhere in those shoes. And we need that desk. We're going to get the desk, remember?'

He began to wonder if someone had set her up, and he began to question the validity of those reports.

'I'll get the desk,' she muttered, seeing no other way to get back to the factory and her car. 'But when we get back to the office, I'd prefer it if...' her voice gave way, and for the second time, she broke into tears.

Unable to help himself, Richard Blake took her into his arms and held her comfortingly close to his pale-blue shirt.

What was he doing, for fuck's sake? After all the things he'd been saying to her?

But it seemed so right.

And it couldn't continue.

It was just as well Jude gathered her self-control. Sniffing, she dashed her hand over her eyes and pulled away from him. 'I'm sorry,' she said. 'I didn't mean that to happen.'

They stared for a long, time-suspended moment into each other's eyes.

Richard's face went blank as he stepped back, giving her much needed space.

The messages they'd exchanged shook him, but his sudden withdrawal was directly caused by the precarious situation between them.

Was Jude telling the truth, or being cleverly manipulative with her tears and denials? Richard was only sure of one thing—normally, he assessed the facts and made up his mind. This time, he was floundering, and he didn't like it one bit.

5

The desk was in the garage, just as Richard had said.

Jude had wondered if it existed at all, or if the whole thing had been a ploy to get her out to the house and throw that stupid accusation at her. In silence, she helped him carry it to the van. He threw some old cloth onto the van floor and, with Jude's help, turned the desk upside down and slid it into the back. Her throat constricted as she saw the carrier bags which had held their picnic still tucked behind the driver's seat, and the easy tears threatened again. She'd no idea why she was so weepy—it wasn't her usual mode. Maybe she was simply tired because of all the work she'd done last week, emotionally on edge because of *Adam*, and angry with Richard Blake for his blinkered stupidity for taking those paper reports so literally. Old man Blake's mistress, for fuck's sake!

Turning abruptly, she went round to the passenger door. Damn the man. If he mixed her up with his father and hated her, choosing to believe those lies about her, there was nothing she could do. There was no need to get into this state. She'd already decided… get away from Aurora as soon as possible and she'd be back to normal. She was used to battening down her feelings when men let her down. She climbed into the van, fastening her seat belt and turning her head to stare out of the side window in blind misery. What a difference from Saturday.

'Right. We'll go back now, and I expect you to stay. Understood?'

It was utterly heart-breaking. Richard apparently believed this rubbish. *Adam* had struck her as understanding and fair-minded. But that was *Adam*... she gave a tiny, pain-filled shake of her head. *Adam* was a mirage, a figment of her imagination.

They drove back to the factory in stony silence. As they pulled up in front of the main entrance, Richard spoke for the first time since they'd left the house. 'Up to the office, please. I'll have a couple of men take this desk up and then you'll be able to get some work done and justify this fat salary you receive. Now my father's dead, you'll damn well work for your money instead of letting everyone else carry you.'

Jude stared at him for a few seconds before she stepped out of the van and slammed its door behind her. Without a backward look, she ran up the steps and disappeared into reception.

Helen was busy typing on the computer when Jude burst into the room. She stopped and looked up.

'Jude.' she exclaimed as she saw the anger in Jude's eyes and the hectic flush on her cheeks. 'Sit down and I'll get you some coffee.' She rose from her chair as she spoke and pushed Jude down into her vacated seat.

Jude sat staring in front of her, tremors of fury shaking her body, her hands clenching and unclenching as she fought to control both temper and misery.

'Better not.' she jerked out. 'Richard Blake is on his way up here and he won't like it if I'm sitting on my backside drinking coffee. This is worse than you could imagine. Someone's been sending him what amounts to hate mail about me.'

Helen looked at her, eyes wide. 'Hate mail? What on earth do you mean?'

Jude replied with an oblique question. 'Do we possess headed notepaper?'

'Used to. Old Mr Blake was an awkward so and so and wouldn't use email. There's probably still some in stores. Why?'

'Okay. So anyone could have gained access to it.'

'Tell me, Jude,' Helen said patiently.

Jude poured it all out, not looking at Helen but staring down at her PA's desk. PA and friend, and someone she trusted entirely. 'So you see,' she finally finished the sorry tale, 'I can't win. But why would anyone do that?'

'To get rid of you?'

'I suppose so, but...' her voice tailed off, and she closed her eyes. 'Surely whoever did it was pushing their luck by saying I was old Mr Blake's mistress? The age difference, for one thing?'

'You'd be surprised—he caught some quite young, attractive women. I suppose they were after his money as much as anything. Maybe they hoped he'd divorce his wife and marry them, and then they'd inherit?'

'I see. So this libel is feasible? Especially to someone who knew old Mr Blake and his string of mistresses?'

'Oh, yes, I'm sorry, but more than believable.'

Shaking her head, Jude sighed. 'Hell. Then there's not a lot I can do, is there?'

'I was trying to think who'd do something like that,' Helen said. 'Hard, though. There isn't much anyone could say about you that's not in your favour.'

'Well, thanks for that. But don't kid yourself that the performance figures have anything to do with me, will you? I'm just a figurehead and someone else has done all the hard work.'

'Jude, no.' Helen whirled round from the coffee machine, slopping hot black coffee out of the cup she was holding over her hand. 'Oh, damn.' She put the cup down and wiped her hand on a tissue. 'What did you say?'

'I'm not responsible for the improvement in the company's performance,' Jude repeated.

Helen leaned on the desk, her eyes seeking Jude's. 'He said this?'

'Yes,' Jude said bitterly. 'Also in the reports, but it seems contradictory. Either I was the man's mistress, and it's my actions which saved the company, or I'm just a figurehead and actually someone else has been responsible for Aurora's success. Richard Blake doesn't seem to see how stupid that last one is. Surely if someone else has made the company what it is today, they'd not be hiding under anonymity? Whoever sent all this poison to him didn't need to try too hard, anyway. His own experience growing up is fertile ground.' She stretched out her hand and picked up the coffee, drinking deeply. 'Thanks. I needed this.'

'Can't you persuade him he's *wrong*?' Helen said, her voice hushed.

'I've tried, but believe me, he's not receptive. Although…' she hesitated, eyes narrowing. 'It's strange, but… I could have sworn when I first went in this morning, he meant to throw me out. Said he wouldn't be keeping me long. I suggested a leave of absence and I'd look for a new job, and then he turned round and implied he'd refuse to give me a reference.'

'*What*?'

Jude nodded, her lips compressed. 'I won't let that stop me, though. I've got an excellent reputation in the computing world and I'll ask round on the quiet. David Eller was talking about needing someone on the marketing side at Master Systems. I can have a word with him at the dance on Saturday, explain the problem discreetly. He won't need a reference because he's very well aware of what I've done here and—'

The whine of the lift alerted them both. Helen whipped away the now empty cup from in front of Jude, who rose to her feet and walked over to the inner door.

'Good luck, whatever, Jude,' Helen said softly, 'but don't rely on talking to David at the dance. He's a refusal this year. He's going down south, something to do with Louise's family, I think he said.' She sat down and began once more to type on her keyboard. 'Have you told Richard Blake about the dance?'

Hand on the door, Jude stopped, giving a brief and bitter laugh. 'There's hardly been the chance. Do I have to? Can't you do it?'

'Yes. No problem with that.' Helen flashed her a glance of sympathy.

Jude looked much better than when she had first come back into the office from her trip with their new CEO, but there was still a rim of white edging her mouth and strain clear around her eyes.

'Although on second thoughts... do *you* have to?' Jude queried, looking pleadingly at Helen. 'Does he have to know about it? Does he have to come?'

His presence would no doubt spoil, for many of them, what was always a most enjoyable occasion. Not only did everyone at Aurora Technology come to the annual buffet and dance, held at the local hotel, but also people from other firms, giving rise to a lot of interesting gossip and exchanges of information.

'Yes. You know I have to tell him about it. Whether he comes will be up to him, but he has to know.'

Jude went into the office as two burly men from Dispatch came through the outer door with the desk, followed by Richard, still looking grim.

They spent the rest of the day in uncomfortable silence. Jude had little to do and, used as she was to working flat out all day, she was bored and restless. A sigh of relief escaped her when the buzzer sounded in the factory to signal the end of the day.

Richard looked up as she rose to her feet. 'Hold on a minute... you may be used to leaving the office as soon as the buzzer goes, but I'm not. I expect you to continue work until I've finished.'

'Mr Blake,' Jude spoke through gritted teeth. It seemed to be the only way she could ever speak to this man. Where had *Adam* gone? 'I'd be delighted to continue working if I had something to do. I sorted the small amount of paperwork you allowed me to deal with some time ago. It's pointless for me to sit here doing nothing, so if you don't mind, I'll put an end to this farce and get out of here.' She turned and walked towards the door.

'Wait.' His voice was commanding. He rose to his feet, tall, athletic in his movements, and crossed to her desk. Picking up the papers there, he flicked through them before muttering an approval, and tossed them back onto her desk.

'Well, Mr Blake? Permission to leave?' Jude's voice was icy, her hand on the door, ready to open it as soon as she could.

Richard Blake regarded her, a frown pulling his dark brows together, his top teeth worrying at his bottom lip. Several seconds passed. Jude met his gaze steadily.

'All right,' he conceded at last. 'You can go. I'll see you tomorrow.'

Jude scowled as she crossed to the lift. Now she knew David Eller wouldn't be at the dance, she had other plans for tomorrow. However, she had little intention of communicating them to her bitter and malevolent boss.

How she wished *Adam* had been someone else.

How she wished Saturday had never happened.

Later that evening, Jude rang David Eller

A moment passed before she heard David's greeting. 'Jude! Hi. How's things?'

'Hello, David. Look, I could do with a chat. I'd hoped to see you on Saturday at the dance, but Helen says you won't be there?'

'That's right. Louise and I are sorry to miss it, but there's a family wedding on. Her cousin, I think. She accepted the invitation weeks ago.'

'Is there any chance of seeing you sometime tomorrow?'

'How could I refuse?' David murmured over the phone. 'Name the time and place and I'm yours.'

She and David had always got on well. Both respected the other's business sense and were good friends. Soon after she'd come to work at Aurora, they'd had a couple of dates, but they'd realised the spark was missing and had instead accepted the good friendship they shared. David, around thirty-five, was now involved with Louise, who also worked for Master Systems, and Jude was glad for him, but it still didn't stop him flirting with her whenever they spoke.

'Huh. Louise will be jealous.'

'Do her good,' David said. 'Keep her on her toes.'

'You be careful,' Jude laughed at him. 'She might turn the tables and you wouldn't like that. Lunch?'

'No can do, sorry. I'm already booked with Louise.'

'David. After all your protestations of undying love. How fickle can you get? The morning? The afternoon?'

'Afternoon. I know I'm free after two-thirty, so let's say three o'clock. I can give you an hour of uninterrupted time. How about that?'

'That's great. Thank you. I'll see you then. Oh...' Jude hesitated. 'Look, if something comes up and you have to cancel... I'm not at work tomorrow, okay?'

'May one ask what this is all about?' David was curious.

'No, one may not. I'll fill you in tomorrow. And David? Thanks again.' Jude put the phone down and Richard Blake's face came into her mind. She shivered. If he did but know it, this would be the first and the only time she'd ever done anything deceitful at Aurora Technology. Not that he'd care or believe her. If only he didn't feel this unreasonable hatred of her. If only... she swallowed, feeling furious... he didn't believe those foul lies about her and his father. Damn the man.

Getting out of Aurora was the only sensible thing to do.

Promptly at three the following day, Jude presented herself at David's office. He ordered coffee, told Anne not to interrupt them, and closed the door.

'Now,' David sat down behind his desk and regarded her with a curious smile. 'I can't wait any longer. Why the urgency? And why have you been at home today? You don't look to be suffering to me.'

As she sat down, Jude sighed. Her primary goal was to get out of Aurora as soon as possible, and find another job, but now she felt uncomfortable coming to David with her story, and the request for a job and maybe a reference. The more she thought about this, the more she wondered if it was a foolish move. Still, too late now, she was here, and David would want an explanation.

'What I say now, I want you to treat it with the strictest confidence. The strictest confidence, you understand me?'

He was quick to reply. 'Of course I will.'

Looking round the room, she wondered where to begin. Eventually, she took a deep breath and turned back to David, to explain what Richard Blake had said to her over the last couple of days and the reasons she was looking for employment.

'So I'm here to ask you about that job in marketing, the one you mentioned two or three weeks back. If it's still vacant, can I have it? I have to warn you, though, that I'd probably have to apply for it without a reference from Aurora Technology.'

'No,' David protested in consternation. '*You*? Asking for a job here, in the marketing division? You can't consider it. Not after running Aurora Technology for three years.' Looking upset, he busied his hands and poured out some coffee, pushing a cup across to Jude.

Jude sipped her coffee, then placed her cup on the desk and leaned forwards. 'Richard Blake has come over from America to take over Aurora Technology, as you well know. Quite what he plans for the company I don't know for sure, but the impression Helen, Ian and I have got is that he intends to close the place down and re-open as a manufacturer of Blake Laptops.'

'Surely not. The Aurora Mercury will sweep the business market at the next tech show.'

'Anything to do with Aurora is to do with his father, and he still hates everything his father stood for.'

'Oh, yes. I know that,' David acknowledged. 'I know pretty well all the Blake history. Everyone knew of old Blake's dislike of Richard, even the fact he didn't believe Richard was his son.'

'Yes, I heard that too, and it's cruel. But now he's come over here full of these reports saying I was his father's mistress, and I can't convince him otherwise.'

David shifted in his chair, a frown gathering on his face. 'That's madness. And paper? That smacks of subterfuge.'

'It does to me, as well, but Richard doesn't seem too worried by that minor fact.' Jude lifted her cup, shaking her head. 'What can I do? I thought he'd suspend me on full pay for the rest of my contract, but suddenly, he wants me to stay and he's had a desk put in the office, so he can "keep his eye on me", he said. And if he won't give me a reference—'

'Yes, you mentioned that earlier. What's this about no reference?'

'That's what he said. I know it sounds weird asking you this, but if the job's gone, I was wondering if you'd mind me putting you down as a referee?'

'No reference sounds like a load of rubbish and I can't see Richard Blake doing something so mean-spirited. Once he realises what you've done, he'll either be happy to offer one or want to keep you. I would've thought you were his sort of person, through and through.'

'Someone who knows what went on before Richard left is being clever and making a lot of innuendos, targeting Richard's insecurities and intense dislike of his father, and I'm telling you, Richard seems to believe it.'

'This can't be true. I can't believe he would take notice of such rubbish without at least seeing for himself what's going on.'

'Well, he has.' Jude was bitter. 'If you think about it, it gives him a reason why I succeeded where, as he saw it, he failed, because I had influence over his father. I'm damned if I'll use the word "mistress"—the very thought sickens me.'

David shook his head. 'I don't understand. Okay, everyone knows he loathed his father, but even so... I suppose if he's got you tied up with him in his mind, then... I suppose...' his voice faded and he stared off into the distance before turning back to Jude. 'You could wait it out?'

'What? Hang around, being insulted at every turn? I don't think you understand how he's behaved towards me so far. He's rude, he's patronising, he's insulting, he hates me. I'm wasting my time, trying to wait it out, as you suggest. I have to leave. And if he won't give me a reference, then I have to do it behind his back.'

He fiddled with his mouse. Pushed his laptop to the back of the desk, then tugged it forwards again. Put his cup on the tray, then leaned back in his chair, hands linked behind his head, looking worried.

'The job, David?' Jude prompted, sensing his discomfort, her puzzlement showing. She'd assumed this would be a mere formality.

'Yes. The job. It's still vacant, but the ad's already gone in. Of course, you can apply.'

'But that would be through the conventional channels,' Jude murmured. 'I'd hoped... maybe you had sufficient influence to let me have it on the quiet.'

'I can't see...' David rubbed his eyes with his thumb and forefinger. 'Maybe I could've just let you in at the back door, but we've sent the ad off and it'll be in all the online tech journals on Thursday. But I'll look at your application myself, and we can ignore the lack of a reference, if you're sure Richard won't...?'

Jude shook her head, disappointment clouding her eyes.

'Look, you've run Aurora Technology for three years and made a damn fine job of it. This will be a comedown, Jude. I have to warn you, everyone will think you're over-qualified, you must know that.' He stood up and held out his hand. 'Jude... reconsider. I think you and Richard could work well together and who knows Aurora better than you now?'

Jude reached forwards and clasped his hand in hers. She knew he was dismissing her and knew she had no right to prolong the interview. 'I appreciate what you're saying, but believe me, it's no good.'

As she walked out to the car park, Jude lifted her chin, anger and disappointment warring inside. That hadn't gone quite as she's expected. David seemed hesitant about the whole thing, although he'd been genuinely appalled by the reports and lack of a reference. But she could tell he thought it was probably something which would blow over, get sorted out.

She shook her head.

Not by what she'd seen so far.

Richard Blake had it in for her.

6

Helen looked wary. 'No. No, Jude almost never takes time off.'

He looked pointedly at his watch. 'It looks as if she's having another day off at my expense.'

Helen gasped. It wasn't anywhere near nine o'clock. 'I think you'll find she's back today, sir,' she murmured.

'I hope so. There's something here I want her to deal with. It's about time she earned her salary.'

Helen hesitated, then overrode her normal reticence. 'That's not fair, sir.'

Richard's head snapped up, and he regarded Helen through narrowed eyes. This was interesting. 'Explain.'

'Miss Drayton has always worked very hard for this firm. Ever since she came here. I've never known her to waste time. She's usually here before anyone else and often stays after everyone else has gone home.' Helen's voice remained level and quiet.

Richard was momentarily silenced. His father had been unfair and harsh in his rule of the company, whereas he took after his mother, a quiet, caring lady. But unlike his mother, he had a core of steel which he wryly admitted to himself had no doubt been inherited from his father.

He remembered coming to learn the factory from the bottom up. There'd been no attempt on his father's part to value him or encourage him to contribute to the firm. After seven years, Richard couldn't take any more of the humiliation, the lack of foresight, the failing figures, the quarrels. His mother was dead. His father, it seemed, would never approve of him, never mind love him. There'd been no reason to stay. To most of the observers, it seemed as if old Mr Blake had been deliberately provoking him to leave. Yet in the end, the will had decreed everything should go to Richard... despite the rumours about his parentage. He wasn't sure yet what he was going to do with the place. His initial intention had been to shut it down and go back to America. What the hell did he want of the place, which only held bitter memories? And yet... he shook his head and let his hands fall from the keyboard, aware of Helen Gresham shifting from foot to foot. He didn't want to be an unreasonable or harsh boss, like his father, and he definitely wanted to sort out the mess surrounding Jude Drayton.

'You're very loyal. Why?'

'Why shouldn't I be?' Helen appeared startled.

'Perhaps I wondered if she might not be easy to work for?'

Helen laughed. 'Oh, Jude's great to work for. She's very understanding, easy to talk to and always clear about what she wants you to do.'

He listened carefully, then, turning away, Richard walked over to the windows, hands thrust into the pockets of his well-cut trousers, shoulders hunched. Here it was again. A complete contradiction to what he thought he knew about Jude Drayton. *More the behaviour he would have attributed to Anna*, a small voice inside pointed out.

Richard prided himself on being an excellent judge of character, and Helen was someone he already liked and trusted, even though he'd only known her for such a short time. Could Jude deceive *her*? A man, yes. A man might be taken in by her... but a woman? Surely that would be unlikely. So maybe Jude was right about those reports being malicious and obviously fake? How he hoped it would be true, even as his insides continued to curl with antagonism towards the woman he'd believed to have been his father's mistress, in whatever capacity. An arch manipulator would be a better way to put it. As Richard sighed, he heard the door behind him opening and swung round to see Jude enter the room.

'You're late,' he said brusquely, walking back to his desk and sitting down, pulling his laptop towards him, pushing thoughts of Anna and innocence to one side.

Jude's eyebrows flew up, and he saw her glance at her watch. A spasm of guilt twisted inside him. She was on time. His comment had been antagonistic.

Without speaking, Jude moved to her desk and sat down, putting what he assumed was her laptop case down by the side of her chair.

'Thank you, Mrs Gresham,' Richard said. 'I'll want you to organise some travel and accommodation for me, for next Monday and Tuesday. I'm going to London and I'll give you the details later. But for now, if you can carry on with what I asked you to do yesterday?'

Helen murmured and withdrew.

For a few moments, there was silence in the office. Through the open windows came the sound of voices and a burst of laughter. Somewhere, a bee droned lazily in the sunshine. A gentle mix of lavender and citrus aftershave hovered in the air.

Jude sighed and sat back in her chair, lifting her laptop onto her desk and opening it. 'This was at home. It's a quote I was working on for a new customer. Perhaps you'd like to take it over, although I've nearly finished it. I've just sent it to you on the company email.'

Still silence. Richard gave no sign he had heard her.

After about five minutes he raised his head. 'You were saying?' His voice was cool. He didn't know how else to speak to her. He couldn't allow himself to treat her as he'd treated Anna, but he hadn't formed a different relationship with her yet. Frowning, he touched the email icon on his desktop. A quick glance showed him the quote.

'I've just sent you the information about a quote I was working on at home for a new customer,' she repeated patiently. 'I've almost finished it and I can keep on with it, if you like, and get it done.'

'Oh, no.' Richard shook his head. 'I'd better look at it. You've probably made a mess of it. I've already noticed Ian Grey deals with orders.'

Jude pressed her lips together and looked down at her keyboard.

Richard opened the file and glanced at it.

A letter from Aurora Technology thanking the firm for their custom and agreeing to work on the terms agreed, which they would submit for final consideration as soon as possible. He clicked on the next document. Ah, here were the terms. He ran his eye over the figures, his attention sharpening. They were good. It was unlikely he would have done as well himself. He looked up. 'Who negotiated this? Ian Grey?'

'No. No, I did. Ian's...' Jude hesitated. 'Ian's good at taking over when something's in place. He isn't so good at setting up new orders.'

'Running him down?' Richard's lip curled. 'I'm sure we'll find he set this up.' He continued to look through the order and went still, his attention caught by another email.

"*Dear Miss Drayton,*

We were delighted to discuss this order with you. Despite our resolve, you have persuaded us to accept your figures and we must add it was a pleasure to concede. We will look forward to dealing with you personally, as you assured us was possible. We are now only awaiting the final confirmation of these figures."

As his mind went over what he had just read, the small seed of hope lodged in his heart sent out a shoot. No matter which way he turned, it seemed Jude was telling the truth and the evidence was there to support most of what she'd been saying. Would he find she was telling the truth about *everything*? Would he, in fact, discover the reports he'd received about her were nothing but lies?

He wished, very much, for them to be nothing but lies.

Closing the file, Richard looked at her. She was staring out of the windows. He took in the defensive set of her head on her slim neck, her stiff shoulders, her arms folded across her waist. Nothing could disguise the attractiveness of her figure, the lively intelligence of her face with those big, dark-grey eyes. He remembered with a sharp pang the feel of that body and the sweet taste of her lips. No woman had ever affected him the way Jude did, from the moment he'd first laid eyes on her last Saturday. That day had been magical, and he'd so been looking forward to seeing her again, taking her out, building a relationship, wondering if he'd maybe found his life partner.

Until he'd discovered she was the very woman he'd been told was his father's last mistress or manipulator—whatever you wanted to call it.

He cleared his throat and said something he hadn't intended to. 'I have some ideas I've roughed out which I'd like you to look at. About some software development I'm thinking of. Let me know what your opinion is and whether you know of a firm who might develop it. I'll send it through now.' He turned to his laptop and tapped a few keys.

She appeared startled.

'Problems?'

'We usually have all our software developed by Master Systems.'

'I know, but this may not be suitable for them. I'd ask them first, but you know the British market better than I do and you might be able to suggest someone more suited for the job.'

He heard himself inviting her to become involved with his ideas for future software developments for his latest laptop and, he'd wondered, for the Aurora Mercury as well, with utter amazement.

Why was he doing this? He'd been going to ask her to pull up the personnel files of the management team and to sort out anyone who was nearing retirement age. A PA job, so why this change of heart? His eyebrow lifted self-mockingly as he acknowledged he was believing her. Which meant there was a lot of business potential there, waiting for him to harness.

He watched as she looked at her screen and tapped the keyboard, obviously downloading the information he'd just sent through. Okay, enough gawping at Jude. It was time for him to get to grips with this place. He started looking at the figures and information about Aurora which he'd asked Helen to send through to him.

An uneasy silence fell in the room, broken only by the occasional tap of keyboards or the ringing of the phone in the outer office. Jude knew Richard had asked Helen to field all the calls for the present time, to give Richard some peace in which to orientate himself with the firm. Richard continued to go over the figures of the order Jude had been working on while Jude became fascinated with his ideas for this new software, which, if he could get it done somewhere, would give any computer firm a distinct edge on the market.

Richard stirred and looked up. 'This quote is all right,' he admitted grudgingly. 'You can complete everything this afternoon.'

Jude's head came up sharply, and she looked across at him, eyes wide. It wasn't really surprising, he thought, in view of his attitude so far. Before he could say anything, the phone in the office rang. Richard stretched out an absent hand and picked it up. Jude could hear Helen's voice.

'No, that's okay, Helen,' Richard said. 'I want to speak to Andrew.'

After the call finished, Richard regarded Jude through narrowed eyes. 'By the way, I forgot to ask. Where were you yesterday?'

Just as he'd wondered if the reports were lies, Andrew had mentioned he'd seen Jude in town yesterday.

When she was supposedly at home, *unwell*.

So, what had she been doing? And her absence backed up comments in the reports about her "frequent absences" from the firm.

'Ill,' Jude said, clearly feeling uncomfortable.

Her obvious unease made him immediately decide she was lying. 'Oh, dear. In bed all day?'

'No,' Jude said warily.

'Tell me the truth,' Richard said, feeling tired. With a dying flicker of hope he wondered if maybe it was all innocent, after all. Maybe she'd been to the doctor. In which case, she'd tell him. Depression swept through him like a black mist as he waited for her response.

'I...' she stopped, took a deep breath. 'I had... something urgent to do.'

'Why didn't you say so and ask me for the day off?'

'Would you have said yes?'

'Probably not,' he admitted painfully. 'What were you doing?'

'I'd rather not discuss that.'

'It was hardly...' Richard paused, fiddling with a pencil on his desk. He raised his eyes once more, fixing her with an icy stare. 'It was hardly ethical of you to take time off for this... urgent business. Time that in effect belongs to me, as I am the one now paying your salary.'

An excerpt from one report danced in front of his eyes. "Miss Drayton is frequently absent from the office. The staff are never sure whether she will be available. This is unsettling, but it is fortunate that the second-in-command is always available if there are any difficulties with production or personnel."

Richard sighed.

True?

Or not true?

Helen said she wasn't often absent, but maybe Helen was covering up?

'If you've finished looking at the software ideas, you can send them back,' he said curtly, still unable to decide which was the true Jude. Arch-manipulator, liar and skiver, or hard-working and brilliant? As soon as he swung one way, something set him off and he went back to his original opinion. 'This afternoon, I want you to pull up the files of the management team and go through them for me, picking out the ones near retirement. You can send them over and I'll take them home and look through them sometime soon.'

'Now wait a minute.' Jude was on her feet, anger blazing in her eyes.

Richard looked at her with surprise.

'I said I wouldn't help you close this factory down. I know everyone here. A lot of them are my friends. I won't be the one to pick them out for the scrap heap. If you want someone to do that, then do it yourself or find somebody else, because I won't.'

'Miss Drayton,' Richard said, his brows snapping together as his hand slapped on the desk in emphasis. 'You haven't any choice. It's becoming very boring to keep on pointing this out to you, but you are in my employ and you will do as I tell you.' He stood up and collected his jacket from the back of his chair, shrugging his broad shoulders into its perfect fit as he walked towards the door. As he reached it, he turned to look at her. He'd almost believed she's been ill yesterday. More fool him. She was still an enigma, and he was still very unsure about her.

Shaking his head, a sigh escaping his lips, he turned, and left the room.

7

The rest of the week passed. Jude was silently miserable in the face of Richard's coolness. Despite her initial protest, he'd made her work through all the personnel files of not just the management, but everyone in the entire factory, tagging anyone who would be sixty or over by the end of the close-down month. He also wanted her to isolate the files of workers who caused trouble or took a lot of time off work, but in all honesty, Jude knew there was no-one who came into that category. Since she'd taken over the running of the firm, most of the workforce was content and if there were those who weren't, they kept quiet.

By Friday evening, Jude could only look forward to the weekend and hope that Richard either didn't know about the firm's annual dance or had decided not to attend.

He shattered her hopes just before it was time to leave.

She'd been aware for some time, as she read through yet another of the files remaining on her computer, that Richard was watching her. It made her feel uncomfortable, but she got on with her work quietly and with dignity, making no more complaints about the tasks he'd had given her. She was pinning her hopes on the job at Master Systems. The job advert had appeared online yesterday, and an application form had arrived in her inbox, courtesy, she knew, of David. The best thing to do was to keep a low profile until she could get away from Aurora Technology and Richard Blake.

It didn't matter about her regrets or her feelings for him. She had to get away.

'I understand it's the firm's annual dance tomorrow night?' Richard's voice cut through her contemplation.

Startled, Jude's hand jerked on her mouse, sending the cursor all over the page, as she raised her eyes to look at his face, angular and shadowed, his eyes an impenetrable cool, golden brown as he watched her.

Running his hand through his thick hair in a gesture which was becoming familiar to her, Richard leaned back in his chair, a faint smile on his face. 'I think we'd better go together, don't you agree?'

Jude could feel her mouth fall open. She was at a loss for words. Under normal circumstances, she could think of nothing she would like better than go to the dance as Richard's partner. Under *normal* circumstances. What was this invite about, anyway? In view of his dislike, she'd been sure, if he was coming, he'd have wanted to avoid her for the entire evening.

In fact, she'd been sure someone as charismatic as Richard would have quite a few beautiful women lined up to go with him, so why on *earth* was he suggesting they go together?

She closed her mouth and found her voice. Inherently honest, she said exactly what was in her mind. 'That's a ridiculous suggestion, in view of the way you feel about me.'

She watched him, a puzzled frown on her face, seeing a variety of expressions flit over his clean-cut, mobile face. Too many to analyse, but enough to show her he was conflicted.

His face ended up denoting confusion. 'Why, indeed? Good question and one I'm not sure of the answer to, if you want me to be honest. Perhaps because we need to show a united front to everyone?'

That was a pretty weak excuse in view of the fact the whole factory and indeed, most of the local area was aware she'd been removed from her post before he'd even turned up. "United front" were the last two words which came to mind. 'I'd rather not.'

'Why?'

'Oh, come on—after this week?' Her eyebrows flew up, and she knew her derision was clear from the curl of her lip and the way she dismissed him, turning to close down her laptop. Out of the corner of her eye, she saw Richard flush, his lids veiling his eyes.

'Well, yes,' he admitted slowly. 'Nevertheless, we *shall* go together, to show a united front. As with everything else, you really have no choice.'

'Oh, but I do,' Jude murmured, a dangerous glint in her eyes. 'Monday to Friday, nine to five-thirty, my time is yours, Mr Blake, but otherwise, you have no claim on me. I do have a choice. And my choice is to go alone.' She stood up and gathered her things together. 'No doubt I shall *see* you there, and no doubt we shall exchange some polite conversation, but I don't want you as my partner for the whole evening.'

It would be unbearable, Jude realised, knowing the memory of the Saturday spent up at that beautiful waterfall lingered on in her brain. What had happened that day had been wonderful and promised so very much—until she'd found out who Adam was and how he really felt about her. To have him calling for her and escorting her to the dance, continually at her side would be a mockery. They might well spend a pleasant evening, but next week he would stride in here, no doubt being cool and withdrawn, and inside, unseen, she would, yet again, bitterly regret her decision. This time, she was forewarned, and she wasn't going to lay herself open to further hurt at his hands.

She walked over to the door and opened it before turning to face him. 'So thank you, but no thanks,' Jude said, and left before he tried to persuade her otherwise.

The following evening, Jude parked her car at the back of the hotel and caught up her long skirts as she climbed out. Her dress was of fine russet silk, fitting close to her slim but curvaceous body, flaring out from the hips to fall in soft folds to her ankles, where it danced and swayed as she walked. Her hair was caught up high on her head, with tendrils falling round her face to soften the severity of the chignon. Heavy gold earrings and a gold necklace completed her outfit, and she knew she looked good. She *needed* to look good. She'd taken quite a battering this past week.

Pausing in the warm, brightly-lit reception area of the local hotel, she slipped her wrap from her shoulders. Andrew French was there, drink in hand, talking to one of the managers from the factory. Jude nodded at them.

The manager smiled his greeting and turned to his wife, who'd just emerged from the cloakroom. They moved off together to find the rooms booked for the night by the firm.

'Jude.' Andrew advanced across the richly red carpet, hand outstretched. Jude looked with affection at the elderly man who'd proved to be her staunchest supporter in the face of old Mr Blake's continued stubbornness. 'You're looking very lovely this evening, my dear.'

'Thank you, Andrew. How are you?'

'Very well and frankly, enjoying my leisure. I haven't seen you for some time. Well, except last Tuesday in town. I waved, but you didn't see me. I mentioned it to young Richard when I phoned him. Asked him to pass on my good wishes and tell you to pop in for a cup of tea sometime.'

So that explained the ending of the truce. It was as she'd thought. Andrew had inadvertently presented Richard with direct evidence she hadn't been ill, as she'd told him. Ah, well, no matter. It had happened.

Jude looked at Andrew with a steady gaze. She didn't suspect him of wishing her harm. Quite the contrary, he'd been one of her strongest defenders during her earlier reforms. But he might know if anyone had been in the habit of sending reports through to Richard in America. Someone might have mentioned that it would be a good idea to keep Richard informed…?

'Ah… Andrew,' she began.

'Yes?'

'Have you… or do you know if anyone else… sent Richard any reports about how the factory was progressing?'

'Good thinking, Jude. Quite. We had to, you know.'

Jude went cold.

'After all, he held his mother's shares, even if his father had thrown him out, so it entitled him to a shareholder's report, didn't it? Must have pleased him to see the profits rising, eh?'

Jude grinned weakly and nodded her head in agreement. Yes, of course. The company's annual report which went to every shareholder. She shrugged. Foolish to think Andrew could have helped her.

'Ah. Talk of the devil…'

With a sense of the inevitable, Jude turned her head and watched Richard approach, immaculate in a well-cut dinner jacket, white shirt gleaming, his brown hair still somewhat unruly despite the formality of his dress. He was stunning. Jude had seen him in jeans, a formal suit, and now black tie, and he carried them all off to perfection. Her heart lurched as she sucked in a quiet breath, her heart rate speeding up to almost twice its rate.

'The devil?' Richard said, a faint smile lifting one side of his mouth. 'Andrew. Good to see you again.' Leaning forwards, he shook the older man's hand. 'It was kind of you to ring and offer your help. Be assured I'll call on you if I need to. Jude... you take my breath away.'

His smouldering look of appreciation made her cheeks stain with colour. What the hell was he playing at, saying something like that and sounding—even *looking*, for goodness sake—as if he really meant it?

'Just talking about you. I was telling Jude here how we kept you up to date with things by sending you the annual report.'

Richard shot her a sharp glance. She flushed again under his scrutiny, but this time in irritation. Was this more ammunition for him, she wondered, that she was trying to find out who'd sent him that rubbish?

'Don't suppose you need to call on me for help, anyway. Jude here keeps everything ship-shape. She can lay her hands on anything, quote you any figures you care to ask her for. Never known anyone who works so hard. Anyway, I'll leave you to it,' he said over his shoulder as he turned towards the private rooms. 'Leave you to it. See you later, no doubt.'

'Oh, but—' Jude stepped forward as if to follow him, and was brought up short by Richard catching hold of her hand. Turning, she found him looking at her, an unfathomable expression in his eyes.

'Two questions,' he said under his breath. 'First, why is it so important for you to find out who sent me those reports? And second, you can "quote me anything about the firm" I might care to ask, eh? Find me anything I might want to know about? And you work harder than anyone Andrew's ever known?'

'Somewhat more than two questions, Mr Blake.'

He shrugged. 'I think you know full well the last three are linked. Well? Let's have the answer to the first question.'

The stupidity of the man. Surely he realised she'd like to confound those damned lies? When she left Aurora, for it was almost one hundred percent certain she would, she wanted to leave with a good reference from Richard Blake—and his apology.

'Of course it's important to know who sent that rubbish to you. If I knew, I might understand what was at the back of it. It might lessen the hurt it's caused me. And I'd know who it was gunning for me.'

Richard stared at her for a full thirty seconds. 'Okay. Now, what about Andrew? Was it true what he said?'

'Why ask me?' Jude's voice was flat. 'Would you believe me if I said yes?'

'I think...' Richard paused, before continuing slowly. 'I think you'd deny it if it *wasn't* true.'

It was Jude's turn to stare at him in silence. Shock made her cold. Was this the start of believing her? If only he would realise what he'd been sent was simply someone who'd got it in for her. Sometimes, it seemed possible, like now, but she couldn't trust him. Odd that, because she felt he was a trustworthy man.

'I think you'd never claim such things yourself, but you'd deny it if it wasn't true,' he repeated.

Jude continued staring. Their gazes met and locked. It was as if someone had knocked all the breath from her body. After a few stunned moments, she turned on her heel and took rapid refuge in the Ladies cloakroom. Once within the safety of its confines, she leaned up against the washbasin and stared at her flushed face in the mirror.

Her hand came up to her throat where a pulse beat wildly. Both hands covered her burning cheeks, but all she could see was Richard's face, Richard's brown eyes steady on her own.

Jude shook her head. She didn't understand what he was playing at. Offensive and distrusting one minute, acknowledging her honesty the next minute. Showing her a glimpse of the man she'd seen that enchanted Saturday. Which was the real Richard Blake? Who did everyone else see? Why was he playing this cat-and-mouse game with her? She knew she was interested in him, fool that she was, and he was hurting her daily. She'd got her feelings under tight control, but if she finally convinced him he was wrong about her, she'd be lost, because Adam would return. Damn it! Damn him! All she wanted was civilised courtesy until she could walk out and take up the job with Master Systems, and never see him again. That would be the best way. The safest way. She'd been burned before and was hesitant about exposing herself again.

She straightened up and flexed her shoulders, grim determination filling her mind. By now, he'd have joined everyone else in the function room, and she could slip in unseen. Deciding to keep a close watch on him, she'd make sure she was on the opposite side of the room for the rest of the night.

Abandoning her wrap, Jude went out into the reception area. As she moved across the foyer, she was aware of a figure straightening up from a leaning position against the wall and falling into step just behind her. She didn't need to look round to see who it was.

She knew.

She knew it would be Richard.

She was acutely aware of the feel of his hand on the small of her back as he went with her into the parquet-floored function room, illuminated by a soft glow from the lights on the flock-papered walls.

There were scatterings of small tables, with chairs grouped around them. A bar at one end of the room was doing a good trade. People moved from group to group, chatting, and a few people were dancing in the middle of the floor.

As the evening progressed, Jude talked to various people with Richard always at her side. Basic courtesy meant she had to introduce him to both working colleagues and guests from outside. Reluctantly, she had to listen as people told Richard how lucky he was to have had someone so able to take over after his father's stroke. She had to be attentive to Richard and smile as he talked easily to the people at the dance, the whole time reminding her repeatedly of Adam. If only he was. Then she'd be revelling in the evening, loving every moment. She'd have pressed into his side. She'd have laughed up into his eyes, exchanged secret looks, held his hand... ah, she was being stupid, stupid, stupid. He was her enemy, plain and simple.

Despite trying to instil common sense into her mind, she was constantly aware of him, *achingly* aware of him, his hand gentle on her arm, the small of her back or her shoulder. She loved his quick grin, his easy laughter, his deep, caressing voice, and wished she could find herself in his arms again. The evening grew increasingly painful.

'Jude.'

She turned to find Ian Grey looking from her to Richard and back again, an air of puzzlement on his face.

'I didn't think you and he...?' He gestured to Richard's broad back, turned towards them as he exchanged pleasantries with the mayor of Crossfield.

'We aren't... we don't...' Jude couldn't answer Ian's question. She didn't understand herself what Richard was doing, never mind explaining it to Ian.

'But all evening... I've been watching. He's most attentive.' Ian's eyes narrowed speculatively. 'If I didn't know better, I'd say you and he are...' he shrugged.

A couple.

The words floated unsaid between them.

Richard turned round.

'Ian,' he said coolly.

Jude hid a smile. It wasn't a very warm welcome.

Ian angled himself between them like a sheep dog trying to cut a particular ewe from the flock. His intentions were obvious. Separate them. It didn't bother Jude too much, because the evening was becoming a trial from her perspective, but she saw Richard frown.

Ian placed his hand on Richard's shoulder, edging him across the floor, away from Jude. 'I'm so pleased you could come to our little do. We weren't sure, you know, if you could make it. Wondered if you had something else arranged, maybe?' He gave a short laugh. 'Now, let me take you over and introduce you to—'

'Thank you,' Richard interrupted, as he subtly displaced Ian's hand, turning back to Jude. 'I'm escorting Miss Drayton. Would you like to take us both over? Or on second thoughts, perhaps just leave it? We're bound to meet up with whoever it is during the evening.' His voice was casual, his attention obviously elsewhere.

Ian directed a look of baffled annoyance at him before composing his face and murmuring his delight in taking them both over to meet his friends.

Richard looked at Jude and shrugged, his eyebrow rising in resigned acceptance, and she turned away to hide her amusement. They followed Ian across the crowded floor, weaving in and out between groups of people, stopping now and then as they were delayed by someone who wanted to speak to them. They came up to two men, deep in conversation. Ian introduced them and for a few moments, the group made stilted conversation before Richard took Jude's hand in his and moved away.

Surprisingly, Ian followed. Dropping in a comment here, a comment there, he implied he was with them, and they were a group. As he knew most of the people they spoke to, it was hard to freeze him out, and it caused Jude to cringe as she witnessed the attempts made by Richard to shake him off, and Ian's total inability to see he wasn't wanted.

Just after the buffet supper, during which Richard had made sure Jude had everything she needed, they announced the results of the Blind Auction. This was an annual event, and the bidding had taken place during the preceding week.

'I didn't know about this,' Richard murmured in Jude's ear as they stood to one side of the small dais which held the band, and, at the moment, Alec Gresham, who was about to announce the winners. 'Who benefits?'

'The workforce decides. There's a small committee who arranges it all and chivvies everyone for prizes. This year, it's for a Women's Refuge but a small amount's going to the local dog rescue.'

Richard listened, his face serious as prizes and winners were named, sometimes laughing at the actual prize itself. 'I like that,' he whispered, his breath touching her cheek. 'A home-made cake every month for a year. And the one before, the thorough spring clean.'

'It's all a bit of fun, but it does good within the community. People donate what they can.'

Ian sidled over. They'd briefly lost him while they had supper, but now he re-attached himself. Once the auction was over, amidst much laughter and applause and the satisfying announcement that this year the firm had raised nearly one thousand pounds, Richard wandered over to Alec and exchanged a few sentences. Jude saw Alec's eyebrows fly up as he shot a look at his new employer, before they shook hands and Richard came back to Jude's side.

'What was all that about?'

'Nothing. Just something I wanted to speak to Alec about.'

Ian looked from one to the other, and as they moved off, he followed.

After fifteen minutes of being shadowed, having their conversations with others interrupted or embellished, Richard frowned, his mouth narrowing into a thin line.

'Jude... would you like to dance?' He gestured to the dancefloor, his tone exasperated.

Jude swallowed. This was impossible. She ought to refuse. To be in his arms again, feeling his hard muscles, taking in his unique smell of citrus aftershave, expensive cotton and warm skin...

But without waiting for an answer, he led her onto the dance floor, slipping an arm round her waist. She burned at his touch and swayed towards him before pulling back. He didn't seem to notice, just settled into the beat and moved without talking, his dancing smooth. Her hands gradually relaxed on his shoulders and the knot in her stomach dissipated. For a few moments, she allowed herself the luxury of imagining the dance meant something.

'I wanted to get away from Ian,' Richard said at last, lifting his head so he could smile down at her.

So don't imagine he asked you to dance for your charms, my girl, Jude told herself, his words acting better than anything to bring her back to reality. Despite that, she closed her eyes and drew in a deep breath of warm cotton, citrus aftershave and...*him*, and her pulse fluttered.

'Does that man ever know when to give up?'

Her eyes snapped open. 'Um, no... not often.' Jude smiled. 'It's better to just walk away from him, mid-flow. He never seems to notice. I thought at first it would seem appallingly rude, but soon realised I was wasting my time worrying about it. But he *is* good at carrying out orders, accountancy, writing contracts. If he has a direction, his energy is boundless, and he saves me an awful lot of chasing about.'

Richard laughed and spun her round as the music picked up pace.

Feeling the softness of his breath on her cheek, she became aware his hands had tightened on her body. She swore she felt the fleeting touch of his mouth on her hair and she shivered. Dropping her eyes, afraid he would see the longing in them, she moved a little closer, melting into his warm strength.

'Let's make sure we're on the far side of the dance floor when the music stops.' Richard grinned at her. 'I shouldn't say it, but the man grates on me.'

'Unfortunately, he seems to grate on most people,' Jude sighed. 'I feel sorry for him sometimes, but then he does something else that annoys me and I forget all my sympathetic tendencies. I just try to avoid him as much as possible, but I warn you, he likes to be told he's doing the job well... at least ten times a day.'

Shaking his head, he laughed again. 'Let's forget him,'

He manoeuvred her to the far end of the dance floor, where the shadows were deepest. As the dance ended, he loosened his hold, and as she backed away, he gently kissed her lips.

Jude's insides melted and her mouth opened to his. They clung together, unaware of the room behind them, the other guests, the music which had started up again. Jude, and it seemed Richard also, was re-living the ecstatic connection made by the waterfall. After minutes, unnerved, they drew apart. Richard turned away, his fingers coming up to touch his lips as Jude lifted her hands to cheeks reddened by more than just the heat of the room. For a few moments, neither of them could move. Eventually, without a word, Jude turned towards the room filled with colleagues and friends and, head high, walked forwards into the throng of guests.

8

Richard arrived home at High Foss Hall, where the Blakes had lived for three generations since his grandfather had made a fortune in the woollen trade, on the Tuesday night after the weekend of the dance.

He'd been in London for a couple of days. During that time, he'd successfully banned all thoughts of Jude Drayton from his mind, but now he was back, and his mind had already started to mull over his confused thoughts and feelings, both of which he felt incapable of getting to grips with.

Stripping off his tie and hanging up his suit, Richard continued to fret. Everyone who spoke well of Jude couldn't be wrong. Yet... was it possible she was a very clever woman who knew how to manipulate people to her own advantage? A supreme con artist? They existed, after all.

His original intention at the dance had been to present a united front, but he knew other motives had driven him. Motives which had caused his resolve to weaken, allowing himself to relax in her company. Motives which had led to the dance, and that pleasing, but very unintentional, kiss.

No wonder Jude had disappeared later. They'd been enjoying themselves, he was certain, although for him—maybe for her as well, he admitted—it was a mixed enjoyment. His mind wasn't made up about her yet.

He needed to concentrate on what he wanted to do with Aurora and to get this mess with Jude sorted.

Richard's father had been unable to rest on the laurels of his own father's success, and he'd opened, in Crossfield, a small factory making electronic parts for radios and televisions. It was this factory which had later been extended and changed direction to become Aurora Technology, making home computers, which were now a thing of the past.

Everyone used smart phones or laptops and because of his father, Aurora got left behind... until Jude had taken over. If it was really her work, she'd done an amazing job in the last several years to bring the company back from the brink of closure to being one of the best business system suppliers in the country—even Europe—and the strong partnership she'd built with Master Systems had to be of benefit to both firms.

Sighing, he pulled on an old and comfortable cotton shirt and well-worn jeans, brushed his hair and ran downstairs. Tonight, he'd arranged to have dinner at High Foss with David Eller, the first time the two friends had met since Richard had come back to Crossfield.

In the modernised kitchen, Mrs Miller, the housekeeper, was putting the final touches to the meal she'd prepared for Richard and his guest. Richard stood by the open French windows of the sitting-room, a glass of whisky in his hand as he looked out across the lawns and flowerbeds, over fields heavy with grass waiting for the foragers, to the hills rising high in the distance. He was pleased to be back home, although his meetings had been interesting. He'd made several good contacts and, in passing, had heard further compliments about Jude.

Stretching and flexing his shoulders, Richard took a sip of the smoky liquid, letting it roll round his mouth, listening to the evening chorus of birdsong, smelling the grass as the dew fell.

He felt almost tempted to abandon his plans for the evening and find Jude, take her to the top of Greenside Fell to watch the magnificent sunset he knew was in store later. And, he admitted, not just to watch the sunset either. He knew the taste of her mouth again. He'd rediscovered it at the dance and it was eating at him.

A frown creased his face.

Jude, Jude, Jude.

Damn it, her name was never absent from his mind these days.

Who hated her so much?

Was there any truth in it all?

How come no-one else had noticed all these problems she was supposed to have?

Those reports... so damned cool and objective, tying her so inextricably with his father, whom he hated so bitterly.

How could they be *all* lies?

Maybe she'd wanted money and a position and saw her chance with an ailing, rich man in need of someone to take charge of Aurora? *Was* she a passenger in the firm? No-one had indicated she was so far. *Was* she someone who talked indiscreetly, giving away information that should be kept under wraps?

Richard put his glass down on a nearby table, the evening and the birdsong turning sour. His usually clear judgement was clouded, his acuity confused, as the conflict continued to rage inside him. The reports, so damning, so concise. Jude, so lovely, so strong.

Jaw clenched, he stared unheeding at the beauty of the evening as the hand in his pocket tightened into a fist.

The sound of a car pulling in through the gates distracted him and he sighed with relief. Just as well David had arrived.

Turning, Richard walked through the sitting-room towards the hall. Strange that David, too, had ended up in the computing world, although in the software sector rather than hardware. Still, interesting.

Richard opened the front door. 'David. It's good to see you again.'

David Eller stepped out of his car, a grin splitting his face. 'Richard. You look good. The States have obviously agreed with you.'

David ran up the steps and the two friends shook hands, regarding each other with pleasure. David stepped back and slapped Richard's shoulder as his friend turned to lead the way into the house. 'So, tell me all. Billionaire yet? If not, you must be damn close.'

They'd both attended the same school in Bradfield and gone on to the same university. After university, their ways had split, but they'd always kept in touch. When Mr Blake parted company with his son, it was to David's flat Richard had gone, staying there for a couple of months before deciding to travel to America.

'I don't bother counting any more,' Richard said dryly, raising his eyebrow and smiling. 'Drink?'

'Please. Whisky.'

'I can't believe we've ended up back in the same patch,' Richard commented, pouring the drink and handing David the glass.

'Mmm.' David took a swallow and sighed in appreciation. 'That's good. Same patch? You intend to stay around?'

Richard looked cautious.

'Hey, come on,' David exclaimed. 'This is me, remember?'

Inclining his head toward the dining-room, Richard smiled. 'Yes, okay. This is you. And this is strictly off-record. But yes, I might stay. I never wanted to go, if you remember.'

'Rumour has it you're going to close the place down, and completely re-vamp it for Blake Laptops or sell and go back to America?'

'Small town rumours,' Richard said, his hand on the back of his chair. 'My email said review, as far as I recall.'

Both men sat down at the table as Mrs Miller pushed in a heated trolley. 'If that's all right, I'll be off now,' she said, taking the covers of the dishes and laying them out on the table.

'No problem. Thanks, Mrs Miller. Come in later tomorrow. I'll make sure I put all this in the dishwasher.'

'I'd appreciate that. Thank you, Mr Blake.' She left the room, closing the door quietly behind her.

'Efficient,' David commented.

'She's the wife of the local farmer. Her children are grown up, and she needs more to do, so she told me. Suits me. I don't want anyone living in, and she's a damned wonderful cook who keeps the place looking beautiful. She's also happy to stay late on occasions like this.'

'You're right about her cooking,' David said, sniffing the delicious smells.

'Help yourself.'

The two men took generous platefuls of aromatic beef stew, full of vegetables, and added soft, floury potatoes. Richard poured glasses of red wine, deep and glowing in the soft lighting.

'Mmm. Good. Now, what was it you were saying? If you think I've forgotten and I'm letting it pass, think again. Staying? What about Blake Laptops?'

'No reason not to open up the British and European markets more. Use the facilities at Aurora.'

'Oh, yes? And what about Aurora?'

'What about Aurora? No reason we can't produce both, is there?'

David stared at his friend and took a mouthful of wine. 'Well, well, well. And why not? It's an excellent machine and well worth keeping it going.'

'I'd have to go over to America occasionally.' Richard shrugged. 'Maybe twice a year, maybe more often. But...' he smiled faintly, studying the play of light through the clouds on the distant hills, 'I never wanted to go in the first place. And now... no reason not to stay, from what I can see. Except...' his voice tailed off.

'Except?'

'I don't know. Every time I go to the factory, the damned memories come back. I lose confidence. No, don't laugh, I really do. I have to lay my father's ghost.'

'It must be hard,' David said slowly, his smile fading. 'The bastard certainly did his best to reduce you to a gibbering wreck. But the place is so different now. That at least must make it easier?'

'I suppose so.' He stared blankly at his glass, his hands clenching before he shrugged his shoulders and attempted to relax. 'But you, David. I find it amazing that not only are you back here but also that you're in computers and so strongly linked with Aurora.'

'Come on. I'm not *in* computers, not like you. I'm a management man. Oh, I'm quite au fait with them, don't get me wrong, but they aren't my lifeblood like they are for you. My next move could be anywhere, as long as it's managerial.'

Once they'd eaten, the stew being followed by an apple pie with rich cream, they moved into the garden, taking coffee and brandy with them.

Once sitting on the wrought-iron chairs, Richard shot a glance at his friend. 'You're quiet, David?'

'Yes. Well... talking of moves. I've been chewing something over for a few days. Honestly, I'm not too sure what to do, but...' David hesitated.

'Go on,' Richard spoke mildly enough. 'Is this a feeler?'

'Heavens, no.' David exclaimed. 'You don't need me for your management team. You need someone who has all the specifications at their fingertips. Your own department's fantastic, but it's well overseen. Which brings me back to what I started to say.' He stirred his coffee, clearly prevaricating as he lifted the cup and took an appreciative sip.

'Whatever it is, you seem somewhat reluctant to spit it out,' Richard grinned at his friend in the deepening dusk, as the sun sank in a soft haze of colour behind the hills and cast dark shadows across the fields. Somewhere in the distance, an owl hooted and was answered by one nearer to home.

'Well,' David explained, now fiddling with the spoon in the saucer of his cup, 'I'm breaking a confidence, but...' his voice tailed off again.

'David.' Richard put his cup down in exasperation and leaned forwards, his eyes alight with amused curiosity. 'This must be real top secret stuff.' A touch of an American accent tinged Richard's deep voice.

'Damn it.' David sounded annoyed. 'You needn't joke. This is serious and involves someone else, as well as you and me.'

'Sorry... sorry,' Richard soothed, sitting back in his chair again, his curiosity aroused. He'd only been back a couple of weeks. What could David want to tell him which involved both of them *and* a third party? 'Come on. You've started this now, so you may as well finish.'

The darkness was now complete. The two men had chosen not to have any lights on outside. Instead, the soft yellow of a couple of indoor lamps spilt out from the open windows onto the terrace. David was just a quiet, dim shape opposite. The soft air was full of the scent of flowers and damp grass.

'Jude Drayton came to ask me for a job.'

Richard drew in his breath, the hiss audible in the night's silence. 'So that's where she was.'

'Richard, please...' David sounded distressed. 'You must understand Jude came to me in confidence. Just as you asked me not to divulge your plans for Aurora and Blake Laptops and said you trusted me, now I'm asking you not to let her know I've spoken to you about this. *I'm* trusting *you* on this matter. I wouldn't be telling you, but I couldn't believe what she was saying to me. It seems you've been receiving some kind of communication about the factory. Reports or something, and they've condemned Jude out of hand. Apparently, they said she was your father's mistress and her position in the firm is just a sham. I shouldn't need to ask, but is this true? Receiving reports, I mean?'

'It's true.'

'And you *believe* them? When they came by post and are therefore untraceable?'

There was a long silence.

'What reason do I have not to believe them?' Richard said, his voice hardly above a whisper.

'Anyone who knows Jude—properly knows her—would realise they're nothing but a pack of lies, and so should you.'

'Why should I believe that? *I* don't know the woman.' A small voice in his head taunted him with what he knew of Anna and what he'd seen of Jude in the previous week, both of which backed up David's comments and make a laughing stock of the reports. 'It's only too easy to accept she might have manipulated my father, with his penchant for younger women and enjoyment of being flattered. Manipulated him to gain the position at Aurora and—'

'So if that's the case,' David interrupted, 'why not let her go? Apparently, she's offered, but you've refused to release her from her contract and refused to give her a reference. Anyway, if she did indeed influence your father into appointing her, who's responsible for the turnaround there's been at Aurora? What's going on?'

Richard shifted in his chair, the legs grating on the stones in protest as his tall frame moved. 'That's a lot of questions.'

'And you're avoiding the answers.'

'I refused to release her from her contract, yes, because she's another seven or eight months to go. She said she'd go anyway, so I pointed out that if I wasn't prepared to release her from her contract, then neither would I be prepared to give her a reference if she breaks it.'

'Why?'

'Maybe because I want to get some value out of her before her contract expires?'

That was his excuse, anyway. Richard wasn't sure he could admit even to David it was the memory of Anna which had made him change his mind about instantly dismissing Jude Drayton, and keep her on. He jolted back to the present moment as David's incredulous voice cut through his reverie.

'Richard, are you mad? Get some value out of her? *Jude*? Are we talking about the same person here?'

'She's had a damn good salary for the last three years and I'd like to make sure I get some return for it. Over the next few months, Jude Drayton will learn what hard work is.' Richard's voice was grim. He might be prepared to admit doubts to himself, but David's interference only drove him back into the position where, for the last few months, Jude and his father had been irretrievably linked by the information he'd been sent.

'*You*? Teach Jude Drayton what hard work is? I agree it would be neck and neck between the two of you, but believe me, Jude knows what it is to work hard. And with little thanks or reward, apart from the rising sales figures at Aurora. Are you blind, man? Have you *looked* at your accounts over the last three years? That's one of my questions you still haven't answered, which was if Jude is just a figurehead, who is allowing her to take the credit for an incredible performance by Aurora?'

Steepling his fingers, Richard tapped them on his chin, looking pensive. Yes, David had hit the bull's eye with that one. The entire credibility of the reports did indeed fall flat with the astounding recovery of the firm.

'Maybe an outsider she's in cahoots with? They might have bought shares when the company was on the verge of going under and they can make a killing now the price of the shares has gone up?'

He hard David sigh, saw him shake his head. 'Dubiously possible, I suppose.'

'Possible, David. Not dubiously.'

'Check the list of shareholders?'

'You know as well as I do if it was the person she's working with, I'd not know, would I?'

'So this... this ephemeral partner, how does he make day-to-day decisions? She'd need to be emailing him and texting him all the time.'

'Perhaps Ian Grey sees where she's trying to go, and steps in to—'

'Ian Grey? *Ian Grey*? Don't make me laugh. Ian Grey is very good at following other people's instructions but he's incapable of sticking his neck out and taking risks like Jude's done.' David stabbed a finger under Richard's nose. 'He likes everything laid down in simple, easy-to-follow steps and he's not intuitive enough to interpret some vague ploy by a supposed collaborator which Jude is apparently trying to instigate within the firm. And if he did achieve something off his own bat, he'd never stop talking about it for days. Sorry, Richard, but no. Jude has to make instant decisions, and she does. She's a decisive and excellent CEO of Aurora. You need to drop these ridiculous ideas and understand her worth.'

'You're a bit scathing about Ian Grey, aren't you? Take the deal with your firm. I was looking at the terms only last week. All the emails are in his name, and a damn good deal it is. I mean to speak to him about it tomorrow. I intend to give him a free hand with contract negotiations from now—'

'I wouldn't. Oh, no, I really wouldn't, if I were you.' David leaned forward to place his coffee cup alongside Richard's, picking up instead his glass of brandy before settling back in his chair. 'It was Jude who thrashed out the terms of our software deal, not Ian. It was only when the terms were sorted out that she handed it all over to Ian to finish, log it all onto the computer and deal with the emails that ensued. Ian was losing your contracts hand over fist until Jude found out the reason and took over.'

'And the reason was what?'

'He antagonised customers. Approached them with a take it or leave it attitude which got their backs up. He was ill or something on one occasion, and Jude went to the meeting instead. I don't know… she got the contract and then they told her that in fact, they'd come along to tell Aurora to forget it, because of Ian Grey. Gave Jude something to consider and after that, she took over negotiating and put Ian in charge of completing everything once the terms were sorted.'

'Jude?' Richard's voice was soft and hesitant, remembering the letter he'd seen regarding one contract she'd been working on.

'Jude.'

A silence fell, broken only by another call from the owl.

David stirred and stretched. 'To anyone who knows Jude, it's obvious these reports are the product of some vicious bastard who's got a king-sized grudge against her.'

Richard sighed. 'The first one or two didn't pick on her. They told me what was going on in the firm after my father's stroke, a formal document.'

'If they were anonymous, and especially as they came by post, why did you take any notice of them? Why not write to, say, Andrew French and ask him about them?'

'Anonymous... mmm, well, there was an indecipherable scrawl at the bottom, I admit, but they were on company-headed paper and the heading said Board of Directors, so I assumed—'

'Oh, come on! It suited you to assume, be honest. No doubt they stirred up a good bit of fault-finding regarding your father and you'd have loved that, wouldn't you?'

Another silence.

Taking this for assent, David didn't let up in his attack. What Jude had spilled out had appalled him, because he cared for Jude, and he sure as hell cared for Richard. 'Am I right?'

'Yeah, yeah, yeah. They went for my father's jugular, making it clear how badly the firm was doing, you're right. Then they itemised everything that was being done to put things right. *Then*... then came the attacks on Jude.'

'Ah.' David pounced. 'So you admit they were just that... *attacks*?'

'I'll admit no such thing.' Richard stood up and took a couple of paces into the darkness of the garden. 'You know what my father was like... he had women all his life, and age was no barrier. The first implication I had that Jude Drayton wasn't what she seemed was a factual statement that the new CEO was only in post because of her connection with my father, which had started before I went to the States. Well, he did have someone then. I can remember him going off to see her.'

'You have no proof this was Jude?'

'No, but—'

'So someone tossed Jude to the lions by linking her with this previous liaison of your father's?'

Richard returned to his chair. He sank down and rested his forehead on his hand. 'Maybe.'

'This is the real root of the problem, isn't it? That she might have been your father's mistress and maybe twisted him round her little finger? I think you could accept she improved things at Aurora—if we forget the mysterious partner. Your logic can surely see the firm was on the rocks and unless someone did something, it would have been liquidated. Okay, Jude pulled it round with Andrew French's support-'

'Yes. He was always behind me, too. Far-seeing, that man.'

'He'd had his stroke before she was appointed.'

'What about the suggestion her appointment was only because of their previous liaison?'

David shook his head in exasperation. 'Oh, come on, Rick. Jude was what, mid-twenties before you went off to the States, the time she's supposed to have been associated with your father. Tell me what a beautiful, intelligent girl like her would be doing with a bad-tempered, old bugger like him?'

'Money?'

'She didn't need that,' David shot back. 'She had a good job with TechDrive. That's where she came from. Come on, does she honestly strike you as being the sort of person these reports make her out to be?'

Richard huffed, a small smile lifting the corner of his mouth as he recalled his first sight of her, flying round the back of his van to confront him, then her pleasure in the walk and the picnic. Her head held high the following Monday, despite the shock of realisation when she found out who he was. Her direct gaze as she refuted his accusations, and her total fury when he suggested she had been his father's mistress... manipulator.

No. No, perhaps she wasn't the sort of person those reports had made her out to be.

But... his father *had* been seeing someone... and Jude was very young to be appointed to such a high-powered job, especially when the firm concerned had been in such a dicey situation... very young and very beautiful...

'Damn it.' Richard exploded. 'I don't know... I don't *know*... no, I suppose not, but—'

'This rubbish has certainly sowed doubts in your mind, haven't they?' David murmured. 'Accept it, Richard. Someone has it in for Jude... very thoroughly. From what Jude told me, and you tonight, this has been a planned hatchet job which to my mind makes it even more distasteful. Use your common sense and realise that, and for God's sake get it out of your head that Jude has ever had anything to do with your father. Forget those reports. Jude is sound, okay?'

9

Richard was already in the office when Jude arrived. He watched as she placed her laptop case on the floor and straightening some technical journals and papers she'd removed from it. As she did so, a printout fluttered from the top of the pile and, in the way paper sometimes could, gyrated across the floor to land almost at Richard's feet. Jude gave an inarticulate cry and stepped forward, but not quickly enough to prevent Richard from shooting her a narrow-eyed look and bending to retrieve the paper himself. He leaned back against his desk and idly glanced at it.

'Excuse me,' Jude said, 'that's mine and you have no right to look at it.'

Richard had only intended a cursory glance before returning it to her, but his attention sharpened as he picked up on the words TechDrive. That had been her last place of employment before coming here. Unintentionally, he read a little more and saw it was a print-out of a job vacancy, as second-in-command of their marketing department. 'Ah. A job vacancy. I assume you'll be applying?'

A flare of colour swept across Jude's face. 'The situation here is ridiculous, and there's no future for me here. I don't want to go back to TechDrive, but I saw the ad this morning and printed it out on impulse. I was curious enough to see what the job offered and maybe to ring and ask about the salary.'

'I've already told you I won't release you, I won't give you a reference and if you break your contract, I shall sue.'

She leaned forward and tapped some keys, clearly ignoring his barbed comment. 'The personnel files are finished. You need to look at them now. I think these are the people we could retire a little earlier than they'd hoped for.' She moved the laptop over to his desk before stepping back.

His hand shot out and grasped her wrist.

She stood very still before raising her head to look into his baffled eyes. 'If we're talking about suing, this could be construed as physical harassment, don't you think?'

'Just who are you, Jude Drayton?' he murmured, releasing her wrist before dropping his eyes to glance at the laptop she'd placed on his desk. 'What did you say these were?'.

'They're the files of people we could ask to take early retirement. They're all over sixty and we might check to see if they'd like an early retirement.'

'Yes, okay. I'll look later. Anyway, this is a diversion. Let's go back to TechDrive. Big firm. Good future. You gave that up for what? A failing, second-rate business that could well have been on the scrap heap within six months. Why did you leave? What did you do there?' Richard stepped back and sat, looking at her with genuine curiosity. What she said next would be interesting.

Jude swallowed, her lips compressing into a thin line. 'What does it matter? Why are you interested? I don't understand why you want to keep me in view of the fact you so dislike me so much. Why *not* provide me with a reference and let me go? What the hell does it matter to you?'

'You,' he shot back, 'have spent three years at this firm drawing a whacking salary and letting everybody else do the work on the strength of the fact my father was screwing you before he had his stroke, and, believe me, you'll spend the next seven or eight months learning what it is to earn your salary. I told you that before.'

Jude whitened and drew in a sharp breath of fury. 'You *bastard*. Not that rubbish again. Stop linking me with your father. I had nothing to do with him. Before I came here, I was living with...' She halted, her hand flying up to her mouth, her eyes widening in dismay.

'Living with who?' Unbelievably, a shaft of jealousy shot through Richard and he turned his head away from her furious glare.

'None of your *damned* business.'

No, it wasn't. Even Richard realised this was something he couldn't push her on. But who had she been living with? Did it have something to do with leaving TechDrive? For all he knew, she still maintained the relationship, although she'd shown little sign of being committed to someone else when he'd kissed her up at the waterfall.

He changed tack again. 'My father—'

'Your father was someone I loathed,' she spat at Richard. 'A stubborn bastard who believed nothing and had to have it rammed in his face before he would accept it, and even then, he often didn't. There were times we had to carry out some of the changes at this place behind his back. Behind his back, Mr Blake. Stubborn. Relentless. Cruel. Disbelieving. Just like his damned son, do you hear me? If he'd offered me his millions on a plate, I would have thrown them back at him.'

Richard recoiled from her utter fury, shocked by the fact she likened him to the man he'd hated. 'You... you think I'm... I'm like my father?'

'Damn right I do! You're stubborn in your persistence in believing those damned lies about me. You're relentless and cruel in your determination to persecute me because of them, despite all my denials. *You* believe nothing I say, either. Your father would take against something for no apparent logical reason. It was enough if he decided he didn't like the colour of the paper it was written on. The pair of you are indeed alike,' Jude snarled, glaring at him through a tangle of blonde hair which had fallen across her face as she leaned towards him. 'Now get it into your head, I am not staying here being insulted daily by you. I am leaving. Do I have to spell that out? L-e-a-v-i-n-g. Got it?'

Richard stared at her and took in a deep breath, repeating with steely determination, 'You are not leaving. You seem to forget, you signed a contract—'

She stepped towards him as he looked up at her from his chair. For the second time in just over a week, her hand came up and cracked across his face with enough force to knock his head sideways. There was a lot of anger in the blow.

'*Fuck* your damned contract.' Jude shouted, moving over to her desk as she started shoving things into her case. 'Sue me. I don't care. I don't care where I end up... back at TechDrive, even with dear Julian, would be better than this.'

Richard's hand came up to his reddening cheek and rubbed it, giving a slight shake of his head. 'Julian?'

A tense silence fell over the room as they stared at each other. It was broken by a knock on the door. Ian appeared, a sheaf of documents in his hand. 'The financial statements you asked for have come through from the bank. I printed them out... oh... I'm sorry.' Ian looked from Richard to Jude, malicious interest sharpening his gaze as he noticed the strained silence in the room and the clear red mark on Richard's cheek. 'Have I interrupted something?'

Jude pulled herself upright and smoothed back her hair, swallowing hard. 'No, Ian,' she answered, her voice harsh. 'You've not interrupted a damned thing.' She turned on her heel, ignoring her still-open case with the last batch of papers she'd tried to stuff in protruding wildly, and her laptop on Richard's desk, and strode to the door, but not before both Richard and Ian had seen the sheen of tears on her cheeks.

'I shall want to see you in a few minutes,' Richard said, panic entering his voice.

His only answer was the slam of the door.

'Umm, something seems to be bothering Jude. Still... nothing new...' Ian's voice trailed off.

Richard shot him a sharp look. 'What do you mean, nothing new?'

'Oh,' Ian murmured, 'she gets het up now and then. No-one takes much notice.' He paused and watched as Richard stared at the door, a frown on his face.

'Now... these statements... I think you'll find...' Ian bent over the desk, pushing Jude's laptop to one side, his finger moving over the papers he'd placed there.

Richard continued staring at the door, his mouth tight. He shook his head, full of discomfort, and tried to pull his attention back to the matter in hand, but after five minutes his concentration wavered. He straightened and ran a hand through his hair. 'Ian... before they appointed Jude—'

'She'd been at TechDrive.'

'What did she do there?'

'Um... she was on the management team, if I remember rightly. There was a rumour she was in line for appointment as head of the marketing department, but Julian Langley got the job instead. It's Julian Langley running it now and I doubt they would have had two changes in three years. She came here after that. Not surprising.'

Julian. She'd mentioned Julian.

'Not surprising?'

Ian regarded Richard, his face expressionless.

'Come on, what do you mean, not surprising? This Langley, did he have it in for her?'

'Oh, no.' Ian laughed. 'No, no. Not at all. They were an item, I believe. But there was some talk at the time... everyone assumed Jude would get the job, but Langley took his ideas straight to the CEO and that tipped the scales in his favour. Trouble was, there were some who said those ideas had been Jude's, and he stabbed her in the back. But then there were others who said she was only sleeping with him to get *his* ideas, that she would use them as part of her presentation in the interviews and Julian got wind of this, hence his visit to the boardroom.'

'What?' Richard leaned against his desk and passed a hand across his eyes. 'She and Julian Langley were *sleeping* together?'

'For two or three years, I believe.'

The relief sweeping through Richard was unbelievable.. Hell, it *had* all been lies about Jude and his father. So, all the rest as well... lies. Had to be.

'And what's your opinion about whose ideas they were?'

Ian looked cautious. 'I don't know,' he said, feigning pained innocence. 'But maybe—'

'What?'

'Why did she leave so suddenly? If they were *her* ideas, there would have been no reason for her to leave, surely? She was the innocent party. But if it was true, and they were his ideas and he knew it, perhaps he asked her to go?'

Richard stared at Ian before giving a slight shake of his head. More likely she was so disgusted with what this Julian had done, she removed herself as soon as she could. That would be more like the Jude he knew so far. If she'd been with that Langley bloke for two to three years, it must have been a serious relationship and a terrible let-down for her if the guy had pinched her ideas.

'Has she had a relationship with anyone here?' He hated himself for pumping Ian Grey for gossip about Jude, but he'd antagonised her so much he knew it would be impossible to ask her these questions himself.

'The ice maiden?' Ian gave a snort of disbelief, still smarting from her rebuff when he'd tried it on with her during her first month or two at Aurora Technology. 'No way. Perhaps she still cares about Julian Langley?'

No, Richard decided. No, she didn't care about Julian Langley, but she cared about being hurt again.

One of those reports he'd received stated Jude Drayton disrupted personnel. She certainly disrupted him. He had to find her. He had to apologise, to explain to her why… Oh, damn, he had to find her. All the stuff he'd been sent was slowly being revealed for what it was—lies—and for that, he was deeply glad, because what he'd seen of her so far had contradicted it all, anyway.

'Okay, Ian,' Richard said, pushing the papers to one side and straightening up. 'Let's leave it for now. I'll look at this online later today and come back to you on it. Send it through, would you? I'm sorry… I've another appointment and I'm running a little late…'

Ian looked after him, puzzled, as Richard moved to the door.

'Mrs Gresham…' Richard hesitated at his PA's desk. 'Miss Drayton… did she… do you know where she went?'

Ian stopped in the doorway's shadow.

'I think Jude needed to be alone, Mr Blake,' Helen suggested, her voice soothing.

'Well, yes,' Richard said, 'I do realise I'm not the most popular person with her at the moment, but I...'

Both Ian and Helen were watching him.

'Perhaps I... it's possible I've... Look, where did she go, please?' All Richard knew was that he had to find her and tell her he knew he'd been wrong and try to explain all his confused and tormented feelings... about her... about his father. Jude was innocent, as she'd claimed to be, as David had told him she was, and he was the fool.

Helen relaxed as if she had come to a decision. 'She went home, Mr Blake. I think maybe she was feeling a little... unwell.'

Richard looked at her, his eyes speaking his thanks. 'Right. Right, thank you. I'll... I'll probably be out of the office for the rest of the morning. I... yes, out of the office.'

Unaware of Ian still lurking behind him, Richard left with only one thing on his mind.

Find Jude.

Apologise to her

10

The sun rose high in the sky and the whole town seemed to celebrate the wonderful weather. Tourists idled up and down the pavements, peering at the heaped market stalls, poking and fingering the goods on display. Cafes burst at the seams. In the main square, coaches were dropping off more trippers, the women gaudy in their bright summer frocks, red-faced husbands in tow.

Jude saw none of it. She was furious, and waiting in the long queue of traffic on the main street wasn't helping. Hell, she thought the town's bypass was supposed to clear the centre of traffic, but it didn't seem to have worked. She automatically edged forward when the car in front of her moved, her hands clenched on the wheel.

She chastised herself continually. Stupid, stupid woman. Her teeth ground together in fury as she recalled his insistence they should go to the dance as partners, her refusal and, at the hotel, his obvious determination he would get his own way. He'd been so damned *nice* on Saturday and she'd kidded herself... fooled herself... especially after that gentle kiss, that maybe all would be well. Why had he kissed her, only to come in this morning being so unpleasant again? The bastard!

Jude changed gear as the traffic moved off. She'd deluded herself before that she'd detected a softening in him, even been mad enough to wonder sometimes about the expression in his eyes... but this time, she wasn't going back. Burned once before with Julian, she'd no intention of allowing her feelings for Richard Blake to develop any further. And they shouldn't have got this far in the first place.

Slamming the car door, she pelted up the steps, her key in her hand, head down, hoping no-one was around. The last thing she wanted today was to meet one of her cheerful neighbours and be drawn into a *normal* discussion about the weather or the number of tourists choking up the high street in town.

Once inside, it seemed almost impossible to cry. Her eyes burned, her throat was tight and her chest hurt, but the tears wouldn't come.

Her mobile rang. She glanced at the screen. David.

'Yes?' her voice was sharp.

'Jude,' David said. 'Did you get the job application?'

'Yes.' Jude she sank down onto the bottom step of the stairs. 'And TechDrive is advertising for someone as well. Richard saw the print-out. He's not very happy. I'm at home. We had a slight disagreement, and he brought up this bloody rubbish about his father again.'

'Oh, hell, I'm sorry. I told him he was being stupid about—'

'What do you mean, you told him? Told him what? Where did you meet him?' Jude interrupted sharply, straightening from her slumped position on the stairs.

There was a strained silence, then she heard his breath release in a hiss. 'Fuck! Let me explain. Perhaps you don't know... Richard and I have known each other for years. We went to the same school and—'

'No, I didn't bloody know,' Jude interrupted forcefully, 'otherwise, I might have been a little more careful in approaching you for a job, *and* in what I said.'

'Look, Jude, I spoke to him about the reports because they seem so far-fetched and it just isn't like Richard to take such tripe into account.'

'Go on. You'd better finish explaining now you've started.' She bit on her bottom lip. She thought David was her friend, and had spoken to him in confidence about the problems she was experiencing. She hadn't known he was a long-time friend of Richard's, and it was becoming obvious they'd talked about her. She felt let down.

'I know Richard. He's not vindictive. He's kind and sensitive-'

'You could have fooled me,' Jude said, her tone sarcastic. 'Do continue.'

'Okay, okay, I know what you think, but he is usually fair-minded. All this with you and Aurora... it's tied in with his father, as you well know. Old Mr Blake was old when he became a father, did you know that? He wasn't the sort of person who was good with children and his decision not to have kids was probably wise. I think Richard must have been one of those menopausal mistakes.' David paused, remembering the unfriendly, forbidding man who'd been father to his friend. He sighed. 'Even when Richard was only a kid, old Blake saw him as nothing but a nuisance. Come on, Jude. Think of growing up with a father like that. Richard could never understand what the problem was, and he was always trying to please him. When he came into the firm after university, Blake made his life hell, and I *mean* hell. He belittled everything Richard did, and not in private, either. The more public his humiliation of his son, the better pleased he was.'

Jude wasn't inclined to comment on what he was telling her. At the moment, she couldn't care less about Richard Blake. She wasn't at all sure she wanted her heart wrenching with this sad tale. 'Go on.'

'He blocked everything Richard tried to do on his own initiative, which as you know, included a desire to modernise the place. In fact, I sometimes think old Mr Blake was so determined to do Richard down he became blind to what was happening to the company... or maybe he'd lost his touch because of old age. I never worked it out. It all seemed so senseless.'

Jude shifted on the step, stretching out her legs and running a weary hand across her still burning eyes.

'And?' Although why she was asking to hear more, she wasn't sure. Maybe that damned soft spot she had for him, despite his arrogant stupidity? Although she shouldn't have slapped him. The first time was maybe excusable because of stress and shock, but this time? It had been uncontrolled anger and she shouldn't have given in to it, especially not at work. Plus, physical violence was never the answer.

David cleared his throat. 'Richard walked out. He had to, for his own sanity. Andrew French was someone who always said old Blake's treatment of Richard was appalling and—'

'Enough of the sob-story stuff, David.' Jude interrupted. 'You can't blame me for not feeling very sympathetic. From what you've just been saying, he's treating me exactly the way his father treated him. It was unjustifiable the first time round, and it's unjustifiable now.'

'I know, I know... but these reports he's been getting have linked you so firmly in his mind to his father, and now he's taking it out on you. You're the whipping boy.'

'Great. Has he never heard of the other side of the story? I've told him over and over again, I had nothing to do with his father. What does it take to convince him? I'm tired of trying, David. I walked out this morning and I'm not going back. He can sue or do what the hell he likes. He's not *my* father... I don't have to hang around and take it in the hope of eventually winning his approbation.'

'He's already coming round to realising it's all lies. Give him a chance. His own logic and honesty will bring him through this.'

'No, this is the end. You're very persuasive, but if you'd been in the office this morning, I don't think you'd be quite so confident. His father has done a lot of damage and I'm getting the fall-out—' She broke off as she heard a knock at the door.

'Jude?'

'Someone at the door, David. I must go. Thanks for explaining. I'll be in touch soon, okay?' Jude sighed as she tapped her phone to end the call.

The door knocker sounded again.

'Okay, okay, I'm coming,' Jude muttered, rising to her feet and putting the phone down on the small table. She opened the door and froze, astounded to see who was standing there. How *dared* he follow her here, to her home? With a flash of fury, she stepped back and swung the door shut just as Richard turned around.

With satisfaction, she slammed it closed.

11

Richard stared at the door in dismay before knocking again. Harder and more persistently than he had the first time.

Nothing.

The door remained closed, and he heard no sound from inside.

'Miss Drayton? Jude? Please. Please listen for a moment. And preferably not while I'm standing here in the street having to shout. I really want to apologise and... maybe explain a little? Please, give me a few moments of your time and then I'll go, I promise.'

'I don't want to see you. I don't want to talk to you. *Go away*! *Now*!'

'Jude,' he said again, sounding helpless. 'I'm *sorry*.'

There was a wealth of agonised apology in Richard's voice. He realised he'd been an idiot from receiving the first printed report. An idiot for not querying its source, for taking the contents so literally without asking around—hell, even asking David would have been a sensible and obvious step to take, but he'd lapped it all up, hadn't he? Gave him a reason for his inability to get reforms through, built on his lifelong dislike of his father—a dislike which had eventually ended up as hatred. And once he'd met Jude—well, he was a complete idiot for allowing the loathing of his father to colour his view of her.

Silence.

It was an impasse. He knew Jude was still there, behind the door—he could sense it somehow.

He leaned his forehead against the door, tiredness and dismay seeping through him. Surely she'd let him in, let him explain?

He tried again. 'Jude? Please can we talk this through?'

Finally, she spoke, her voice an angry hiss. 'Why are you here?'

'I told you... I need to explain. To apologise...' He swallowed and felt his hands ball into tense fists. 'To talk to you away from the factory.'

Nothing.

He began again. 'Last night... I was having dinner with David, and he queried why I believed those reports and what they'd said about you, and I told him... Jude... *please*? Do I have to stand on your doorstep and share this with your neighbours?'

Another long moment passed.

At last, the door opened. His relief flooded through him and for a moment he had to place both hands on the door frame as he staggered forwards on weak legs. Standing to one side, Jude allowed him into a long, narrow hallway, then led the way into a sunny kitchen at the back of the house. She gestured to the table in the middle of the room. Richard pulled out a chair and sat down, his elbows on the table, his fingers splayed through his hair as he gazed down at the polished surface, uncertain what to say now he was in, actually sitting at her table. He peered through his fingers. Jude was leaning back against the sink, arms folded tightly across her body, waiting in silence, glaring at him. She wouldn't give him any help.

'I'm sorry,' he repeated, helplessness lacing his voice. 'I thought... I shouldn't have goaded you this morning. I come in every morning swearing that this time it'll be different. And every morning the same bloody thing happens. I tense up and I want to lash out. At my father. But it's you who suffers, because... because...' His voice roughened and briefly, he covered his face with his hands before removing them as he exhaled heavily.

Jude remained silent, her face unfriendly.

'Would you... come and sit down?'

A tense and silent moment passed before Jude crossed to the table and sat down, her face turned away from Richard, her toe tapping impatiently on the floor.

Eventually, Jude looked at him, a frown on her face. 'Well? You forced your way in here with a load of excuses about not wanting to discuss things on the doorstep... but you don't seem very inclined to discuss much now, Mr Blake. Perhaps you'd better go after all?'

'No!' His head jerked up, troubled eyes meeting hers. 'No,' he said again, his voice quieter this time. 'Miss Drayton... Jude, if I may.' his voice softened. 'I want to apologise to you and... to ask you if you'd—'

'Apologise? For what exactly?' Jude asked, her turn now to drop her gaze to the table.

'A lot of things,' Richard murmured. 'And yet—'

Normally such an articulate man—at Blake Laptops—here, and at Aurora, he found himself inarticulate or saying totally the wrong things. The sort of things he might have expected from his father. He scrubbed his hands over his face and let them drop onto his thighs, giving a slight shake of his head at the whole situation. Yet he had to get through it and explain at least a little of his perplexities when it came to anything associated with his dad.

'Itemise them,'

He looked startled. '*Itemise* them?'

Jude stared at him. 'Yes. I think perhaps I deserve an itemised list, don't you?'

'It's not so easy to itemise everything,' Richard protested.

Jude remained silent, her eyes unrelenting as she continued to glare at him.

He sank back in his chair, misery clear on his face. 'Okay, our initial meeting was bad—'

'Our initial meeting was, on the contrary, rather good,' she interrupted.

He glanced at her, wondering if he could detect a softening in her attitude, but her face was unforgiving, her voice cold. She was, it seemed, just stating a fact.

'Our *first* meeting,' Richard corrected himself with an audible sigh, 'was good. Our second meeting was bad, but if you'd been receiving, for some months, official-looking reports purporting to be from the Board of Directors which damned you to hell and back, I think you might've found it difficult to be polite—'

'You were far from polite, Mr Blake. You were insulting and, at times, verging on being violent. Your behaviour was unacceptable and uncivilised.'

Richard flushed, his top teeth catching his full bottom lip, biting down hard. Hell, but she was making this hard, but the violence had been more on her side than his. He opened his mouth to point out she was the one who'd slapped him, but was prevented by Jude continuing to speak, her voice angry as her hand slapped down onto the table.

'I doubt *I* would have given quite so much credence to untraceable reports. I'd have preferred to find out some facts for myself, maybe emailed someone I knew, such as Andrew French or David, to get some corroboration... or otherwise... of what was going on here. I might even have stopped sulking and come over to deal with the factory myself, in view of the fact the previous enemy was powerless and I could now do what I wanted.'

There was a long pause before Richard admitted a truth he'd only just acknowledged within recent months. 'I wanted to see Aurora fail, and I was angry with you because you rescued the place.'

Now he'd accepted she was probably innocent, it became important that he redeemed himself.

He wanted her back.

Jude. Jude Anna Drayton.

Yes, he wanted her back.

Another long silence fell between them.

Jude sighed. 'Do you want a drink?'

'I... yes, I... thanks.'

'Tea? Coffee?'

'Coffee. Thank you.'

Richard's eyes followed her as she picked up the kettle, slapping the lid down on the worktop and filling it with the full force of the tap. Next, she opened a cupboard to take out a cafetière and a bowl of sugar, shutting the door with a decisive smack. When she yanked open the fridge door to remove a carton of milk, she set it down with such abruptness that milk slopped out of the top of it. Swearing under her breath, she swung round to pick up a cloth from the sink and mopped up the milk with sharp, stabbing movements which betrayed her inner tension.

The kettle boiled. Spooning coffee into the cafetière, Jude poured in the water. Taking it and the mugs, she placed them on the table, returning to pick up the milk and sugar.

'Here.' She sat down in the chair opposite Richard and pushed the cafetière and a mug across to him. 'And help yourself to milk and sugar.'

'Thanks.' He reached out for the milk but ignored the sugar.

The smell of the coffee rose, mundane and comforting in the midst of the conflict. Grateful that adding milk and holding the mug gave him time to collect his thoughts and let the atmosphere cool down a bit, Richard took a careful sip from his mug, then put his mug down and ran a finger round the rim.

'What else?'

Goodness, but she was relentless. He'd hoped for a few more moments of grace.

'Mainly the way I behaved on the first day, even though I had some excuse—'

'But we also worked quite well together, during the following week, and then, at the dance, you...' She jumped to her feet and took her mug to the sink, where she poured away her undrunk coffee. 'Your behaviour has been disgusting and unfair.'

'I'm sorry.'

Very sorry if she couldn't even sit and have a coffee with him. His own drink tasted suddenly bitter, and he pushed the mug away.

'It makes sense for me to leave, but you won't release me. Why not?'

Because he didn't want to, he knew that.

He watched her back as she remained at the sink, her hands gripping its lip.

Because he couldn't eradicate that Saturday and the effect she'd had on him.

'I'm very regretful of the things I've said and done. My father wasn't an admirable man. He treated my mother badlybadly and flaunted his affairs in her face. I hated him, but I also wanted his approval, because he was my father.' His hands clasped and unclasped as he spoke, his eyes staring into a past long gone.

He saw Jude was watching him, but there was no sympathy on her impassive face. 'And?'

Richard's eyes were full of pain. 'I think you already know. I never got his approval. No matter how I tried. Then, when I came to work for him, I got tired of trying to please him and tried instead to save the factory. He trampled my ideas into the ground. Frequently and publicly.'

Rising to his feet, he paced the floor as the remembered pain writhed inside him, as raw now as the day he'd finally given up and walked out. 'I got away. Of course I got away. But how do you forget a lifetime of being belittled and knowing your mother was being humiliated? How do you dissociate yourself from reports which corroborated everything I knew about him and linked you into it as well?'

Swinging round, he held out his hands in appeal before letting them drop to his side as he saw her expressionless face. 'I've made a success of my life and sometimes think I did it only to spite him, not that he ever cared. Now I've come back and I have to stop hating you, and stop hating that damned factory. I have ghosts to lay. A lot of them.'

'And?' She still stood with her back to the sink, arms folded.

He peered at her and noticed her eyes were over-bright, detected a sheen to them which looked like tears.

For *him*?

'I came to apologise, of course I did, but also to ask you if you'd come back... if we could try to work together. I promise I won't... Jude, please? I accept the reports were lies, and I want to start afresh with you. Because of Anna. I... liked Anna.' He sat down again, looking exhausted.

Her bottom lip rose to cover her top lip as she stared at him. After a few moments, she shook her head. 'It won't work, Mr Blake. It won't work. You see, I don't trust you anymore.'

'Jude, please—'

She held up her hand to stop him. 'Look at it from my point of view. Forget Anna. Forget that Saturday. One minute you're sneering at me and accusing me of being your father's mistress. Next minute my work's okay and you're sharing some software ideas. Then we're back to the distrust. *Then*... then the dance, damn you! The dance and that *kiss?* This morning, you were thoroughly nasty and yet now, here you are, begging me to come back, saying you're sorry and you want to start over. Well, it won't wash, Mr Blake. How am I to know you won't be abusive towards me again tomorrow? Or on Thursday? Or next week?'

'I know,' he admitted, his voice despairing.

He'd lost her. What did he expect? She was quite right in what she said. A pang of pain shot through his heart.

'I know,' he repeated. 'I suppose it was foolish of me to try, but at least I've apologised. And I mean that, most sincerely. Yes, I can understand why you won't come back, so apply for what you like. I won't stop you and you'll get your reference.'

Jude regarded him with obvious surprise, her eyebrows climbing and her mouth open. She'd clearly not expected his offer of a reference and saying she could leave, but what else could he do? He'd blown it and it was better she left before he became more enmeshed.

Slowly, he levered himself upright and turned towards the door.

He was halfway down the passage when he heard her voice behind him, wry and resigned. 'Damn you, Richard Blake. I don't know why I'm doing this, but one more chance, you hear? One more only. If you blow it this time, it's the end. Okay?'

He turned to face her, his voice tentative as hope fluttered inside and his body trembled slightly. He hoped she didn't notice. 'You'll come back? You're sure?'

Because in view of everything that had happened, it was almost unbelievable she was generous enough to give him a second chance.

'More fool me. Yes, I'll try it.'

'Thank you. Jude. Thank you.' He stepped forward and stretched out his hand. Hesitantly, she took it and they shook hands on the agreement.

12

Jude couldn't believe it. Here she was, back where yesterday she'd sworn she would never, ever be again. She hoped Richard would keep his promise to her and be civil, professional and respectful. That would be a start. If things developed from there… a shiver of hope ran through her. Not the time or place to harbour such thoughts. Today was going to be busy because amongst all his other work, Richard had organised a tour of the factory.

Just as she was thinking of this, he strode into the office and dropped the laptop bag he was carrying onto his desk. 'Mrs Gresham, can you spare a minute, please?'

Jude looked up from a journal article she was reading online as Helen followed him into the room. He glanced impatiently at his watch. 'Where's Ian Grey? It's nearly nine-fifteen. We're supposed to be going round the factory soon.' He shot an uncomfortable glance at Jude as he riffled through some print-outs on his desk and pulled out one paper. 'Good morning, Miss Drayton.'

'Good morning,' Jude replied. 'I've seen him. He'll be here in a moment.'

Richard's eyes crinkled with almost imperceptible amusement before he glanced down at the paper in his hand. 'Mrs Gresham... can you tidy this up and put it into an email for me and I'll check it after the tour? Nothing to do with here... America, if you don't mind. You'll find all the details you need in the Blake folder in my online documents.'

'No problem.' Helen smiled at Richard.

'This tour...' Richard turned to Jude, who had resumed reading.

She stopped and looked up again.

'I believe it's something dear to your heart, the factory?'

'Well, yes, it would be,' Jude replied, fighting back the desire to speak sharply. It seemed a rather stupid comment for him to make, because surely by now he knew how she felt. Then she felt ashamed of herself and took a slow, careful breath. He was trying. He was trying to talk to her and find out what she was thinking, perhaps about how she hoped... *had* hoped, she corrected herself... to further develop the factory.

'Okay, yes. I'll try to be honest with you. It worries me, what's going to happen to Aurora. You've had me going through personnel files to see who we can retire early, and... and your email upset me as well, saying you would close the factory down.'

Richard took a step forwards, his eyes flaring wide in shock. 'I'm not aware of saying this place would close,' he said.

'Your email said the factory would be converted to the manufacture of Blake Laptops and everyone's jobs had to be reassessed. I assumed that meant the end of Aurora.'

He rubbed his hand over his chin and mouth, his eyes narrowing. His hand dropped to his side as he nodded. 'I see. This is one of the things that's been bugging you. Well, yes, I'd like to have a British base for manufacturing Blake laptops. But most people will keep their jobs, Ju-Miss Drayton. By changing the direction of the factory, I only intended to get rid of any dead wood, anyone who's not carrying their weight. I was uncertain what to do about Aurora, but now I think I intend to keep on with the manufacture of the Mercury after all. I've been looking at the machine... and the sales figures. They're both good. I'll be cutting back on the Mercury production, but there will be places on the laptop side of things for people to move across into jobs there, and probably room for employing a few more, too. When I've been round the factory and talked to the department heads, I'll be in a better position to plan how to re-organise things. The factory will have to close for a month or two while we sort out the new production lines, maybe alter the interior structures. I've been thinking we could re-open under the name Blake Aurora. How does that sound?'

Jude stared at him, her mind whirling. He intended to keep on manufacturing the Mercury. He would make the laptops alongside. 'It rather seems I owe you an apology. But your email wasn't very clear—'

'No, I agree, because when I sent it I wasn't sure what I intended to do.' He stared at her, almost pleadingly, she thought. 'You know this place has bad memories for me and I know I implied I wanted to close it, but now...' He shrugged, looking tired, and sighed. 'Maybe I can see it continuing.'

Jude nodded and her heart lurched. She was first to turn away, to look at the article she'd been reading, her fingers playing with the mouse under her hand.

Maybe she was an idiot, but she still fancied the hell out of him, despite everything. He seemed to be keeping to his side of the bargain they'd agreed on yesterday. No sign, however, that he returned her feelings. No sign of "Adam". Ah, well... she was at least grateful for the civility and professionalism.

'Now,' he said, turning back to his desk, 'I want you to come round with us and take a few notes if you don't mind. Only bits and pieces to act as an for me later, okay, so we can discuss things together. Let's see if Ian's arrived yet.' He led the way to Helen's office and Jude heard him greet Ian as she hastily collected her notebook from her document case and checked she had a stylus, firing it up as she followed.

As they toured the factory, Richard asked many shrewd, searching questions. However, it also seemed Jude couldn't have arranged a better testimony for herself if she'd tried. It became embarrassing to notice how attentively Richard listened to the many people who spoke in her favour.

They'd all heard rumours, their future was uncertain, and as far as they were concerned, they had nothing to lose by letting the new boss from America know what an asset he had in his previous CEO. Jude found it embarrassing, to see how carefully Richard was listening, and every now and again his eyes would turn towards her, darkly inscrutable, but there was a small smile lifting the corners of his mouth.

It seemed Ian was the only person who wasn't pleased. As they progressed, Jude noticed a frown gathering on his forehead and wondered what was bothering him.

On the production lines, Richard watched the process of the boards being placed into the cases. 'Are there any labour troubles here?' he asked as he lifted one of the complicated electronic circuits for a closer look.

The shop floor manager shook his head. 'Miss Drayton's always prepared to listen. If she thinks we've got a problem, she tries to sort it out. Because she's fair, the workers do their best for her. See, it's not a case of having to go through someone to get her ear. We've always been encouraged to go direct to her.'

'I think,' Ian interjected sharply, 'you have to remember I do a good bit towards sorting things out.'

Jude's mouth opened in amazement but the shop floor manager beat her to it as he glanced scathingly at Ian before directing his attention back to Richard.

'We go direct to Miss Drayton,' he repeated firmly.

Design and Development also offered nothing but praise.

'Was there ever a time you couldn't keep up with developments in the computer world?'

Alec Gresham, Helen's husband, scratched his head. 'Not in the last three years,' he admitted. 'Before that, maybe... but now it's okay. We cost out a new project and Miss Drayton, she tries to get the very latest at the very best price, so our product will be competitive. She does a damn good job, too.' he added, grinning at Richard.

'If you recollect, there was a move to updating production before Miss Drayton arrived,' Ian suggested. 'I seem to remember I had some ideas along those lines after old Mr Blake had his stroke, but before Miss Drayton arrived.'

Jude shifted from foot to foot as she stood at the back of the small group of people. She was perplexed at Ian's sharp interventions. Yes, he'd been the acting CEO until she arrived, but not effectually. What was he trying to do now? Undermine her? Imply he was doing a lot within the workplace to ensure its smooth running?

'Aye,' said Alec, sounding sarcastic, 'but they weren't carried through, lad, now were they?'

'Mr Blake was obstructive and still considered himself in charge of the factory,' Ian blustered.

'Aye, he did that,' Alec repeated. Then, in a damning tone, he continued. 'And nowt changed when Miss Drayton arrived, neither. Just that she had the balls to push things through, eh?'

They moved on to Stock Control.

'Are you ever held up because of lack of parts?'

'Heaven help the firm that can't deliver on time here.' Jenny Andrews laughed. 'Jude would be on their backs so fast they wouldn't know what'd hit them.'

'Oh, come on, Jenny.' Ian laughed derisively. 'Not that long ago we were held up on that big order for Fitness Footwear because the software wasn't available.'

Richard looked from Jude to Ian to Jenny, his keen eyes missing nothing. Jude was feeling furious about Ian's constant niggling. It wasn't directly aimed at her, but the purpose was clear enough, as far as she could see. Still, it didn't seem to matter because everything he said was being refuted, and Richard was listening to his workforce as well as Ian's rather petulant comments. But still... a shiver ran through her. She still felt tolerated rather than liked—nothing Richard had done so far had reassured her of his respect.

'Yes,' Jenny replied, 'but only because it was a rush order. They'd asked for twenty computers and then upped the order to fifty *and* changed the software requirements. We wanted to meet their request if possible,' she explained to Richard, 'because they'd suggested there'd be more orders if we could do what they asked. Jude put the factory on overtime to up the production and drove over to Master Systems herself and waited until the new software was ready... they were apologetic about the delay but we'd only given them very short notice to alter the requirements and let them know we wanted extra. *No-one* could have foreseen such a large rush order, and we *have* had more orders from Fitness Footwear so it was worth it,' she finished, glancing triumphantly at Ian.

He bit on his bottom lip, looking annoyed, while Richard narrowed his eyes, rubbing a hand across his chin as he stared at Ian. It seemed he, too, had finally noticed Ian's attempts to claim credit, and also to put her down. Jude wondered who he'd believe—herself, or Ian? She was sufficiently uncertain of the truce to be sure.

The Software Installation Department was hushed, only the hum of computers breaking the reverent silence.

'Master Systems provides all our software, I understand,' Richard commented as he stopped to watch the familiar logo of their office software come up on the screen of a Mercury. 'A bit pricey, maybe?'

'Now there I agree with you,' Ian nodded. 'I said we should keep with our original supplier but I was overruled.'

'Well,' the chief technician answered, 'yes, if you look at price per package, then it is expensive. But consider the reliability of it and the fact it's so universally used. We used to use cheaper software, Mr Grey's right there, but Jude negotiated a great deal with Master Systems and since we swapped over, our sales have gone up. Firms have said they'd wondered about buying from us before, but our software put them off, even though our complete package was cheaper. They're much happier now we use mainstream software and the increase in sales has more than compensated for the increased cost. Jude had to push it through with the directors as usual, but like everything else, she managed it.'

'Everything else?' Richard's voice was idle, his attention apparently on the screen in front of him as the operator checked the installation was properly completed.

Only Jude noticed his subtle sharpening of interest.

'Why, yes.' The man stopped, remembering to whom he was talking.

'Go on,' Richard said in a neutral tone, leaning forward to bring up one of the menus.

'Well,' the technician shifted from foot to foot. 'Your father didn't want a CEO brought in—'

'Oh, come on, Mike. Mr Blake was more than happy to see Jude in the job because they—' Ian cut himself off, as he glanced around furtively, almost hopefully, Jude thought, to see if there had been a reaction from anyone.

She turned away, now furious. Were these bloody rumours common knowledge, then? Had she blindly gone day-to-day, not realising half the work force were speculating on how she'd got the job? How could she have been so stupid? No wonder Richard had come over from America so full of doubt about her. Jude felt like weeping but instead her face froze, her lips thinned and she hid her distress behind a cool façade, turning back to watch the exchange.

Richard was still looking at the screen. 'What was that, Ian?' he asked, his voice abstracted. 'Sorry... I lost you for a moment.'

'Mr Blake was happy to see Jude take up the position, as he was no longer capable of overseeing things for himself,' Ian muttered, realising Richard had completely missed the barb he'd aimed at Jude.

As well, Jude realised the technicians gathered round were looking at Ian disgustedly.

Maybe everyone hadn't been sniggering behind her back, and she was just letting Ian's comments get to her?

Then her spirits lifted even further as she heard the determined voice of the head technician as he denied Ian's words. 'That's not what we heard, Mr Grey,' Mike said. 'We heard the firm was only a matter of months away from total collapse. The directors were in a panic and wanted someone modern to take over. They were out of touch with recent developments in the computer world, which were happening so fast. We weren't selling much... a few systems for home use, and spares, but no contracts or office machines. They advertised the job against Mr Blake's wishes.'

'Advertised?' Richard asked sharply. 'Where advertised?'

Jude understood Richard was hearing absolute proof she hadn't been put into the job as a figurehead on the whim of his father because she was his current mistress. Her fears about the workers were unfounded, and she relaxed, shooting another quick look at Ian from under her eyelashes. He stood, tapping his foot, looking even more annoyed. What on earth was wrong with him? She suspected he resented her, but what did he hope to gain by bad-mouthing her like this?

'Online, on all the important technical job vacancy sites. As I said, it was against Mr Blake's wishes. Mr Grey here applied for the job,' Mike added, clearly annoyed by the other man's interruptions, 'but he wasn't successful. Miss Drayton was working for one of the big national companies and the directors took her on. I believe your father was furious to hear they'd taken on a woman... so furious it caused a second, minor stroke. And from then on, he gave her hell.'

Richard straightened up from the computer and transferred his attention to Mike. 'I'd heard,' he said quietly, 'that my father had known Miss Drayton long before she got the job, and she was a frequent visitor to the house to discuss... business with him.'

Jude was aware the entire department, now aware of the subtle nuances of the conversation, had come to a standstill and was watching the three men with interest. She knew the rumours of her demotion and the tension between her and Richard Blake would have raced through the factory, and no-one was happy about the uncertainty surrounding their jobs. Now, they were regarding Richard with suspicion, and Ian with an active dislike. It seemed she had the general support of the factory and it brought a lump to her throat.

'Well, I don't know if she knew him before she came here, but if she did, it didn't do her much good. I told you, when he heard they'd appointed a woman, it brought on a secondary stroke and she was never, ever allowed in the house. Never. Those were his strict orders. Everything went through Mr French. Even after the funeral, she wouldn't go to the house. I overheard her say to Mrs Gresham that it would be awkward going in when the old gentleman had disliked her so much.'

Richard directed his keen gaze to Jude, standing a little apart from the group. She felt colour flaring in her face but she met his gaze calmly. A few seconds of utter immobility followed before Richard pivoted on his heel and strode to the door, stopping there to turn and address the immobile personnel. 'Right, thank you, everyone. I'll let you know what we intend to do as soon as possible, but roughly, I hope to close in about two to three months' time and alter the premises to accommodate production of the Blake Laptop. Then we'll run with the production of the Mercury, but there'll have to be some re-shuffling of jobs, hence everyone having to re-apply. I'll analyse what we need where and if your job's gone, there'll probably be an alternative we can offer. I hope that's okay.'

He left the room, and as Jude followed, she was aware of a buzz of talk rising behind them.

13

The sun rose over the eastern hills, as soft as melted butter, and the long shadows of dawn spread over the patchwork fields, green where there was grazing stock, yellowed and sere where they'd been cut. Jude stretched in bed and opened her eyes. What a glorious day. She lay there watching the sun rise higher in the blue sky, while through her open window she could hear a multitude of birdsong punctuated with the harsh cry of rooks wheeling above the trees. Over it all there was a smell of dew-soaked grass and flowers creeping into her room. Not a day for staying at home, this Saturday morning. She'd have to go somewhere, do something.

Flinging back her duvet, she leapt out of bed and within twenty minutes had showered and was downstairs, the kettle boiling, bread cut and in the toaster. Jude leaned back against the worktop, arms folded as she waited for the toast to be ready, her mind drifting over the last few weeks.

It was just over three months since Richard had come here to apologise, begging her to come back and try again. Three months in which he'd kept his promise to her and treated her with professional courtesy and a degree of easy friendliness. What a joy it had been to work with someone like him. So sure of himself, so visionary, he inspired her as no-one else had, and the ideas they had bounced off each other had been fruitful and interesting.

What a difference to working alongside Ian Grey. She could almost feel sorry for Ian. He'd had such hopes that when Richard arrived, he would become a valued second-in-command or even be in charge, should Richard have returned to the States. As it was, he'd been relegated to the accountancy department with some subtle manoeuvring, which Jude found breathtakingly admirable.

The toast popped up. Jude carried it to the table and buttered it, paying little heed to the radio, playing popular classics in the corner of the kitchen, as her thoughts continued to dwell on Richard.

How he took her breath away when she looked up and studied him when he was unaware, deep in some online article or typing notes. If she'd been attracted to him before, when he'd been flinging insults at her almost hourly, she was surely attracted to him now. Sometimes he would look up as she watched him. Their eyes would meet in a long, unsmiling moment that left her heart pounding and her hands trembling, and it seemed... it seemed maybe he wasn't indifferent to her either. Sometimes they bumped into each other, or his fingers brushed hers, and a frisson of pure electricity fizzed through her body.

She thought their initial attraction to each other was resurfacing, and Jude knew she wanted him as much more than a co-worker. After a long time, she was ready to fall in love again. Yet she was hesitant. She'd fallen in love with a co-worker once before and that hadn't gone well, leading to a break-up and her having to leave her job. Richard, though, was as different to Julian as...

Someone knocking on the front door interrupted her daydreams.

Jude chewed and swallowed her mouthful of toast as she rose to her feet, glancing at the clock in surprise. It was still very early, so maybe it was the postman. The knock came again as she walked towards the door.

'Hang on,' she called, groping for the key on the table. All thumbs, she dropped it, and then had difficulty putting it into the lock. Finally, she jammed the chain as she was sliding it out. 'Hang on,' she called again, although the noise must have made it obvious she was on her way. At last, she swung the door open.

Not the postman.

Richard Blake.

Her stomach flipped and her knees went weak. In view of the recent thoughts she'd been having about him, she could feel herself blushing. What on earth was he doing here at this time of the morning, on a Saturday?

He turned as the door opened and gave her a tentative smile. 'Jude. Good morning. I was worried I might get you out of bed. After all, it's Saturday. But unless you can dress in record time, it looks as if you *were* up, which saves me some embarrassment.'

Jude realised he was nervous. She could see him rubbing his thumb and forefinger together. 'No, no. I got up early... it's such a beautiful day, so I thought I might go somewhere... have a day out, you know. I thought I—'

'That's what I was planning,' he cut in. 'A day out. I wondered if you... I thought you might... that is... oh, *damn*.' He ran a hand through his hair, looking miserable.

'Look,' Jude said, gathering her wits at last, 'I'm just having some toast and coffee. Would you like to... would you like to come and join me?'

He gave her a wide smile and stepped with alacrity into the cool gloom of her hallway, following her through to the sunny kitchen, its windows flung wide to catch the glorious day. A pleasant smell of toast and coffee filled the room, the radio still murmuring in its corner.

'Coffee okay? And toast? Do you like toast? I might have some bacon and eggs if you want more. I'm not sure...' she wandered over to the fridge and pulled open the door, her turn now to feel nervous, aware of his lean height behind her. She wondered again what he was doing here. Was she jumping to wild conclusions thinking he was going to suggest they went somewhere together... but why else was he here, and what else had he meant when he'd been wittering on about going out?

'Toast would be fine. I never eat much in the mornings. Toast and some coffee. Thank you.'

Taking the loaf out of the bread bin, Jude cut two substantial slices. Slipping them into the toaster, she turned next to the kettle, re-filling it, remembering with clarity the last time she had done this, with him here in the kitchen. What a long way they'd come in such a short time.

'Sit down... please.' Jude waved at the table.

He sat opposite where she'd been sitting. 'This... it's a nice room,' he said.

'Mmm.' Jude turned her back on him, resting her hands on the edge of the sink to hide their trembling, staring out at her long, narrow back garden.

Why was he here?

It must mean he was going to ask her to spend the day with him. Her legs felt weak and her heart was hammering in her chest. Taking in a deep breath, she exhaled slowly and as quietly as she could, then repeated it.

The toast popped up, and the kettle boiled, forcing her to move, to spoon coffee into a cafetière and pour on the water. Putting the toast on a plate, collecting a knife and some butter, she carried everything over to the table and set them down in front of Richard, who was watching her.

'Jude...' He buttered his toast. 'When you and I met... I mean *first* met,' he ducked his head, but not before she'd caught sight of a quick look of shame on his face, 'we had such a wonderful day. I asked you then if I could have your mobile number because I wanted to see you again. I know there have been a few rough patches since then and I *know* all my fault, all of my making. But over these last few weeks... I feel maybe we've both... I feel... oh, damn it, Jude.' He laid his toast back on the plate and pushed his mug backwards and forwards with restless fingers, his eyes following every move the mug made. 'I don't have any right to ask you after the things I've said and done, but I'd like to start again. I'd very much like to wish a lot of things unsaid, but that's not possible. I apologised to you once before and asked if, on a business footing, we could try again. Now I'm asking more of you. I'm asking if maybe you could forgive me and... and... I'd really like it if... if we could start again, go back to the first Saturday, Anna and Adam, and go on from there? Recently, I feel we've... I think we're both reconnecting. But I might be wrong?'

My, my, my. The sophisticated Richard Blake struggling to find words. Jude stared at his bent head, thinking about what he'd said. Oh, yes, he attracted her, but as she'd been thinking earlier, what if something set him off again? If she allowed herself to become involved and then he turned on her, she didn't think she could bear it.

But if he really meant it, if he really was over his hang-ups and believing the report rubbish, then this relationship could grow into something very special.

'Jude?' At last, he looked up, his face ashamed, his eyes pleading. 'I... I'm sorry... maybe I'm expecting too much. Maybe it's still too soon, but we've been working so well together, become friends... I don't think I ever stopped caring about you, even though I hated you for a while.' He slid his chair back and half rose from his seat. 'I'm sorry. This isn't what you want to hear. I better go—'

'No.' Jude held up her hand. 'No. I'm sorry. I was just thinking about what you said.'

He sank back down, his eyes widening, not daring to speak as he waited for Jude to continue.

Jude tightened her lips before raising her head and looking at him with pain on her face. 'This could be a dangerous game we're playing. I know we had a great day together, but it was an unbelievable shock to realise Adam and you were the same person, and that as Richard Blake, you hated me so much.'

'Please, don't. Don't remind me of how awful I was. I'm not sure I'll ever forgive myself for being so easily swayed by those damned reports. It's not me, not the way I usually approach business matters. But Aurora spooks me. It's stupid, I know, but even now, even though I'm settling in, the ghosts are lurking.' His hands on the table clenched until the knuckles turned white.

'Yes, I know. I accept what you're saying, but you must realise you upset me.' Jude glanced down and ran her finger round the rim of her mug. 'Then the dance... I didn't know whether I was coming or going. You were so pleasant at the dance, and you *kissed* me, Richard. I came back into work so full of hope, but it was wasted. You were at it hammer and tongs again, and, okay, that's ended up with our truce and I admit since then it's been all right since then. But now? You're asking me to commit myself to a personal relationship with you and that's a different scenario altogether, isn't it?'

'The dance. Yes, I'm sorry. I saw you as Anna and I forgot who we were and where we were. No excuse for the kiss, I know. But I enjoyed that evening and it made me realise I couldn't ignore the fact I still found you attractive despite everything I thought. Another apology, I suppose except... I can't regret the kiss. But the next morning I was angry with myself and I took it out on you. I shouldn't have done, and you were right to walk out. It was appalling behaviour and I know I'm asking a lot from you when I ask if you could erase those first days?'

Standing up, Jude collected her mug and plate and took them over to the sink. Turning round, she crossed her arms as she leaned back, regarding Richard, her eyes sombre. 'I'll be very honest. There's nothing I'd like better. Yes, I still have feelings for you despite everything that's happened, but I have to say I'm wary. For the last few weeks, we've managed a good working relationship. But if we go out together today, and maybe after that, more often, I'm still frightened that something will make you turn against me again. I could end up being very hurt, do you understand? Because I care for you a lot and I think we might...' Jude tailed off, before asking, 'Are you sure—*absolutely* sure—you've exorcised this thing about those reports and linking me in with your father? You mentioned the ghosts still lurking?'

Richard nodded his head as his lips tightened. 'Jude, Jude, *yes*. They're lurking, but I think—I hope—I've got control over them and I can rationalise things. It's better now we've been working together, and the plans are in place to amalgamate the two companies. It's becoming my firm, no longer anything to do with my father. The whole organisation is so far removed from anything he'd planned or wanted, so all of that is helping me. I know was a little insane when I first arrived, and you've no idea how I regret my stupidity.' Richard rubbed his hands over his face, looking sombre.

Jude moved forwards to clear the rest of the things from the table. 'That's honest of you. Okay, yes. I'll come out with you today. I can't think why, in the teeth of everything you've thrown at me, but there you go. No accounting for taste, is there?' She gave him a shaky smile over her shoulder as she dumped their plates in the sink and reached over to close the window. Her insides churned. She was taking a gamble, especially after what he'd just said. She was undoubtably an idiot, but she found she cared about him too much to worry.

He smiled back and stood up, sliding his chair under the table. 'I thought... maybe the Lake District? A walk, or rowing on one of the lakes. I've... I've made a picnic. What do you think?'

'Sounds okay to me. Come as I am?'

Richard looked her over, slim in her denim jeans, her short-sleeved tee-shirt cool and practical, sandals on her feet and the mass of tawny blonde hair caught up in a lime green scarf on top of her head. 'Good,' he said with an admiring grin. 'Perhaps some shorts, and maybe a jersey or a jacket in case it cools down later?'

14

Ten minutes later they were in Richard's car, heading through the town. Tourists thronged the pavements and the market stalls. Traffic was, as usual, queuing from one end of the high street to the other, but they edged forward until they came to clear roads and, in a half mile, broke free onto the bypass. Richard drove with concentration and speed, changing gear with economical movements which brought out the best in the car, keeping well back from traffic in front of them and only overtaking, with a series of quick gear changes when the way was clear. Every now and again he glanced sideways, stealing a quick glance at Jude. He knew he was lucky she'd agreed to go out with him and knew he needed to treat her carefully. He certainly intended to—while working with her, observing her with the personnel, listening to her ideas—he'd fallen hard. That day with Anna had hooked him, anyway. Admittedly, when he'd discovered she was the hated Jude Drayton, he'd been confused, hurt, uncertain how to proceed, other than with anger, seeing in her the embodiment of everything his father had stood for. Once he'd come to terms with the fact someone had tried to cause trouble between them, begged her forgiveness, apologised, he'd allowed himself to hope.

Today was the fruition of his hopes.

'It's getting close, now, the factory shut down,' Jude observed, sitting at a slight angle in the passenger seat so she could look at Richard as well as the passing scenery, which was a delight at this time of the year.

'Yeah. A fortnight until the Midlands computer exhibition starts, then all go the week after that. Exciting times.' Richard shot her a quick smile. He felt relaxed and happy. He felt like Adam. Yet now, it was even better because there was nothing but truth between them.

He caught glimpses of campion, cow parsley and chamomile tangled on the verge, swaying and dipping in the rush of air caused by the passing cars. There were lambs, now half grown but still silly, which ran and leapt in that endearingly stiff-legged way, collecting in wide-eyed gangs by the gates, tossing their heads and spinning away as the traffic passed. The leaves on the trees were all out, fresh, thick and vibrant, and the few remaining uncut meadows were filling with sorrel and buttercups, destined for hay. A warm glow spread through him and he flexed his fingers on the wheel, thoroughly looking forward to his day.

'Do you think you'll get down to the exhibition?'

'I'm hoping to, but only a day visit. Too much to oversee up here, I'm afraid. Then you and I will be deep into all the planning and logistics once the alterations start. It would've been good to have a month's holiday like everyone else.' Richard reached out to push a CD into the stereo and the sounds of piano music filtered into the car. 'I think the workforce feel as if it's all their Christmases rolled into one, with a month's paid leave. I've been hearing some of the plans about what they'll do. Made me feel quite envious.' Again, a quick grin before his attention returned to the road.

He was aware she was watching him and hoped he'd caught her interest to re-start their relationship. It was looking good so far.

'How's the software coming along?'

'Great. David finally set up a meeting next week. Monday morning. His software engineers have had a look at my proposal and been discussing it. I'm looking forward to it. This could be worth a fortune, you realise?'

'Do you need any more money?' Jude sounded slightly amused, but a quick look showed her with tightened lips, turning her head away to look of her side window.

'Not for me, no. But I don't just accumulate wealth. I have sponsorship programs in place for poor students and support various charities.' He spoke gently, knew he was deliberately playing down the full extent of his philanthropy, not wanting to paint himself as too much of a champion. At the dance, he'd doubled the amount the blind auction had made, but that was between himself and Alec Gresham, and if Alec had told Helen, she'd not prattled about it to Jude, of that he was sure.

They continued to chat on the journey, but the occasional silences in between weren't in any way strained. Sometimes Richard pointed something out... a hawk hovering at the side of the motorway, or a range of distant hills. Sometimes Jude made comments about the beauty of the scenery, lacking now in lushness and verdancy of the summer dales, but compensating with breathtaking grandeur.

In time, they turned off the motorway and travelled along a winding road that led them deeper and deeper into mountains splashed with green bracken, moss-covered rock, and dark spikes of evergreens.

They drove through Keswick, with grey stone houses tumbled along narrow roads, reached a lakeside carpark and the engine died. Richard rested his wrists on the wheel and turned to look at Jude. 'Walk? Rowing? Steamer trip? Shops?'

'Not shops.' Jude exclaimed with a shudder. 'It'll be jam-packed in the town. Unless you...?' she hesitated.

'No, not me. Same reaction as you.'

'And the steamer trips... they'll be pretty full, I suspect. I think I'd prefer it if we could get away from the crowds?'

'That means effort either by foot or arm power.'

'It would be nice on the lake,' Jude said wistfully, 'but I can't row very well.'

'I'll do two-thirds. You can do the rest.'

They grinned at each other.

Richard carried their picnic down to the lakeside, where they queued to hire one of the dumpy wooden rowing boats. Various people were already afloat, and shrieks of warning and laughter flew across the water. Arrogant swans fluffed their wings and eyed these antics with disdain, floating past with cool superiority. Ducks quacked and quarrelled on the lake shore, snatching at any morsel of food thrown by the tourists. In the distance, green hills rose high into the blue sky. The day was perfection.

It didn't take long to reach the head of the queue.

'Two, sir? For the whole day? We shut at seven tonight, all right?'

Richard steadied the boat as Jude climbed in, then stepped in himself, settling with familiarity, lifting the oars and pushing off from the jetty with a strong shove. As soon as they were clear, he dipped the oars into the water. He'd done a lot of rowing in America, single sculling. Being on the water with the rhythmic dip and pull of the oars went a long way towards soothing his troubled mind in his early days, and given him the courage and confidence to strike out on his own and start up his company. He enjoyed the flex of his shoulders, and relaxed as he swept the blades through the soft water. The boat pulled swiftly away from the bobbing flotsam of boats around the shore. Soon, they were by themselves, heading out into the centre of the lake.

Jude trailed one hand through the water, twisting to look back as the shoreline receded, then turning forwards to see where they were heading.

'We could have a look at the islands. This is the only boat hire place on the lake, so if we row as far as possible, we should be able to find one that hasn't got anyone else on it. We could eat there, maybe swim, if you feel it's warm enough? You *could* land on most of these little islands once,' he added, his voice now uncertain. 'I suppose it might all have changed.' It had been over eight years since he'd been in the Lake District and he'd no idea if there were new rules about accessing islands.

'I doubt it.' Jude leaned an arm on the edge of the boat, stretching out her legs, looking completely relaxed and happy. He was glad he'd remembered what she said about liking water and silence.

She was looking at him again as he pulled smoothly on the oars of the boat. He was very conscious of her gaze as he felt sweat bead on his forehead and upper lip, his muscles flexing in his arms and thighs, bracing himself against the force of the water.

He lifted his head, allowed his eyes to meet hers in a long, burning look, and swallowed. Letting the oars rest, the boat drifted, carried by its own momentum as messages flickered between them and he thought a shiver ran through her body. After a few moments, Jude turned her head to gaze at the enduring mountains that lined the lake, a touch of colour staining her cheeks. Without a word, Richard shifted on the seat before he dipped the oars into the water and continued the steady rhythm of his rowing.

They landed on the gravelly shore of a small island. The gravel gave way to rock, and then to moss and grass. A few trees topped the highest point. Gorse, smelling of butter and coconut, gave perfect shelter from the slight breeze that ruffled the still waters of the lake. Richard pulled out a rug from the large rucksack he'd put into the bottom of the boat and laid it on the smooth turf in the shelter of the bushes. There was a view down the lake to the mountains at the far end.

Tired after the long row, Richard flung himself full length, his arm over his face to protect his eyes from the sun. His body relaxed in the warmth, and he relaxed. He knew Jude would wait, content to sit in the warm sun and let the peace and tranquillity of the scene wash over her.

After a few peaceful minutes, he sat up and grinned at her, reaching for the rucksack and pulling it closer. 'Right, I've got my breath back and now I'm rather hungry. Let's see what we've got.'

He dug into its depths to produce the food. Crusty granary rolls filled with salad and chicken, juicy apples and peaches, a bottle of water.

Jude was hungry, too. They ate in silence, leaning amiably against each other. The scenery, the lake, each other's company was, for the moment, enough. He had a lot to think about and suspected Jude was sharing some of his doubts and apprehension. This development was impetuous in some ways, inevitable in others. Sexual tension had been simmering away, Richard realised, alongside their growing friendship and working relationship.

Tacitly, it'd been acknowledged this morning.

When he'd eaten enough, he lay back in the sun's heat, and slowly held out his arms. Jude stared down at him before easing herself down, allowing him to cradle her. Pressed against her soft body, he delighted in the shivers of excitement running through him, the reaction of his body to her closeness. His fingers gently combed through her hair. There was the sound of the small waves breaking on the gravel and the sigh of the wind in the gorse, and he relaxed even further, not quite awake, but not asleep either... simply enjoying the sensuousness of it all, letting the tremors of anticipation build, feeling the longing deep inside. It had been a long, long time since he'd let go enough, trusted enough. Most of his dates over the last few years had been fleeting, a release, with little in the way of feelings.

He was aware of Jude watching him as she lay in his arms, and knew she understood what he was feeling and was reciprocating.

As he smoothed his hand over her cheek, she sighed and turned towards his fingers, her breath soft on his palm. His heart contracted as her thumb gently brushed his full lower lip and his body stirred with longing. He knew the attraction between them wasn't one-sided. He'd seen her looking at him when she'd assumed he was immersed in his work. He'd seen her prop her chin on her hand and gaze out of the windows and knew whatever she was thinking about was nothing to do with business.

Now, Richard's hand slowly started stroking her arm, her thigh, and she shifted and moved closer. He was longing to take more, have more. It was consuming him.

He opened her eyes and stared into her face, now so close to his. He smiled, his breathing quiet and even, his dark lashes fanning on his cheeks as he slowly blinked. His lips were slightly parted, and he placed one long-fingered hand on her arm, slid it up to her neck and cupped her cheek.

Gazing at him, Jude's lips parted, and he saw a delicate flush bloom on her face. Tentatively, she raised her finger and brushed it against his mouth a second time. With his eyes still on her, he caught it between his teeth and his tongue caressed the tip. He wanted to free himself from his clothes and feel himself skin to skin with her.

'Jude?' His voice was soft. 'Must we waste any more time? I so want you. I fell in love with Anna that day. And you... I think you feel the same. Be honest with me, please? We've been good friends this last couple of months and my feelings are back. I want to know if you... if you feel like me?' His eyes were pleading, his words beseeching as he slipped his hand behind her head.

Her eyes locked with his. She swallowed, her lips parting. The pressure of his fingers brought her head closer to his own. Their eyes remained open, fixed on each other.

Lashes, skin, lips became a blur.

Softly, their lips touched.

An explosion of feeling rocketed through Richard, and of their own volition his hands caught her shoulders and slid round her back as she made a stifled, inarticulate sound, almost a sob, admitting the truth and giving in to the feel of him, the touch of him, the smell of him, the taste of him.

'Jude... Jude...' he murmured against the skin of her neck before his mouth found hers again, caressing, biting, invading, and his hands smoothed over her back, slipped round to cradle her breast, slid up to caress her face, moved down to pull her even closer.

Their breathing quickened as clothes became a barrier. They pulled back from each other, a silent question given and answered before fingers moved to unfasten, unbutton, unzip, and soon everything lay scattered around them on the soft grass.

There was no stopping, no holding back, other than adding protection. Jude seemed as impatient as he to be close, their bodies pressed together, tongue against tongue, with the sun beating down, adding to the sensuousness of their lovemaking.

'Jude...' he couldn't stop saying her name, his breath soft against her skin. 'I love you. I *love* you. Hell. Can you ever forgive me?'

He felt her as she breathed in, her eyes wondrous as her hands explored him with delight, smoothing over the hard contours of his back, the softness of skin and hair on his stomach, making him so tight he thought he might lose it before he'd even pleasured her.

'There's nothing to forgive... hush...'

She pulled his mouth to her own and stopped his remorse with her lips and tongue. There was no need to talk after that. They touched and explored. Body arched against body. Richard sucked in a breath as Jude slid her hand down and curled it possessively around him. Feeling his willpower waning again, he used his fingers to enter her and tantalisingly stroked until he saw intense feelings build then break and cascade through her, causing her to cry out. This was Richard's signal to move onto her, slide inside, and take his own exquisite pleasure.

Silence fell. Sweat-slicked body rested against sweat-slicked body as their breathing slowed to a normal rate. With a gentle hand, Richard pushed Jude's hair back from her face and kissed the corner of her mouth. He looked shaken by the experience they'd shared. Jude smiled up at him, her mouth looking soft and swollen from his kisses.

'Hey,' he said, his voice quiet as he ran his hand over her shoulder and caressed the pliant warmth of her breast, 'all okay?'

'All *very* okay,'

'I'm not sure I meant that to happen, but it was... good.' Richard swallowed, his gaze tender. 'Maybe we better get dressed? Someone else might row out here, you know.'

'Who cares,' Jude murmured in reply, pulling his head down and kissing him sensuously on his mouth. He felt his stomach contract as her hand smoothed a downward path, her lips moved over his, demanding entry.

He returned her caresses, sliding once more over the swell of her breasts, half laughing against her mouth. 'Again? Dammit, woman. What have I landed myself with? An insatiable hussy, it seems.'

Their shared laughter mingled as he rolled over and looked down at her, then the laughter faded as passion took its place for a second time.

Later, Jude lay with her head on Richard's shoulder, lazily throwing pebbles into the water.

Richard squinted up at the sky. 'Time's passing,' he said, reluctance in his voice. 'We ought to get the boat back.'

Jude sighed. 'Do we have to go back?'

After their second intense session of lovemaking, they'd swum in the clear, cold waters of the lake, allowing the warmth of the sun to dry their bodies before dressing. Abandoning the rug, they'd explored the tiny island, ending up in another little bay full of pebbles that crunched and slithered under their feet but had proved a surprisingly comfortable place to lie.

There they'd stayed, talking, skimming stones, holding each other, delighting in renewing the personal discovery of each other, an extension of their conversation the day they'd first met. Where they'd travelled, what they enjoyed doing in their time off, which books they liked, and which music they enjoyed. The conversation wandered idly from one topic to another, even on occasions touching on work.

Sitting up, Richard ran his fingers through his hair before clasping his hands round his knees. He smiled down at Jude, still lying on the pebbles, warmth spreading through him because she didn't want the day to end.

Neither did he.

'I said we had to take the boat back, but we don't have to go home. We can eat out, go for a walk round the lake, or something.'

'Mmm, quite like your suggestion of a walk round the lake... except for the fact I'm starving. What's the time?'

'Nearly six.'

'It can't be.' Jude sat up, shoulder to shoulder with Richard, and turned to look at him, eyes wide. 'We've got to get the boat back by seven.'

'Keep your distance,' he warned huskily, 'or we'll be here another hour at least.'

She leaned over and kissed him gently on the mouth. 'Sounds like a good idea to me. I wouldn't care if we stayed here forever.'

He could understand that. He felt warm, loved, lazy, and in no hurry to get back to reality, and by the look of it, Jude felt exactly the same.

'You would when it started raining.' He stood up and reached down to pull her to her feet. 'Jude, I promise... it'll be all right now. It's been all right, hasn't it, for the last couple of months? And we'll find out who sent those damned letters. I won't be swayed again, I promise.'

She smiled at him. 'I hope so, I really do, sweetheart.'

But he thought he could detect a note of doubt in her voice, and was worried she might think he'd turn on her again. Oh, well—he sighed internally—the only way was forward, and as time passed, her trust in him would grow. He hoped.

Back at the other bay, they packed up the remains of the picnic and folded the rug before climbing into the boat and pushing off towards the town. The sky was still a clear and placid blue, and the sun hadn't yet lowered itself behind the mountains. This time, Jude sat next to Richard, and they rowed together. Their progress was slow and erratic, caused by Jude's lack of skill in keeping in time with Richard, and punctuated by their laughter and kisses.

The man who hired out boats wasn't very pleased. 'We shut at seven, you know,' he said, looking cross as he glanced at their happy, sun-flushed faces before looking pointedly at his watch. 'It's twenty-past now. Where on earth have you been? We were thinking of sending out the motorboat to look for you.'

As it was clear to everyone they'd been visible for the past twenty minutes, his complaint was gratuitous.

'I'm sorry... um, something came up,' Richard said innocently. Jude turned away, her shoulders shaking with laughter. 'Look, I paid for the day, but let me give you something extra.'

There was a rustle of notes as Richard handed the man more money.

'Aye, well then, I suppose that's all right,' the man grumbled. 'But I have to get home, you know.'

Still muttering and mumbling, the man padlocked their boat up to the others as Jude and Richard strolled away along the shore, arm-in-arm and still laughing. They came to the town and ambled down the main street, stopping to look in windows, deciding what to buy from the genuine to the ludicrous.

'Do you like that sweater?' Jude asked, pulling him to a stop and pointing at a rich, dark sweater in the window of a shop which looked very expensive.

Richard stepped back, looking at the front of the shop. 'Oh, yes,' he murmured after a moment. 'But only if it costs at least one hundred pounds. The name alone must put at least fifty percent onto everything.' He nodded his head upwards at the name, "The Discerning Man", emblazoned in gold script on a dark blue background.

'I hope you *are* discerning,' Jude replied. 'If you're not, I'll have to send you back for a different model.'

He grinned at her.

'But it is a nice sweater,' she added, looking back over her shoulder as they walked away, hand in hand. 'I feel hungry now. You said you'd feed me.'

'Do I detect a whinge in your voice?'

'Oh, no, sir. Not really, sir. But it's like this. I had to work overtime this afternoon. The boss wasn't happy with my first attempt, so I had to repeat my work.'

'The boss wasn't happy with your work? That's not the impression I got. Are you a liar as well as a hussy?'

Then Richard's laughter died away, his face filling with dismay as he realised what he'd said.

He'd come close to repeating one of his original accusations.

Now, he stared at her, his eyes reflecting his anxiety, his mouth turned down. 'I'm sorry,' he whispered, dropping his forehead to rest on hers. 'I'm *sorry*.'

'Leave it. You can't keep apologising every time you say something that might be misconstrued, for heaven's sake. What's past is past. Let it be, okay?'

The day slowly ended.

They ate an aromatic fish and chip supper out of paper, rank with vinegar and sharp with salt, wiping their greasy fingers on the papers afterwards before dropping them into a bin. In the park beside the lake, they found there was a brass band playing and sat on the grass listening, Richard's arm round Jude's shoulders.

As the sky darkened, they made their way back to the carpark and reluctantly slid into the BMW.

Richard paused and turned towards her, one hand on the keys. 'You don't have to go home,' he suggested in a low voice. 'Come back with me?'

Jude stared at him, looking helpless.

'We can have tonight… go for a walk tomorrow. Jude… what does it matter now?'

He knew why she hesitated, but his relief when she finally spoke was tremendous.

'Okay,' she murmured, looking at him, her heart in her eyes. 'Okay.'

15

Monday morning found Jude still at Richard's house. She didn't know how, hadn't intended it to happen. Somehow, Saturday night had passed in a daze of sleep and making love and sleep again. There was an unspoken assumption on both sides that she would spend Sunday with him as well.

The weather that day had continued to be beautiful, and they'd taken another picnic, returning to the waterfall where they'd first spent time together, which was called, Richard told her, High Foss.

'But the house is called High Foss Hall.' she'd exclaimed.

'Of course. It's named for the falls.'

It surprised her they could walk there from the house. Surprised and intrigued. The falls were hidden in a fold of the hills which rose behind the house, and the river ran along the edge of the gardens and, at one point, had been cleverly integrated.

'Picnics, water and you.' Jude laughed as they'd walked up the grassy slopes beside the river. She breathed in deeply, feeling so happy it shocked her. Could happiness like this last? She surely hoped so…

'Do you mind?' He shot her a quick look, his obvious concern causing a frown to mar the smoothness of his face.

'No. I like it. I'm not into very sophisticated pleasures, I'm afraid, although I like the ballet, a concert or two, eating out now and then. Generally, I'm happy with a good book, some fresh air, whatever.'

'Easy to please.'

'So what makes *you* happy?' Jude asked with curiosity. 'Apart from the usual stuff we've mentioned, like books and films and such like? Really, ever after happy?'

He shrugged and stopped to look down the hill at the house, now some way below. 'Like you, I don't ask a lot. I grew up here and always enjoy walking in the hills. It was an escape for me.'

He was evading an answer, she knew that.

Not really surprising because she wasn't sure what she was asking him, anyway. When they first met, he'd seemed relaxed, but there had been something casual in his pick-up, as if he was interested, but expected little. Now, she felt he was more invested in her and she liked that. Did he see this as long term? Did she even want to ask a question like that? She knew it was her own insecurity, after the Julian affair, which made her wonder what the future might hold, but it was too early for such a serious discussion. She needed to drop it now. Shrugging, Jude turned away. Richard said nothing, following her up the hill.

The falls were not deserted, as they had been previously, and all afternoon there was a steady stream of visitors. Jude and Richard were content, lying near the pool in the sun until it lost its warmth, and they'd reluctantly come to their feet for the descent to the Hall. He'd persuaded her to have something to eat and after that, one thing had led to another until they found themselves back in Richard's large bed with no thought of anything but the here and now.

So here she was, with only her jeans and tee-shirt, plus a borrowed jumper from Richard.

'Won't do,' she said, arms akimbo, fixing him with a severe look.

'Will do, very nicely, too,' he grinned at her, turning from the mirror where, bent at the knee, he was knotting his tie, his white shirt gleaming, legs long and slim in their well-cut, dark wool trousers. His jacket lay on the bed. Jude picked it up, holding it ready for him. He approached, kissed her on the nose and turned his back, slipping his arms into the sleeves and shrugging it onto his broad shoulders.

'Tell you what I'll do,' he conceded. 'At least, if you're nice to me.'

'Nice to him, the man says.' Jude shrugged, appealing to an invisible audience. 'Okay, I'll be nice. What will you do?' How quickly, how easily, had she slipped into loving Richard. Yes, the attraction had started the very first day they'd met, but had been interrupted by his idiotic belief in the anonymous reports he'd been sent. Now, after several weeks of working side by side, it had started to grow again. And yet, a suddenly apprehensive shiver chased away her happiness, and she wondered again if something terrible would cause it to all come crashing down. If it did, she thought her pain would be far greater than when she'd walked away from Julian.

Aware Richard had said something, she dismissed her black thoughts. 'Sorry. What was that?'

'I said I could drop you off at your house, so you can get changed and I'll let the boss know you'll be late in, so he doesn't fire—' He stopped in abrupt dismay.

Jude sighed. 'I've already told you, you're going to have to stop being so sensitive. Okay, we got off to a poor start. You weren't given much choice, were you, with all that rubbish you were sent? Now we have to forget it. We can't watch every little word we say, every nuance.

You're making a joke, okay? Finish what you were going to say and I promise I'll laugh.'

'He doesn't fire you,' Richard finished slowly. 'You're very forgiving.' He slipped his arms round her waist and looked down at her, his eyes dark with remorse.

'We can't watch every word we say,' she repeated. 'Now look, even you're going to be late. Come on.'

He drove into town, pulled up outside her door and leaned over to kiss her. Even though one hand stayed on the steering wheel and one on the gear lever, his kiss alone dissolved her into melting longing, making her recall every passionate moment of their weekend, every breathy whisper and touch, every kiss and caress. Damn, but she'd got it bad.

'I'll be coming in with you at this rate,' Richard joked. 'Hey... why don't you take your time... pack some stuff? Stay with me tonight... the rest of the week?'

Jude remained silent for a few moments before replying. 'No. No, not yet. I... I'm not sure I want to take that step just yet, okay? Give me some space here. Maybe next weekend, if you still want me, I'll stay again?'

She saw his face fall, heard his sigh. 'Okay. And yes. I think—just maybe—I might want you to stay.'

Getting out of the car, Jude flashed a quick smile, walked through her tiny front garden and let herself into her quiet house. Leaning back against the door, she wondered why she'd refused to return to the Hall. Partly because she felt this was all moving rather fast, no matter how intense her feelings were. She wanted time to catch her breath before taking the next step. And there was still a small but ever-present niggling fear that he might turn on her again. Oh, hell! She'd think about it all later.

Arriving at the office just after ten, Jude found Helen sitting at her desk skimming through something online, a cup of coffee by her side.

'Hello, Jude.' Helen looked up. 'Some coffee?'

Jude glanced at the closed inner door. 'Yes, I will, thanks. Is Richard in?' Even speaking his name made her stomach flip.

'No. He went off first thing to see David about his software. He left a message for you, though.'

A cool message, despite the new look in his eye and the energy sparking out of him today. Helen had wondered why he hadn't wanted to know where Jude was, despite the improvement in relationships over the last few weeks.

'What was his message?' Jude asked, studying the toe of her shoe.

'Just to tell you where he'd gone and that he'd be back before lunch, and when you came in, not to give up on him. He wanted to talk something over with a couple of the Master Systems software engineers, before David goes off to the exhibition next week. Very vibrant, he was. Seemed… I don't know… different somehow.' Helen looked at Jude curiously, but could only see the top of her head.

'Mmm, yes. No doubt he'll want to discuss it when he gets back.'

'It worried me he'd want to know where you were this morning, and I didn't know. You usually ring in if you can't make it.'

'And did he ask?'

'Well, no, he didn't. To be honest, I didn't understand. He said he expected you'd be in by lunchtime, but how did he know that?' Helen looked rather helpless and shook her head. 'But yes, he's different today. Pleasant, buoyed up.'

'Good.' Jude grinned at her. 'And don't worry. Richard knew where I was. He spoke to me early this morning. Anyway, I better try to get some work done. At least show willing.'

The lift whined to a halt and footsteps approached the office.

'Too late,' Helen warned, obviously concerned for Jude, maybe wondering if Richard might be unpleasant. Jude could have reassured her on that score but for now decided on discretion.

'Miss Drayton,' Richard said gravely. 'Good morning. Is everything well with you today? I hope you had a good weekend?'

'Mr Blake.' Jude inclined her head and stood up. 'Yes. My weekend was surprising but very enjoyable, thank you.'

She was aware of Helen looking at them, her eyes widening, and a small smile creeping over her face. It already looked as if she might be reaching her own conclusions. She sighed and gave a slight shake of her head as she followed Richard into the inner office.

'Jude...' Richard pulled her into his arms the minute he'd kicked the door shut behind them. His mouth claimed hers as she wound her arms round his neck and returned the kiss with as much passion as he offered. 'That was too long,' he murmured, raising his head. 'Too long since I saw you last.'

He leaned his back against the door, Jude still held within the circle of his arms. As he spoke, he dropped kisses on top of her head, on her forehead and eyelids, then took possession of her mouth again in a kiss that went on and on, leaving them both breathless.

Eventually, he drew back. 'Can we go home?'

Jude smothered a laugh. 'I've only just come in. What on earth would Helen think if we both disappeared again?'

'Nothing, probably. She doesn't realise yet what's happened. She was on edge this morning, waiting for me to ask where you were.'

'I know. She was worried for me in case you decided to eat me alive, but you can dismiss the idea she doesn't know what's going on. Her face, just then, said it all. She's guessed.' Jude laughed as Richard made a growling noise and bit her neck, forcing her head back. 'Put me down.' Jude pushed against his chest as he tried once more to cover her face with kisses. 'I'd love to go home with you, Mr Blake, but I'm going to say no. We already discussed this, remember?'

The intercom made them both jump, startled by the intrusion into their own private world.

'Mr Eller on the phone, Mr Blake. He'd like to speak to you. Shall I put the call through?'

Richard sighed and ran a hand through his hair, breaking away from Jude. He moved over to his desk and depressed the button to reply to Helen. 'Yes, thanks, Mrs Gresham.'

He grinned at Jude as she moved over to her own desk and dumped her case down, unzipping it and pulling out her laptop, taken home with the intention of doing some work. Jude smiled secretly, a feeling of warmth spreading through her. Fat chance she'd had of that.

Richard perched on the edge of his desk as he waited for Helen to connect David. 'David? Yes, I've only just got back. They've already decided they can do it? That's great, and thanks for letting me know. I wasn't expecting to hear from you so soon... oh, they did? Let them know I appreciate it, won't you? What was that? Oh, Jude.' Richard grinned across the room at her. She looked up and crossed over to stand by him, head on one side. He slipped his arm round her and she laid her cheek on the soft wool of his dark suit, running her hands under his jacket, over the fine cotton of his shirt, revelling in the feel of his body under her fingers, the aromas she'd come to love. Richard kept the phone to his ear, his hand covering the mouthpiece as he bent to kiss her, his arm pulling her more tightly to his side. She could hear David on the other end of the phone.

'... meant to ask when you were over here if you're behaving in a more civilised manner to her these days? I haven't heard from her since she rang to tell me off after you let me down so badly, betraying my confidence like that, and I'm worried about her, because that's some time ago now. I was ashamed of you and I hope you're behaving better now. Jude's got a lot of go in her and—'

Richard choked off a sudden splutter of laughter as Jude dug her fingers into his back and his hand slid off the mouthpiece.

'Ouch. You little—'

'Richard? Are you all right?' David's voice came down the phone again.

'Ye-yes. Just a... a rather voracious creature whose appetite... um, sorry. Yes,' Richard said gravely, holding Jude back with his arm and grinning at her. 'Yes, she's got a lot of go, I agree with you there... but her enthusiasm can wear me out.'

Jude renewed her attack.

'Eh?' David sounded puzzled.

'Sorry, David.' Richard sounded breathless. 'I must go. There's someone in the office who's being rather demanding. I think I'm in trouble about—'

The phone fell with a clatter on the desk as Jude broke free of his restraining grip and launch herself at him.

'Richard? *Richard*?' David was shouting, his voice faintly tinny. Richard picked the phone up with one hand and fumbled it back onto the cradle, then slid his arms round Jude.

16

In the outer office, Helen picked up the ringing phone. 'Mr Eller? But I just put you through. Did you get cut off? There's only Miss Drayton in the office with him... You think in view of the previous animosity between them I should just check...? The phone *fell*? Are you sure? But Mr Blake... he wouldn't... Jude wouldn't... Yes, all right. Just hold on, please.'

Helen stood up and crossed to the office door. She tipped her head to one side. Unable to hear anything, but because David Eller was adamant that Richard had sounded strange and had dropped the phone, she knocked on the door. No answer. Helen paused. What was she to do? Surely... nothing could be wrong? There was total silence from the office. Her knock remained unacknowledged and David was waiting at the other end of the phone.

Helen opened the door and peered through the crack. She gasped, smothering a laugh as everything became clear. Richard Blake's happiness, Jude's relaxed manner, the dropped phone. Her boss and ex-boss were locked together in a passionate embrace, oblivious to the rest of the world. Helen pulled the door shut as quietly as she could.

'Mr Eller?' Helen picked up the phone, a grin on her face. 'I can assure you everything is all right... No, I haven't spoken to either of them but... How do I know? Because I *saw* them, Mr Eller. They didn't want interrupting... No, believe me, they don't want interrupting... It was amicable... very amicable, I think you could say. Yes, yes, you could say they've settled their differences very thoroughly.' Helen put the phone down, still laughing at David's loaded comments.

Helen propped her chin on her hand, a smile lingering on her face. Something had obviously happened this weekend. Good for them. They were ideally suited. The only thing left was to sort out the small matter of those anonymous reports. Ian Grey was due to go down to the exhibition soon, and when he did, she intended to do a little investigating. That man had been bitter ever since Jude had been appointed and she would be prepared to bet a penny to a pound he had something to do with them. It was just his sort of thing... spewing out his poison under the cover of official reports on the progress of the company. If they were on Ian's computer, Helen knew it would take her some time to locate them, which is why she'd been prepared to wait until he was out of town. Just as soon as he'd gone, she'd start looking. As the senior PA, she had every right to be in his office—no-one would query her.

Her mind made up, Helen got to her feet and collected the travel folder for her husband's trip to the exhibition in London. She might as well give it to him now... she wouldn't be needed for a while in there, that was for sure.

Before she could leave, Ian came in.

'Is Richard here?'

'Yes, but he's busy. Jude's in with him and I don't think they want any interruptions.'

Ian's face twisted and Helen was shocked at the flash of hatred which briefly showed. Already discontented, she knew he didn't like seeing Jude and Richard working well together, but this looked more than unhappiness. What was going on in his mind? Helen had never really liked Ian and her thoughts about him being the instigator of the all the trouble was now firmly embedded. She watched him now as he brought himself back under control, but it was obvious that annoyance still lurked in his narrowed eyes as he stared at the inner office door.

'Jude always seems to be *in* with him,' he remarked sourly. 'I don't understand—when that email arrived, he said Jude had to go but now they're as thick as thieves. I thought with Jude gone, Blake would go back to America and leave me in charge.'

His voice had descended into a frustrated mumble and Helen shivered at his animosity, which for once he wasn't trying to hide.

'*Mr* Blake, Ian. Mr Blake,' she reminded him acerbically. 'And obviously, once he'd seen and heard enough about Jude's work here, he reconsidered.'

The door between the two offices opened. Richard's head was turned as he finished something he was saying to Jude.

'...and I'm so pleased David can make a start on that new software. We better keep it under wraps for now. I'll see you later, okay?'

Turning, he saw Ian and paused, looking annoyed.

Helen, watching, hadn't missed the flash of interest on Ian's face when he heard the comment about new software and keeping it quiet. She saw his inner battle as he debated speaking, and her guess was it would be to question Richard in a congratulatory way about the proposed development—it would be just the sort of smarmy opportunity he loved. Oddly, he didn't, but stood silently watching his boss.

Oh, she was worrying unduly. After all, what good would it do to know something was being developed? Things were always being developed in the IT world.

'Ian,' Richard's voice was cool. 'Can I help you?'

'Just wanted to let you know everything's under control in Accounting.'

'So I should hope—and you don't need to come and tell me personally. An internal email will be fine in the future. Now, please excuse me because I want to go over to the assembly lines.'

Helen allowed herself an inward smile as she saw Ian's mouth tighten. He gave a baffled look at the now closed inner door, shrugged and turned on his heel.

But she swore she heard him muttering, as he left, about sorting things out once and for all—and somehow, she didn't think he meant the Accounts department.

17

The week passed peacefully. It leaked out round the factory that the old boss and the new boss had reached an amicable partnership in more ways than one and it was proving popular, with several jovial comments being made as one or the other of them passed through the factory for various reasons.

'This is good,' Richard commented, coming into the office after talking to Alec, one of the unfortunate personnel not getting the month's holiday. 'I'm finding everyone's stopped regarding me as an ogre. I seemed to have gained in popularity and humanity by taking up with you.' A surprising warmth flooded through him, and a sense of wonderment at the transformation there'd been in him from arriving a bitterly angry man, still curdled by the treatment meted out to him by his father, to now. The company was becoming *his* company. Jude had come into his life—strong, warm, vibrant, loving. He knew she was very much his equal, and sometimes he thought she was a better person than he was. She wasn't burdened with baggage from childhood and was more forgiving.

He dropped a quick kiss on Jude's head as he passed her desk, his hand on her shoulder.

'Mmm?' Jude covered his hand with her own as she looked up from her computer screen.

Taking advantage, this time Richard kissed her on the mouth and for a few moments neither of them gave any heed to work.

Sighing, Richard pulled himself upright, stepped away from her, and sat down at his own desk. 'I said it seemed I was gaining in popularity. I assume it's because I've taken up with you?'

'Oh, no, not just that,' Jude grinned. 'They all wondered, you know, when you came over here, what would happen. They're happy now they know their future is secure.'

'I suppose.' He gazed into the distance, chin on his fist, before dropping his hand onto his mouse and looking at Jude, a smile lightening his face. 'Are you coming home with me tonight?'

During the last week, Jude had returned to her own home each evening, hard though it had been. She was trying not to get too involved. Then all that happened was that she lay in bed at night, wishing she was with Richard, so keeping away seemed counterproductive.

'Oh, yes,' she said now, looking at him from under her eyelashes. 'If I'm wanted?'

'Brat. You know full well I've been pining for you all week and trying very hard to keep my hands off you here at work.'

'Same here, but I think it was a good idea, really. Gave us both some space, time to reflect, and be sure of what we want, didn't it? But yes… about this weekend. I already packed some stuff, and it's in my car. I can follow you out to High Foss. Wasn't sure what to bring, but I packed some stuff for walking.'

'There's a satellite live performance on at the local cinema on Sunday. The Bolshoi. I recall you enjoy ballet. I booked us two seats and we could eat out afterwards. It doesn't finish until about seven, or maybe even later. Is that okay?'

Jude stared at him in astonishment. 'You're prepared to watch ballet?'

'I like ballet.'

'Then great. I'd love to, thanks. Nowhere posh for dinner, I hope? I've only got jeans.'

'Indian suit you? There's one just behind the cinema which has a great reputation, so Ian tells me.'

'Oh, yes. I know the one and it *is* good. I've eaten there before.'

'Great. Um... would you mind showing me where this dog rescue place is, on our way? I've got their cheque from the blind auction, and ought to drop it off. I did the Women's Refuge last week. It's an interesting place. They have a room open for any women who wants to drop in just for a chat, whether or not physically abused. Women whose husbands don't treat them very well.' His mouth tightened. 'My mother would have enjoyed something like that, although...' His voice trailed off as he rubbed a finger over his lips. 'I don't know. Maybe she was just too proud and private. She might not have wanted to admit to her humiliation.' He recalled her silence about her husband, her dutiful attendance at formal dinners when she'd been told to be present, her quiet withdrawals if one of his father's women had turned up at the house and his insides churned with the same distress he'd felt as a young child. What a strange, unpleasant and bitter man his father had been.

Jude's face softened in sympathy. 'Things have changed in the last fifty or so years. Women have more determination and courage to speak out about what's going wrong in their relationships. Not all of them, though. Which is why we still need that refuge, and others like it. So sad.' Resting her chin on her hand, she stared out of the window before giving a small shake of her head and turning back to Richard. 'Yes, we can go round by the shelter. I enjoy going there.'

He smiled in response, but his eyes returned to his screen. He didn't often allow his personal feelings to show and even though this was Jude, he automatically shut down. If he concentrated on his work, he'd calm down and return to the present, where he was happy and was beginning to feel love and trust were possible. He was aware of Jude looking at him for a few more moments before she returned to the article she was reading and was grateful for her understanding the subject was closed. One day, he'd tell her everything, but it was still too raw and he preferred to push it to one side—the treatment of his mother, his own suffering at the hands of a man who was supposed to have nurtured him, but at every step tried to destroy him. Sometimes, he wasn't sure how he'd come through it, to be honest.

The rest of the afternoon passed peacefully as they sorted out various tasks. Finally, when the five-thirty buzzer sounded, Jude and Richard looked at each other, a silent question given and answered. They both closed their computers and within seconds were in an embrace, passion spilling from both.

'Home.' Richard breathed, as he dropped soft kisses on Jude's eyelids, cheeks and mouth. 'Home now. I can't bear it a moment longer.'

'No. You've forgotten the shelter. You said we'd call in at the dog rescue?'

Pulling back, Richard gave a quick frown. 'Damn. So I did. I don't suppose we could put it off—'

'Let's get it done. It won't take long. Come on, follow my car. It's not much of a diversion, I promise.'

They were soon there, but it wasn't so easy to just leave a cheque for five hundred pounds and get away without effusive thanks and the offer to tour the premises. The cat cages were large, with a cat ramp leading from the ground to a platform where there were the beds and toys, and from there, access to an outside space. This was because, the organiser informed them, the cats would forget all the smells and sounds of being outside, and be nervous when introduced back to a garden when they were re-homed.

The sheds which housed the dogs were similar. A large cage, but no upper platform this time, just access to an outdoor pen. They'd divided the pens with solid fencing. Explaining this, the organiser said there would be too much barking and growling if the dogs could see each other or see the personnel. They ambled round, glancing in at the animals. Some were looking resigned, some jumping and barking, others asleep.

Walking in front of Jude and the organiser, Richard stopped, immobile, staring into a pen. He sank down on his haunches and held out a tentative hand towards the wire. Jude stepped forward. She saw what appeared to be a tangle of wild grey fur propped against the wiring. Two sad, supplicating eyes had fixed on Richard. A pink tongue came out and touched the outstretched hand, and Jude saw Richard swallow hard as he slipped a finger through the wire and scratched at the top of the dog's head.

He stood up. 'This dog...' he cleared his throat, the pain in his eyes obvious. 'This dog. Is it up for adoption?'

'Yes, she is. Actually, she's—'

Richard's hand rose, silencing the organiser. 'I know who she is. She's my old dog's pup. She had a litter just before I left. I came home and found my father drowning the pups.' He sighed and looked defeated. 'But... I took my dog and the only remaining pup to a friend of my mother's. Mrs Hardcastle. I knew I could trust her, so what happened? Why's the pup here? Well, hardly a pup. She must be six going on seven by now. But she's got a few years left in her. Her mother was ten when she had that litter.'

'I'm sorry, Mr Blake. Mrs Hardcastle died about four months ago. The older dog was put down because she'd got cancer. There was no-one to take this one in, so she ended up here.'

'I want her,' Richard spoke decisively, bending down once more to touch the dog gently through the wire.

'Of course. But... not tonight? You must get a bed for her, a lead, some food. We have to process the paperwork and she needs another couple of injections. Mrs Hardcastle spayed and chipped her, so no problem there.'

Jude stood next to Richard. The dog's eyes were bright and loving and she pressed up against the wire, almost as if she knew Richard had been her saviour once before, and would be again.

'What's her name?' Jude asked.

'Scrap,' the organiser smiled, 'because she was so tiny.'

'Hello, Scrap,' Jude whispered, reaching through and scratching at her head. She turned her head and saw Richard knuckle first one eye and then the other before standing up and turning away, shoulders hunched.

After a few moments, while Jude crooned to the scruffy grey dog, Richard turned back. 'When can I collect her then?'

'Monday. Would that be okay? If we haven't managed her injections by then, you can take her to the vet yourself, I imagine?'

'Monday,' Richard murmured. 'Monday. Yes. Good. I'll see you then.'

Turning, he strode away with a brief word of thanks thrown over his shoulder, leaving Jude to say their goodbyes. When she appeared at the driver's side window, he saw her concerned look and attempted to smile as he wound down the window.

'See you at the Hall?'

Jude nodded. 'Off you go. I'll follow.'

Richard was sitting in the kitchen, moodily staring out of the window, a mug of coffee in front of him, and a second mug waiting for Jude. His shoulders were hunched defensively. There'd been too much emotion today. Talking about the refuge had brought back bitter memories, then to see his old dog's pup sitting miserably in the pen at the animal rescue had almost broken him. His past was weighing heavily on him and just at the moment, it was winning against his new life here, his optimism about the future, even winning against Jude. He couldn't stop his mind returning to the day he'd found his father drowning the pups, his unexpected tears and the sneers the older man had directed his way because of his reaction. Scooping up the last remaining pup, calling his dog, he'd turned and walked away from the Hall, unsure of where to go or what to do, but knowing only one thing was now definite—he was going to leave. Mrs Hardcastle had met him in the village. Kind and observant, she'd questioned him, taken his dog and the pup, promising to look after them. He was sorry she'd died, too, and he'd not known.

'Give it a minute in the microwave if it's cooled down too much.' His voice was flat.

She sipped, nodded, and sat down. 'It's fine. I'm sorry it upset you back there.'

'Ah... not upset exactly. I was glad to see Scrap. Well, not glad, but glad I found her and can give her a suitable home. Just that it brought back that dreadful day when I got back from the factory and found she'd had the pups that afternoon and he... hell.' His fist smacked down on the table and it remained there, the knuckles white. 'I only saved that one pup. Jessie was looking at me whimpering, and the pain in her eyes was awful. She knew what was going on. Why was he so awful? Why did he have to be so bloody unkind all the time, Jude?'

She laid her hand over his tense fist and rubbed softly. 'I can't answer that. He wasn't a very nice person towards anyone, you know. You got the brunt of it, though. I suppose it was just his character. He's gone, sweetheart. Gone. I'm sorry about the other puppies and glad you saved Jessie and Scrap. Try to let it go, love.'

'I was doing okay, but seeing Scrap—she's so like Jessie—brought that horrible day back. I knew after that I had to go. I hated him by then, but what he did to the pups sickened me. It must have been only another couple of weeks before I left.'

'And look at what you achieved.'

'Yes.' Richard turned anguished eyes on Jude. 'But sometimes I worry I'll end up like him. This hatred has been burning in me since I left.'

'You don't have to hate any more. He's gone. The factory has changed. You yourself have said you feel better about it all. It's only when something like this brings it back, it hurts. But you've won. I don't think you'll ever end up like him,' Jude murmured. 'He would never have rounded off and then doubled the money from the blind auction.'

Richard looked up, startled. He hadn't been aware she knew of that. 'Helen told you?'

'Yes, but on the side. She wasn't trumpeting the news to everyone. And I asked, anyway. I was curious why you'd gone to speak to Alec just after the auction finished. It was a lovely gesture. Certainly not one your father would ever have made. You saved Jessie and Scrap, and now rescued Scrap again. And I never heard the workforce say a good word about him. They spoke better of you, on your return, even though they were wary about what you intended to do with the place.'

Richard sat, absorbing her words, then his hand curled round hers as he lifted it to his lips and kissed her knuckles, his eyes alight with hope and love. 'I hope you're right. I hope everything is behind me. Him, my hatred and those reports.'

They spent the evening lazily, with passion ebbing and waning. Richard and Jude, Adam and Anna, who cared, now?

Finally, they ended up in the kitchen, exhausted and laughing.

'No more,' Richard said, as he chopped onions for a Bolognese sauce. 'I think maybe it was a good idea of yours not to stay every night. Uncertain we would've had any energy left for work.' He shot Jude a grin as she sat at the table nursing a glass of white wine.

There was a long pause.

Richard slowed, then stopped his chopping. 'Jude?' He glanced over his shoulder to see her fiddling with the wine glass.

Jude sighed. 'I love you, but... I still worry this is all moving too fast, even though I'm not sure how to slow things down. I worry, still, about what you said earlier, about hoping it was all behind you.' Jude paused and sipped her wine. Putting the glass down, she looked at him. 'Richard... what if something happens which leads to... oh, I don't know... you losing faith in me again? Blaming me for something? I warn you, if you do—if you doubt me—I'm not staying around to take it, understand?'

'Oh, Jude...' he put the knife down on the board, and sighed, staring into the far distance. 'I don't think I will. I really don't.'

Jude shook her head. 'Sorry. I've put a dampener on things. Sorry.'

Richard resumed his chopping. 'No,' he said. 'I can see it worries you and I can understand why. I think we have to speak of it occasionally. My behaviour to you was appalling and you know I'm sorry. And... maybe one way to slow things down *is* for you stay at home during the week, like you said you wanted to anyway. But leave some stuff here and keep on coming for the weekends? Maybe later, when we know each other better, you'll move in with me?'

'Okay.' Smiling, Jude stood up and came behind Richard, resting her cheek on his back, her arms snaking round his waist. 'Any plans for tomorrow? We need to get stuff for Scrap, don't forget.'

'Unhand me, brat, I need to get these in the pan,' Richard said, a touch of laughter in his voice as he turned in the circle of her arms to kiss her, his mood lightening. He moved to the cooker, and Jude sat down again as he continued speaking. 'Yes, we do, but there's time for a walk first. This time, no picnic, but lunch at a rather good pub I know. Then on the way back we can stop off in town and pick up the stuff I need for the dog.' He stirred the pan's contents, lifted the spoon and tasted, then added a quick shake of salt. 'Have you ever walked the Fossdale circuit?'

'No. Is it round here?'

'Further afield. There are a lot of Fosses or Forces round here. Viking influence. This one takes in a waterfall, though. Two, actually. And a limestone pavement and cove.'

'Sounds interesting.'

'You'll enjoy it,' Richard spoke with confidence as he continued making the sauce. 'Okay, job for you. Can you measure out some pasta and set it on to cook?'

The rest of the evening passed pleasantly and the following morning, after a tender session of making love, Richard and Jude drove to Fossdale village.

The walk and lunch were all Richard had promised. Starting from the village, they went up a river valley with bluebells and wild garlic flowers lacing into the grass. The path eventually reached the Fairy Foss, a sheet of water running over a curve of rock, which Richard explained was called tufa. It fell, bubbling into a deep pool before spilling over and running down the way they'd walked.

'It's a limestone which has built up from deposits in the water. Well, weird as it sounds, it's built *down*.'

'*Down?*'

'Mmm. As the water flows over the lip of the fall, tiny amounts of limestone get deposited on the rock and then the moss, calcifying it and forming a lip which increases with time. It's probably taken a few hundreds of years, although I'm hazy about the timescale. You can cross over and look behind it.'

They stepped over the natural dam to the far side, where Jude, in fascination, could see how the tufa had formed its own "stone waterfall" with the original rock behind, where hart's tongue ferns grew in profusion.

'Wow. Limestone is weird,' Jude commented. 'Weird, but magical.'

From there, they followed a stream into a narrow limestone gorge, similar to the one that led up to High Foss. Another waterfall loomed ahead.

'We climb that,' Richard grinned at her.

'*Climb* it? How far? Come to that, how *can* we, anyway?' She shot him a doubtful look. 'I walk, Richard. I'm not a climber.'

He laughed and put his arm round her to bring her to a standstill. 'Look.' He pointed. 'Only the first bit and you can get about a third the way up that, on the rocks at the base. There's water running there, but it's easy enough, when the stream's low, like it is now, to step from rock to rock. When we get there, you'll see it's almost like a staircase and what you can't see from here is the path veering left away from the fall, so we don't have to go any higher than that first lip, okay?'

Unconvinced, Jude shot him a doubtful look, but realised when they reached the fall that he was right. With him behind her, she managed the climb and as he'd promised, they turned left into a small valley before rising onto the moors behind.

After crossing a wind-blown moor and rough grass meadows, they dropped onto the limestone pavement. Rough ribs of whitish rock, with deep fissures between, streaked across in front of them, in which grew more of the hart's tongue ferns like those seen behind the waterfall. It was attractive, but very difficult to walk over, and Jude was glad they only had to cross a short stretch. Before descending a series of steps combined with a path down the side of an amazing white limestone cliff, they stopped to look at the view, which on a clear day, seemed to stretch for miles. At the bottom of the cliff, Jude found the clearest stream she'd ever seen, magically bubbling up from its base. From there, a straightforward path led back to the village and the pub.

Once seated and having placed their order, Jude sat back, looking utterly contented.

'That,' she said, smiling at Richard, 'was about the best walk ever. I loved it. But I'm starving hungry now, for sure, hence my choice of the Yorkshire pudding.'

After lunch, as they drove into town to buy the things Richard needed for Scrap, Richard felt an overwhelming happiness, which it seemed Jude shared. Surely, nothing could come between him and Jude now? As far as he was concerned, he loved this woman and was sure it would be forever.

18

Ian was becoming increasingly anxious. He still had to finalise his plans for Jude's ultimate downfall. It'd been impossible recently to find the office empty of both Richard and Jude, and it worried him he wouldn't be able to fulfil what he intended—a search for evidence about a new software development, which it seemed only Richard and Jude knew about. His tentative idea meant it was imperative he found something before he went down to London, because that was where he was going to set off a chain of events he hoped would mean the end of Jude Drayton. He'd bided his time for a very long time, sure that within months of Jude's arrival, she'd fail miserably and the CEO's job would be his, but instead finding she turned everything round and make the company a success. His resentment and bitterness grew alongside, and seeing how well Jude and Richard were now working together had tipped him into a determined crusade fuelled by his warped personality and hatred.

The week of the exhibition, when the Mercury would be unveiled to the IT world, arrived. Alec Gresham had already gone down to set everything up for the opening day, and would stay until Wednesday evening, returning the following day when he'd had a chance himself to have a good look round. Ian was taking over on Thursday, before closing their stand down on Friday evening, and knew he had to get into the shared office before he left, otherwise all his careful planning so far would be wasted.

He'd needed a willing accomplice and this he'd found, as he'd thought he might, in Julian Langley at TechDrive, but it took until the very last moment to complete the rest of it.

On Wednesday, Richard had driven south to have a look at the exhibition himself, leaving the newly-acquired and deliriously happy Scrap in the competent hands of Mrs Miller, his daily help.

Jude, after spending most of the morning in the office, had gone off for lunch with one of their customers who wanted to upgrade to the Mercury. Ian hovered in the vicinity of the office until Helen also took herself off for lunch. Once she was out of sight, he slid through the door and into the inner office. Going over to Richard's desk, he moved the mouse. Damn. The man had shut down, and Ian hadn't a clue what password he'd be using. Jude, then. His hand trembling with nervousness, he touched Jude's mouse and exhaled in relief when the desktop came up. Quick, quick... run through her folders. What would it be under?

It was almost an anti-climax when he spotted a folder entitled Blake Software. Neither was the folder password protected, as he'd feared it might. Opening it, he selected all the pages and sent them to the printer. Hearing the LaserJet begin its quiet whirring, he rushed into the outer office, hand outstretched, ready to collect up the incriminating document, page by page. Once he had them in his hand, he whipped back to Jude's computer and sat down, opening, this time, her email account. Using the address he'd been given last week by Julian Langley, he typed a message, added an empty folder he'd created, also called

Blake Software, and pressed send. Breathing fast, he deleted the folder, put the computer to sleep, gathered the papers together and stood up.

His heart pounded, and he shook with relief and triumph. Done it. Nothing would stop him now. Nothing would save Jude. He had her right where he wanted her and it was even more amusing that she didn't know, hadn't a clue what was coming. No turning back, even if he wanted to, which was most definitely not on the cards. He had no remorse. He intended to see this through and wreck Jude, whether or not he gained..

Having returned from lunch, Helen was just opening her desk drawer when she heard a sound from the inner office. She froze. Who was in there, with Richard away and Jude out with a customer?

She threw open the door between the offices. 'Ian!'

He saw her shocked look and knew Helen wasn't a friend. She was too close to Jude. Watching, Ian saw her looking round the office. Her eyes narrowed, looking for anything untoward. He knew it would all appear as normal, but she still stood there, looking cross and shaking her head.

'What are you doing?'

'Wasn't aware I couldn't come in here.' He fought to make his face blank, give her no ammunition, nothing to accuse him of later.

'What are you *doing*?'

'Some papers I need for tomorrow,' he answered, inwardly laughing as he waved the precious documents in her face. 'Richard said they'd be in here.'

'Oh. Well, in that case…' she moved back from the door. He crossed towards her, unable to stop a huge grin from crossing his face.

'You look very pleased with yourself,'

'Oh, you know... couple of days at the exhibition... makes a change... and you never know what will happen, do you? You can meet a lot of useful people.'

'Hmph,' Helen turned to her desk and sat down.

He knew she was still watching him as he lounged in the doorway, in no hurry to go.

'Well, if there's nothing else,' she added pointedly, 'some of us have work to do, even if you haven't.'

'Oh, I have, I have,' he assured her, a glint of malicious amusement in his eyes. 'I have a phone call to make.' To let Julian Langley know it was all successfully in place. The call was the last part of his Machiavellian jigsaw. On Friday, all the pieces would fall in place and bingo.

The end should be pyrotechnical.

Pity he wouldn't be around to see it.

Ian felt her eyes follow him as he nodded at her and left, knowing the whole encounter had disturbed her. But what could she say? What could she do? He clenched his suddenly trembling hands round the sheaf of paper he carried and swallowed convulsively. This time next week... he, Ian Grey, would be the one conferring with Richard Blake, making decisions about the company. And his final step would be to encourage Richard's return to America.

The exhibition in the Midlands was a big one. Ian Grey took charge of the Aurora stand on Thursday morning and was enjoying his autonomous position, feeling very pleased with himself. By the weekend, Ian would be where he should have been for the last three years... in charge of Aurora. Blake-Aurora, in fact. Even better. He rubbed his hands together and glanced at his watch. Nearly time for the final part of his plan to be put into place. He didn't know why he hadn't done something like this long ago. It would have been more effective than—

Ah!

There he was now. Julian Langley, drifting along, looking at this stand, that stand. Clever. Very clever. This way, it wouldn't look as if they had planned the meeting. Ian bent down, pulled the envelope of the printed pages from his document case, and laid them ready on top of the Aurora stand.

His time-bomb.

He sniggered in delight.

Julian Langley stopped by the Aurora stand. 'Ian Grey?'

'The same, the same,' Ian said affably, holding out his hand.

Julian Langley looked at it for a moment before rather reluctantly reaching out for a brief shake. 'You have the documents?' he asked.

'Here.' He handed the other man the brown envelope. 'Did you get the email?'

'Here.' Julian touched the breast pocket of his suit.

'And you know what I want you to do?'

'Make sure these get passed to David Eller of Master Systems, together with the email.'

The two men smiled coldly at each other.

'What you do with them before they get passed to David Eller is up to you,' Ian said. 'But... that marketing job? If I need it, maybe you could see to it I'm appointed? In exchange for this?' He nodded at the envelope, determined to cover his back in case anything went wrong.

'Of course. I didn't doubt you'd ask.' Julian gave him a veiled look of contempt. 'Anyway, it'll be good to see Jude get her comeuppance at last. Sanctimonious bitch.' Julian Langley glanced around as he spoke, picked up the envelope and tucked it under his arm. 'Just before I go, a bit of gossip, okay? What will happen to Aurora Technology now that Blake's come over from America? Is he going to sell up, do you know, and go back to the States?'

'Not as far as I know... yet. He intends to keep Aurora up and running.'

'And no doubt run production of his laptops as well?'

'Yes.'

'Damn it,' Julian said with tight lips. 'He'll be able to drop his price now. Still, inevitably, he'd use Aurora to give him a European outlet for his laptops, so we won't go breaking our hearts over that one. How come, if he's staying, that doesn't take care of your problem with Jude after what you told me about those reports you sent?'

Ian frowned. 'When Blake came back, I expected her to be given the boot. I'd put in enough groundwork for that to happen. But somehow it all went wrong. Too many people saying too many things in her favour,' Ian added bitterly. 'And even worse, now.'

'Worse?'

'It looks as if the pair of them have taken up together.'

Julian Langley whistled. 'No wonder you need a lever to get rid of her. I wondered just why you'd set this up... it all seemed rather drastic.' He shrugged. 'Should do it, I think. I'll dump it on Eller late on Friday, just before we close, okay? That do you?' One eyebrow went up as he dismissed Ian and turned to wander casually off to look at another stand nearby.

'Great. Great, thanks.' Ian's voice cracked with relief. A tremor swept over him. So easy. So damned easy.

If it was only Richard, Jude, David and his engineers who knew about this software, then he'd done it. The Master Systems people wouldn't talk. They were all carefully screened and paid well. They threw anyone who was indiscreet out without ceremony, and the security there had always been top-notch.

Richard Blake wouldn't say anything to anyone, close-lipped bastard that he was. David Eller was no more likely to speak out about it than Richard. A CEO who spilled news of recent developments would last no longer than milliseconds.

So—*Jude* would get the blame. Humming tunelessly under his breath, Ian tidied the stand, well-satisfied with his plan so far.

*****

Friday evening came. Julian Langley kept his eye on Master Systems, and just as David Eller shrugged into his coat and picked up his laptop case, Julian closed in.

'Mr Eller?'

David looked up.

'My name's Julian Langley. I don't believe we've met before. I work for TechDrive and admire your company's software, sir. Excellent stuff.'

David raised an eyebrow. TechDrive did their own software. He couldn't see what this man wanted with him. It was late, he still had to drive north, and the motorway at this time of night on a Friday was horrendous. He sighed. 'Can I help you?' he asked, hiding his irritation at being delayed.

'Mmm, well, yes. I think maybe you could.' He nodded at the chairs left stranded by the now empty stand of Master Systems. 'Could we sit down for a moment?'

'Please do.' David indicated one chair and hooked the other with his foot, pulling it closer.

Julian sat down and opened his briefcase. 'I don't know if you're aware...' he began, then stopped and gave a boyish grin. 'Hope I'm not speaking out of turn here,' he said disarmingly.

David gave a silent sigh. Having started out in marketing himself, he recognised a softening up gambit and wished this Langland or Langley or whatever they called him would recognise this was like meeting with like and get down to the basics. 'I'm sure not,' he said now with courtesy.

'I gather you have something to do with Aurora Technology?'

'We do their software, yes,' David admitted. Now what?

Julian shook his head, projecting sorrowful regret. 'Jude Drayton and I used to know each other... very well. Very well indeed.'

'Oh, yes?' This wasn't the person he would have picked out for Jude.

'I've sometimes wondered... over the last three years, you know, since she left TechDrive... whether she hasn't regretted it...'

Not that he'd noticed. Happy as a sandboy. David gazed at Julian Langley, carefully keeping an expression of neutral politeness in place. Where was this leading? Apparently not to a hard sell. 'Regretted what?'

'Leaving our firm... leaving me. It was very sudden when she left. I know she'd hoped to be appointed to my position, but then, she didn't have the necessary ideas for a company like ours...' Julian shrugged, rolling his eyes and sighing.

David was not feeling cooperative. There was something funny here, and he wasn't sure he liked it. 'I thought your marketing department had lost a bit of sparkle in recent years.'

Julian frowned. 'Not at all. We're aiming for a more conservative market these days.'

Settling himself with resignation in his chair and wishing the man would come to the point, David sighed. In which case, they would lose sales. No-one wanted a *conservative* computer company. 'I see,' he commented dryly. 'And how can *I* help you?'

'Ah... well, this takes us back to Jude... As I said, I've often wondered if she didn't regret her move... we had a query from her a few weeks ago about a position within the marketing department. Sent her the information pack. I don't know if she applied, but... Look, I don't quite know how to say this...'

'Straight out would help.'

Julian's look was frankly murderous this time. He knew David was not impressed and somewhat disbelieving that he had anything of importance to communicate. Well, he'd soon shift the bastard's polite smile.

'Right,' he retorted. 'Look at this.'

From the envelope, he pulled out and slapped down on the table between the two chairs, the print-out of Richard's ideas for the software development, and an email. David picked up the photocopies first. Keeping his face expressionless, he hid his utter shock at what he was looking at. 'How did you get hold of this?' he asked.

'Attachment sent with this email.' Julian indicated the remaining sheet with a flick of his finger.

David reached forwards to pick it up. 'Dear Julian,' he read, 'I think this should prove of some interest to you and I send it for old time's sake. Looking forward to working at TechDrive again. With love, as always, Jude.' David swallowed, dismayed. What on earth was Jude playing at? Was she mad? Was she *mad*?

19

By the end of Thursday, Helen had found no trace of the reports on Ian's computer. She was discouraged but knew she hadn't given herself much time. Alec had been due back from the exhibition in the Midlands and she'd wanted to be at home when he'd arrived. Today, Friday, she intended to try again.

During the afternoon Helen went into Richard's office. Jude and Richard stood close together, looking at some online catalogues as they discussed the presentation of their own computers. Richard was planning to incorporate his own laptops into their present marketing policy.

'I like this,' he said, smiling down at her. 'You're a woman of many talents, Jude my darling.' He saw Helen waiting by the door. 'Yes, Mrs Gresham? Look, could I call you Helen, as Jude does?' He gave her his charming smile.

Helen could see why anyone would think this man attractive, now he was so relaxed. 'By all means call me Helen.'

'Mrs Gresham sounds so formal. And will you call me Richard? Everyone does in America, and I'm finding all this formality over here daunting. Well,' he turned to Jude, 'except they all seem to call you by your first name.'

'Give them a chance, Richard,' Jude said. 'They've known me three years. You've suddenly come on the scene again. Now you've announced your plans and they realise you're not like your father...' she paused and grinned at him, 'well, they'll come round to you soon. Give it another year or two.'

Richard laughed. 'Only that long? Anyway, sorry Helen. You wanted something?'

'Just to say,' Helen said, 'that if you've nothing for me to do, I've some bits and pieces I promised to sort out for Ian while he was away.'

Jude shot her a sharp look of surprise. Helen had very little time for Ian. Why this sudden cooperation? Helen avoided looking at Jude, her eyes fixed on Richard, waiting for his reply.

'He's not imposing on you, is he?' Richard asked rather absently, as he moved the mouse and brought up a new page.

'Oh, no. I'm up to date with everything you wanted me to do, and nothing to organise for anyone else. I said if I finished up, I'd help him out,' Helen said, her voice innocent. Help him *out* just about sums it up, she thought with some satisfaction.

'Then by all means.' Richard glanced up at her. 'I only hope he appreciates it.'

Helen withdrew as quietly as she'd arrived and walked along the corridor to Ian's office. Like everyone else had a habit of doing, as she'd found out yesterday, he'd neglected to log off before leaving his office. They were all at fault here, Helen realised, shaking her head as she sat down at his computer.

She went back into his documents. There were hundreds of folders in there, work-related ones common to everyone which she could ignore, and many she'd already searched yesterday. His hard drive must be just about on its knees. All the remaining documents still needed checking, and it would take her some time. She glanced at her watch, bit down on her bottom lip and set to work with determination.

Some two hours later, she leaned forward, her eyes lighting up. Yes. *Yes*. She'd found it. Buried in a folder within a folder within a folder within a... she had lost count and had nearly shrugged her shoulders and given up on this line of investigation. It was only her steely determination to open everything until there was nothing left to open which had led to it. She breathed in and scanned the contents of the document on the screen. This was it.

Helen clicked on the print icon and heard the laser printer hum into action. Closing the document, she opened the next one in the obscure folder. Again, it was what she wanted. There was no need to look further. There were five reports in total and she printed out the lot. She didn't read them in detail but caught sight of enough to make her whistle under her breath.

It was no wonder Richard had arrived hating Jude and linking her in with his father. What a bastard Ian had proved to be. Although Helen had suspected he was behind the maliciousness Jude had been the victim of, it was still a shock to realise it was true and that he could be so unprincipled and vicious in such a subtle and professional manner. She couldn't blame Richard for reading and believing these reports. They'd started innocently enough. Even when the innuendos about Jude had been inserted, they'd been couched in very careful terms, showing concern only for the well-being of the firm which made what they said even more believable and shocking. The picture they had built up of Jude wasn't pleasant at all.

Collecting the final print-out, she shuffled the papers together and slid them into an envelope. Here was all the proof she needed to get Ian Grey the sack, and she had every intention of using it. Helen switched off the printer, closed all the programs on Ian's computer, and, after a quick look round which showed no sign of disturbance, she left, feeling thoroughly satisfied.

Now the only decision she had to make was whether to deliver these papers to Richard now, or wait until Monday. Checking her watch, she wondered if he might still be in the office, but when she got there, it was to find him gone. She shrugged. She'd take them home with her and give them to Richard on Monday.

Nothing would happen over the weekend.

20

David Eller was frowning as he pulled off the motorway on his last leg of the journey home to Crossfield. He glanced at the clock on his dashboard. Late though it was, he had the most uncomfortable task yet of phoning Richard, for to ring him tonight was unavoidable. It was a conversation he'd postponed until he got home. Not one suitable for hands-free while driving in Friday evening traffic.

The software development pages and the email from Jude lay on the seat beside him. Now and then David glanced down at them.

Julian Langley, eh? Claimed to be Jude's ex-boyfriend. Implied Jude was still interested in him and wanted to return to her old firm. Well, maybe. He knew, who better, that Jude hadn't been happy with Richard and had been looking for another job. However, over the last three months things seemed to have settled down, and the previous week Helen had implied there had been a startling personal development between Richard and Jude. David, for one, could see that was a definite possibility.

So how come, if that was true, Jude had sent Julian Langley such a startling email *yesterday*?

Jude was fiercely loyal. If she'd decided Richard was the man for her, David couldn't see her stabbing him in the back. She was devoted to Aurora Technology and had taken great pride in restoring the firm's fortunes. If Richard and she were now working together, there was no way she would do the firm down.

The more David considered this, the more he thought there was something strange going on. Why, anyway, had Julian Langley approached him? Why not go to Ian Grey on the Aurora stand and inform *him* of the perfidy of his previous CEO?

Come to that, why not keep quiet about the software leak, and get his own firm to develop it? No-one could prove this to be solely Richard's idea. In the computing world, software ideas flew about all over the place. Similar pieces of software could appear on the market almost simultaneously because the developers had been thinking along the same lines, triggered by a previous development or market trend.

It would have been an excellent piece of software to keep quiet about, and nor was David naïve enough to think Langley had handed the only copy over to him. He would most definitely have made a second one. But that was strange in itself... handed over with this email, it was an open admission someone had leaked the idea. Quite what the CEO of TechDrive might say about that, David wasn't sure. If it happened to his company, he'd put a stop to any idea of using it, so if Langley hoped to profit, he was out of luck... and probably knew it. So, *why*?

His mind went round and round as he drove on. He didn't like this. He didn't like it at all, and he knew Richard would be angry. As it stood, it all pointed to Jude. There were only a handful of people who knew about the software... himself and two of his development team, Richard, and Jude.

But David couldn't, knowing Jude as well as he did, believe that she would have done this. There had to be some reason behind it. Some set-up.

But who?

More to the point, *why*?

At last, David pulled into the driveway of his house. First things first. He wanted to fortify himself with a stiff whisky before calling his friend. This wasn't a job he was looking forward to at all. Climbing out of the car, David stretched before leaning in to pick up papers. Dread in the pit of his stomach, he ran up the steps and fitted his key into the lock.

*****

At High Foss Hall, Richard and Jude lay entwined together on the sofa in the sitting-room, eating crackers and cheese, a glass of wine to hand, with Scrap curled up on the rug in front of the fire. They'd left work as soon as it was possible and Richard had swept her off with him back to the hall, dropping her car off at her house in passing. There had been no thought of food or anything else in their heads after a week apart and, once inside, they'd gone straight upstairs. In the rays of the evening sun pouring into his room, they had made love twice, passionately, breathlessly, tenderly, before falling asleep curled up together. It was less than half an hour ago that they'd they woken up and gone downstairs in search of something to eat.

The ringing of Richard's mobile startled them both.

'Eh?' Richard straightened up on the sofa, laying his book down on the table next to him. 'It's nearly ten. Who could that be?'

Jude sat up, her own book on her lap. 'No idea. You aren't expecting to hear from anyone?'

The mobile continued to ring.

'Not that I know of.' Richard got to his feet. 'Anyway, we'll never find out by mere speculation.'

Richard went over to the small table near the window and scooped up his phone. 'It's David,' he commented. 'Hi, David. What on earth do you want at this time of night? Surprised you're even back home by now. Did you enjoy the exhibition?'

'Hey.' David's voice sounded flat and tired. 'Yep, I'm back.'

A silence fell.

'David? You still there?'

'Sorry to break into your weekend when it's so late.'

Richard raised an eyebrow. 'Yeah, okay, no problem. I asked if you'd enjoyed the exhibition? Are you all right?'

'Yes...' David spoke with slow reluctance, acutely uncomfortable.

Richard waited again. The silence continued from the other end of the line. Shaking his head with some impatience, he said, 'Look, is this something important? I... I'm sort of rather heavily engaged this weekend, if you get my meaning, and if it's just something about the exhibition, do you mind... could it wait until Monday?'

'No,' David said. 'No, it can't wait. Look... just as I was about to leave, someone from TechDrive approached me, by the name of Julian Langley. Do you know of him?'

Richard looked startled. He'd heard that name only two months ago and would have no cause to forget it, for with the speaking of it a burden had lifted from him and he'd finally abandoned his senseless hatred of Jude.

'I've heard the name, yes,' he said now, with caution.

'I don't quite know how to say this... he showed me the ideas you have, for that software. Copies of the same documents you emailed through a few weeks ago for our initial consideration.'

'Wha-a-at? How the *hell* did he get hold of that?' Richard snarled. 'What's going on here? And why did he bring it to you?'

'He said because he knew I was friendly with you. He said we ought to know about it.'

'So how did he get it?' Richard asked, his voice soft. 'Come on, David. If he was being so virtuous, it must have been with a reason.'

'Well, that's just it, Richard. I think he had a reason, but I'm not so sure it's all as simple as it appears—'

'Cut the waffle... *how did he get hold of it*?'

'He said it was sent as an attachment to an email he received...' David swallowed, an audible gulp which reached Richard.

'And?'

'Richard, there has to be some explanation for this. It's not what it seems. It simply *can't* be what it seems, as you'll realise. I think Langley maybe has it in for—'

'*Who sent it*?' Richard's voice was tight. Already the knuckles of his hand, where it gripped the phone, showed white as the anger built within him.

'The email supposedly came from Jude, but—'

'*Jude*?' His voice breathless with shock.

On the settee, he saw Jude straighten as her gaze shot towards him, a query on her face.

'Yes, but, *listen*, will you? I can't see it. I think Langley has—' David pulled back from the earpiece in surprise. The call had just been cut off.

*****

Damn. He'd ruined Richard's weekend thoroughly, judging by the fury he'd detected just then. Ruined... oh, hell! What had Richard said? That he was heavily engaged this weekend...?

David froze.

Heavily engaged... and Helen had assured him there were serious developments between Jude and Richard. Did that mean Jude was *there*? There *now* at High Foss Hall? And he'd pretty much just told Richard she'd supposedly betrayed the firm with her ex-lover? He bit his lip. There was nothing else for it... he had to get over there and get over there fast.

David was convinced there was something odd about this whole affair. He'd known Jude for three years and had known nothing but good of her. Richard had known her for about four months, give or take, and had come over here hating her with no justification other than libellous and anonymous reports. David didn't understand what had caused enough of a truce between them for a relationship to develop, but he wondered if it was yet strong enough to withstand this. He knew Richard would more than likely react with anger. It might be someone else at the Hall with Richard. He could be wrong, Helen could be wrong. Nevertheless, he had a gut-feeling there was serious trouble now at High Foss, of which he was the unwitting cause. Jude might need some support. Yet surely Richard could surely see this was a strange situation. A definite set-up, although quite how, quite what, David wasn't sure. Throwing on his coat, he raced out of the house. The sooner he got there, the better.

21

Richard leaned against the wall, his hand over his eyes. This was madness. David had just told him Jude had sent Julian Langley an email with an attachment. The attachment was the software development idea he'd had. His mind was a whirlwind of conflicted thoughts.

No. She couldn't have done this. She couldn't.

But this was *David* telling him. About an email from Jude. He vaguely recalled, through the shock of hearing who had sent the email, David also saying things about it wasn't what it seemed... maybe a set-up... a set-up? He tried to grasp it, but it slipped away in the confusion.

If Julian Langley hadn't had a fit of conscience, Richard would never have known about it. Yet... why would Julian Langley have had a fit of conscience?

The reports...

His mind couldn't accept her betrayal after the last few weeks and the glorious days they'd spent together. Their love-making...

Those reports had said...

No.

Jude contradicted them. All the people at the factory had contradicted them. He'd promised... *promised*... he would never be influenced by them again. *David* was saying it wasn't what it seemed...

Only a week or two ago, he'd *promised*.

He stood upright, cold, his heart beginning to pound in slow, painful beats as the insidious messages in the reports resurrected themselves foremost in his mind. Cool and objective, the sender of them had nothing to gain. Otherwise he would surely have identified himself as the hero who was saving the factory.

An email. *From Jude*. With the software attached. To her ex-lover.

How was it possible to deny such concrete evidence?

Richard stood still, his body consumed by an agony of doubt, his insides churning with sick dread sitting uneasily with doubts and disbelief.

He'd *promised*.

She couldn't have done this.

He walked back across the sitting-room and looked at her, feeling tired. After all, what did he know about her? He'd only known her for about four months. It was entirely possible she might be a brilliant and manipulative woman who, on the surface, fooled everybody and use everybody for her own ends.

A conman.

No! He shook his head, distress rising in him like lava. It couldn't be Jude. It couldn't be true. He'd tell her what had happened and watch her reaction. It would be all right. She loved him. She would never betray him. She could never have made love with him the way she had and then betray him like this.

But... who had sent that email if not her? David himself had said it was from Jude.

What was he to *think*?

Aware of her startled face and questioning gaze, her book now put to one side, Richard turned away. Fumbling with a bottle of whisky, the neck clattering against the glass, he attempted to pour himself a drink. *Hell*. This was a nightmare. It couldn't be true. It was simple… he should ignore it. He'd promised he'd never doubt her again.

Yet despite his promises, all the doubts, fears and insecurities of his past life reared up and assaulted him from all sides.

Richard tipped the tumbler to his mouth and swallowed, once, twice, the burning spirit searing his throat. He upturned the bottle a second time. The spirits hit his stomach and clawed into his body. Scrap whined uneasily and sat up, looking worried.

'Richard?' Her voice came as if from far away. 'Richard? Are you all right?'

Turning, he saw her half-rise from her seat, and he could see concern shadowing her eyes 'Was it bad news?'

'Bad enough,' he said, putting his glass down with a crack, and sitting down on a chair opposite. 'That was David on the phone. He's been at the exhibition. A man called Julian approached him. Julian Langley—'

As he saw Jude gasp and her skin flush, Richard stopped immediately, sensing her reaction to the name he'd just mentioned. His face tightened, the knuckles of his clenched hand showing white. 'I see the name means something to you?' he asked.

'He and I… when I worked at TechDrive, he and I—'

'Yes?'

'We went around together. Have you had no previous girlfriends before me?' Jude queried, her voice sharp.

She looked wary as he stared across at her.

'That's not all, though, is it?' He saw Jude recoil from the sharpness of his voice and let a silence fall, watching her.

Dropping her eyes, Jude thought furiously. What was wrong? What could he be implying? Okay, she knew Richard had seen the advert for that job at TechDrive when it had fallen from her pile of papers. However, it was no secret she'd wanted to leave Aurora at that point, and Richard of all people knew that.

What she *had* kept quiet about, however, was the fact that when she'd rung TechDrive, no-one had been available to speak to her about the job and the next day Julian himself had rung her back, to talk to her about it. It had annoyed her he'd chosen to do that. She knew he'd been trying to wind her up.

Her head shot up as she heard Richard's voice. 'Have you been in touch with him?'

Jude stared at him, confused.

'*Have you been in touch with him?*'

So Julian, damn him, had mentioned to David she'd rung and asked for the application pack. Why had David bothered to ring Richard to pass on that rather useless bit of information? Why did it matter so much? More to the point, why was he so angry now, when everything was so good between them?

'Well, yes, I—yes, yes, I—' Jude stammered, shrinking back as Richard swore.

By now, the little dog, upset by the shouting, slunk off through the door, looking for her bed in the kitchen.

'Why?'

'Richard—'

'*Why did you do it?*' His voice hammered at her, relentless in its anger.

Jude came to her feet, her hands clenched at her sides. This had to be more than just making a query about a job there.

'Do *what*?' she cried out.

Richard, too, came to his feet with cold eyes, his jaw tight. Part of him knew he should stop. Part of him remembered his promise to her, but inside he was dying.

It seemed he'd been fooled by her, as everyone else was fooled by her, except perhaps one person, who had been astute enough to see through to the real Jude Drayton underneath and try to tell him about her. He'd allowed himself to fall in love with her. No doubt a clever plan on her part. A way to keep her job. A way to get financial security for life, if he'd married her. She had to know how rich he was. She had to know, being in the computer world.

'You told him about my software development idea. He came to David this afternoon. He came to David and showed him copies of the same notes I'd emailed to you and David... the very same notes. He knows every detail of my ideas.' Richard's voice was shaking with anger and pain. Not for losing his ideas. He could bear that. It was the knowledge that it had been Jude... *Jude*... who had betrayed him and destroyed him, after he'd worked so hard to trust her, to overcome what he'd believed about her when he'd first come to Aurora. He swayed and put out a hand on the chair back to steady himself.

'Richard...' Jude's voice was horrified. 'Richard... I *didn't*.'

'He showed David an email. The email came from *you*, with the documents attached.' His voice was deadly quiet.

'I didn't. I didn't send the documents. I didn't send him any email.'

'You said you'd been in touch with him.'

'Y-yes,' she stammered, upset by his anger. 'Yes, but not for that. Not for that. I wouldn't—I *wouldn't*—how could you think it? I rang them about that job—you saw the advert—and Julian rang me back the next day to tell me about it. He-he knew I wouldn't want to speak to him... our break-up was acrimonious. He did it to annoy me, but that was all. I have never been in touch with him at any other time and certainly not to do this... I *wouldn't*.'

Richard had stopped listening. He was incapable of reason. He could see only one thing... the reports must have been telling the truth. 'How often do you ring him up? When there's something worth leaking? Dear God, how *could* you—' His voice broke, and he turned away, his hand covering his eyes.

'*Listen* to me.' Jude grabbed his arm and pulled him round to face her as she tried to interrupt his bitter tirade and make him see reason.

His hand dropped, and he glared at her. 'Was this just a way of safeguarding your back? Ensuring there was always a way back to TechDrive? You must have suspected this cushy berth would have ended after my father died, and you must have known he wouldn't have that long to live. It always puzzled me why you'd thrown up what was a good job at TechDrive for such a risk as Aurora. I wonder how much money you got out of dear old dad? *Hell*.' He turned away from her again, his head bowed, his voice bitter, as he lashed out mindlessly. 'How could I have let myself believe in you? Those reports were right all along, but you stared at me with your big grey eyes and I fell for it, didn't I? Like a damned idiot, I fell for it. And all the time, you were planning to stab me in the back.'

'I didn't pass on your ideas,' Jude said again, with steady desperation.

'Damn, Jude, what do you take me for? Do I look that stupid, or have you always found you can manipulate men? My father? You had it all worked out, didn't you? Use him to get this job. Use Julian Langley to keep your foot in the door at TechDrive. See if you could manoeuvre the new boss into having sex with you, so you could be kept on here in the same capacity as you were before? Or were you planning on marriage and retirement?'

Richard was consumed by his ghosts and the thought Jude had let him down seeped like an evil mist into his mind.

His heart was breaking.

Jude recoiled. How could he denigrate what had happened between them and call it *sex*? There was no way she could ever use such a thing to manipulate... but then, he didn't really know her, did he?

Her heart began a slow disintegration.

He didn't know her... and he was again choosing to believe some poison he'd received while in America, not his own experiences with her, despite his promises. It was only last weekend she'd expressed doubt about his belief in her and he'd sworn it was all behind him. Now look how easily he was reverting to his distrust and dislike of her.

'What did the email say?' Jude demanded. 'Tell me. What did this email say?'

'Eh? I-I don't know.'

'I'd like to see it. I'd like to check my email on my computer and see when it was sent.' Jude was realising someone had set her up. 'I think,' she said, eyeing Richard to gauge his reactions, 'this might have been planned deliberately. Perhaps by the same person who sent those reports to you?'

'Conspiracy theory? Spare me.'

'You can't believe this of me... surely you know me better than that by now? Why couldn't it have been planned?'

'I could almost applaud,' he said scathingly. 'There's one thing you seem to have forgotten about all this. *Who knew about this software?* *I* did. *David* did. *His team* did. *You* did. Now who, out of all that lot, would want to conspire against you, tell me that? Who, out of all that lot, had access to your computer, eh? *Tell me that?*' His words were thickly spoken, cold and bitter. They fell like hail stones into the silence of the room.

Jude stood indecisively. Her world was collapsing around her. This was a living nightmare. Her unknown enemy was succeeding beyond his wildest dreams. Jude was sure he hadn't intended her to die by inches. Or perhaps he had... he'd shown no mercy so far in his attempts to oust her from the company.

'Ian?'

'Ian? *Ian?*' he said with amazement. 'Why pick on Ian? He was down in the Midlands, remember? How could *he* have set this up? And how could he have known about this software, anyway? We kept it a secret, Jude.'

'Isn't it possible he heard something? *Saw* something? Some of the ideas you roughed out? Or talked to the engineers?' She knew she sounded desperate. She knew she wasn't fighting for anything as mundane as a job here. She was fighting for Richard. Her love. Her whole life. Because she'd warned him... if he let her down again, that would be the end.

'Yeah, yeah, yeah.' He waved his hand. 'What an imagination. Hell, Jude. Why not admit it? Cut your losses and scarper off back to Langley.' Voice breaking, he turned away, unable to look at her..

Despite a small voice inside him saying the Jude he now knew might not have... no, *couldn't* have... done this, the insecurities caused by his father's behaviour, and the reports that had come at him four times each year, rose up and overwhelmed him.

Oh, yes, the ghosts were knocking at his door with a vengeance.

'I can only repeat, I didn't do this. I can't make you believe me, but I hoped... I hoped after what we'd shared...' Her voice gave way as despair ran through her like an icy stream, dismayed that he really appeared to believe what was happening, with no sign of questioning it, no sign of listening to her.

But... *her email*. It was some justification for Richard's reaction. And yes, there was also the puzzle how someone else had found out about the software. But Jude knew that might have happened, whatever Richard was saying.

'*Shut up.*' He whirled round to face her. 'Shut up!'

She stared back with steady pride. 'I hoped,' she repeated in a careful voice, tears threatening at every moment now, 'that you would at least listen to my side of this and maybe conclude the whole thing stinks, but it seems I was mistaken... and this...' she gestured with her hand, encompassing herself, Richard, the house, 'didn't mean the same to you as it did to me. I *warned* you. I said if you lost faith in me again, it would be the end, okay? The *end*... so don't... don't do this to us... to what we have...'

Waiting for a moment for an answer which didn't come, she turned away, unable to continue speaking. Her throat was choked with tears she wouldn't allow herself to shed in front of him. Jude kept walking, out of the sitting-room, out of the house, into the gathering dusk of the summer evening, her heart aching with the pain of his rejection, his breaking of the passionate promises he'd made, that he'd laid his ghosts to rest.

Left alone, Richard sank down into a chair and dropped his head into his hands. 'Yes, go,' he whispered. '*Go.* Do you hear me? Damn you... get out of my life.' His words fell like stones into the silence of the room.

22

David pulled his car to a stop outside Richard's front door. Funny... it was standing open, light from the hallway spilling out onto the gravel.

Uneasily, he stepped out of his car and went up the steps. 'Richard?'

Silence.

'Richard?' he called, more loudly now. Still no response. David moved into the hall, shutting the door behind him, and went into the sitting-room, to see Richard, slumped into a chair, head in hands.

Crossing over to where he sat, David laid his hand on his friend's shoulder. 'Hey,' he said lightly, 'it's not the end of the world, is it?'

Shocked, he recoiled as Richard turned and looked up at him. His eyes were black holes in a white and strained face.

'David.' His voice was flat.

'Where's Jude?' David asked, dread filling him. 'Was she here when I rang?'

Richard laughed, a shocking sound in the quiet of the room. The laughter gave way to a harsh, wracking sob. 'I don't know. I don't know where she is. She walked out. She always said she would, if I doubted her again. But fuck, David, what am I to think? You rang me and told me she'd sent the software down to Julian Langley. Did you know she used to be an item with him?'

David castigated himself for ringing Richard up. He hadn't realised that things between Richard and Jude had moved so fast, although after what Helen had said, he should have read between the lines. Damn it. How could he have been so stupid? He knew how bitter Richard had been about Jude. It seemed he'd reverted to that same bitterness and was back to accepting what had been said in the reports instead of trusting her. David blamed himself for whatever had transpired between the two of them. If he'd waited and talked to her on Monday, this could have been sorted, and the identity of the sender established.

Of one thing David was sure, it couldn't be Jude, and Richard was a fool for not realising that, too.

'Richard.' he said urgently now. 'Whatever it looks like, I don't believe Jude would ever do something like this.'

'I think I'm realising that,' Richard said tonelessly. 'But I let the ghosts take me over, David, and I said some unforgiveable things to her. I should have listened to her. We should have talked it over together and—'

'Where *is* Jude?'

'I don't *know*. She walked out, I told you. And I don't blame her. I've let her down. Again.' Deep inside was a bitter ache at her disappearance, and Richard wondered where she'd gone.

'Has she got her mobile with her?'

'I don't know. Probably not. I think it might be... upstairs...' Another shaft of pain shot through him as he recalled why her mobile was upstairs, what they'd been doing for most of the evening prior to David's call.

'Why the hell did you shut your phone down on me?'

'I hardly wanted a pleasant chat with you after the bombshell you dropped in my lap, now did I?'

David shook his head. 'I was a fool to ring you,' he said, dropping into a chair. 'I should have left it until after the weekend.'

'No,' Richard said, his voice grim, his eyes dark with the pain which was clawing at his insides. 'The sooner I knew about it, the better.'

'Hell, you *never* learn, do you?' David stared at his friend, shaking his head. 'You believed all that rubbish you were sent, then realised it was a load of crap when you saw with your own eyes the brilliant job Jude's been doing. It's all there in front of you. The workforce, the profits, the esteem we all feel for her, her own integrity. Then the first sign that sick bastard, whoever it is who has it in for Jude, is at it again and you don't keep calm and question it, oh, no. You flip. This is a set-up, Richard. You know it must be. Jude would never, ever do something like this, to you, or to Aurora Technology. I tried telling you when I rang, but you bloody well cut me off instead of listening.'

Richard stirred uneasily. 'A set-up? Jude said it might—'

David shook his head, looking exasperated. 'Of course it is! It's odd Julian Langley should so virtuously approach me, bearing in mind he held in his hands leaked software ideas which would have benefited his firm. With a few tweaks, it would've been very hard to prove it'd been nicked from somewhere else. Think about it. And how come, of all people, it was *Julian Langley*? I know little, because Jude's never told me, but I know they used to go out together and there was something funny about his promotion. He used her. He had his knife into her even then. In fact, he might have been the author of the reports.'

'But not the sender of the email with the copied software file.'

'No, obviously not. But it wasn't Jude. Damn it, you don't deserve that girl, you really don't.'

'I don't... look, it's all very well for you to lecture me about all this, but it's only after I came here, I realised maybe I'd been fed a line. I'd had long enough being told that she was a useless tramp and at first it was hard to throw that off. And when you... *you*, of all people... ring me to say you've got the leaked software, apparently sent in an email by Jude... what the hell was I supposed to think?'

'Ah, but that's my point. You didn't think, you reacted. A bloody knee-jerk reaction.'

There was a long pause. Richard's hands clenched and his face twisted. 'I know I've let her down,' he said in a low voice.

'I'll say.'

'But that email? And... who else knew about the software?'

'Oh, come on, don't be so bloody naïve. You know as well as I do, in industry, how easy it is to overhear things, look at other people's machines, email from other people's machine. How often do you close down every time you leave your office? How often does Jude? If her computer wasn't shut down, all the perpetrator had to do was have a good look at her files for anything interesting, and that might have happened any time. We're too damn careless, all of us. This has been a set up. Now... I think you better tell me what happened between you and Jude, and then we better see if we can track her down. I don't like to think of her wandering round, probably distressed. We need to find her.'

In a few brief and bitter words, Richard related the exchange between them. He didn't spare himself.

David swore. He stood up and pulled his friend to his feet. 'You're coming with me,' he said with anger. 'We'll find her. And we'll sort this mess out once and for all. But you've lost Jude this time. You know that, don't you? You've thrown her away without realising the value of what you had. I wanted her, you know. I think I told you that. Before

I met Louise, I wanted her. But she wasn't interested in me that way. I decided I'd rather have her as a friend than not at all, but *you*....' His voice was accusing. 'You had her and you've thrown her away.' He turned away and shook his head in disgust. 'Get into the car. We'll find her.'

David's words assaulted him, lacerated him. He knew what David said was true, because Jude herself had told him—if he let her down one more time, she was gone from his life.

23

Jude continued to walk into the soft summer evening, tears now streaming down her face, hardly able to catch her breath, so great was her distress. She didn't know where to go, what to do. Her unknown enemy had destroyed her. Standing at the bottom of the drive, she couldn't think, couldn't move. Like a rabbit caught in the glare of oncoming headlights, she stood frozen and bewildered.

Stumbling, tripping, she eventually walked forwards, uncaring of direction or destination. How could this have happened? Three months ago, she hadn't even known Richard. Then she... then he... oh, dear God. He'd warned her that the ghosts were still present, and although he said he was trying to let it all go, he admitted being fearful that something might set things off again. It was devastating to discover how easily his promises and protestations had been forgotten, how easily he'd turned against her. Her caution, her fears... both had been justified, and she should have listened to them and not let the relationship develop so quickly, until he'd built up his trust in her. If she'd held back, *this*... his rejection.... wouldn't be hurting so much.

Even though her pain, she could still see how it looked from Richard's point of view. An email, supposedly from her, with his software papers attached. Sent to Julian Langley, of all people. But he should have at least *listened* to her, been prepared to investigate. He shouldn't have been so easily swayed into judging her like that, however bad it looked. Her fist came up to her mouth and she bit on her knuckles, staring along the road in the dusk. As if she hadn't learned her lesson with Julian.

Stumbling, Jude almost fell. She turned off the road and clutched the bars of a gate. In the field were some cows, their breath blowing, soft tearing sounds reaching her as they cropped the grass. A car swept past, heading out from the town. Jude watched its lights, her head turning to follow its progress. The lights slowed, turned into the driveway of the hall. Jude had no curiosity or interest. She dropped her forehead onto the top bar of the gate and her tears fell hot on her hands as they slid out of her eyes.

Uncertain how much time had passed, Jude straightened and stumbled into the road again, one foot in front of the other, one foot in front of the other, going who knew where, who cared where. Home, she supposed. The neighbours had a key. It was all too much to bear if she stayed still.

Another car, this time coming up from behind, slowed, passed and disappeared round the bend. Jude didn't care. Sobs still occasionally wracked her body. She swiped her eyes with the back of her hand and pulled at some tissues in her pocket to blow her nose.

Her world had just ended… how was it possible to feel so much grief, even after knowing Richard for only such a brief time, and keep on breathing, moving?

Going round the next corner, Jude saw a lay-by, and in it was the dark shape of a vehicle, easily discernible in the moonlight, now risen from behind the hills. As she came near, a figure swung out of the driver's door.

'You're out late, bitch.'

Jude didn't reply, but kept putting one foot in front of the other, one foot in front of the other... she would get home and then maybe she would know what to do.

''Ere... I just spoke to you... can't you be civil?'

She stopped, dazed. 'What?'

'You got a fag?'

'I don't smoke.' Jude moved off again.

A rough hand grabbed her upper arm. She turned to see a narrow-eyed youth staring at her, unshaven, mean-lipped and ugly, with greasy hair.

'Give us your bloody money!' he shouted.

Jude just continued to stare at him, unaware of the danger surrounding her.

'Stupid woman.' He slapped her across the face, a backhander that snapped her head round, a ring on his hand cutting her lip.

He needed money.

He needed a fix, and she would provide it for him.

'Hey.' She twisted in his grasp, brought back to a semblance of awareness by his slap.

'Bloody well give us your money, all right?'

Fear stirred in her guts. He would hurt her. She knew it, she could feel it, and there was nothing she could do. She struggled in his grasp. 'I haven't-I haven't got any money.'

'Come off it, you silly cow. You'll have some in your pockets. Do you take me for bloody daft?' He twisted her arm up round her back so viciously she heard it crack and an intense pain shot through her shoulder.

She kicked backwards with her foot, trying to connect with his shin. Anything. Her arm was numb.

The youth attacking Jude thrust his hands into her pockets. He pulled out some tissues. '*Hell*! Is that fucking *all*? Then give us your watch.'

He could sell it. He knew someone who'd give him something for it. Better than nothing. Might be enough to get him... to get him... he pulled at the strap on her wrist, had to release her arm to get a proper grip on it, yanked it off and shoved it in his pocket.

Jude swung her fist at him in desperation. It grazed past his shoulder. Her other arm hung uselessly. She screamed again.

'*Shut up.*' For the second time, he slapped her across the face.

Staggering, Jude would have fallen had he not caught her by the shoulder.

'Sod you!' He swore, slapping her until her head was reeling and she could only see a red haze in front of her eyes.

As he let go of her, she staggered again.

He followed her, hitting her, punching her anywhere on her body as withdrawal symptoms clawed at his insides. Jude fell to her knees and rolled over against the wall, her one working arm shielding her head.

In the lay-by, the youth kept shouting, his voice reaching a crescendo of hatred as he lashed out with his boot. Jude rolled away even as she picked up another sound, above the youth's heavy breathing, and her own whimpers.

A car.

Her attacker froze.

He could hear the car, too, approaching along the lane behind him.

He glanced around wildly and leapt towards his battered vehicle. In seconds, he'd slammed the door and started the engine. With a spurt of gravel, he pulled away from the lay-by and shot off into the darkness.

It was only when he was round the next bend, he turned his lights on, then broke the speed limits until he was on the motorway and south bound.

Jude was aware of lights passing by on the road, a car going slowly. Frightened in case it was someone else out to hurt her, she turned her head away and curled into the wall.

24

As David drove, he peered out into the darkness on his side of the road as Richard looked out on the other side. Richard's face was grim and his clenched hands lay on his thighs. As they drove, the full enormity of what he'd done overwhelmed him. Without considering the matter at all, he'd condemned Jude out of hand and had said things to her which were unforgivable. Now, he realised this had to be a set-up, this whole thing. It was too pat, too slick, and David was right... he'd been an utter fool to react as he had.

As a result, he'd lost Jude.

'See anything?'

'No.' Richard's voice was dull. He wanted to weep.

'By now, she could have reached town.'

'You think so?'

David shrugged. 'Someone might have given her a lift. Would she have gone the other way, do you think?'

Richard was silent. The glimpse he'd had of Jude when she'd walked from the room, he wouldn't like to say where she'd gone. Shame burned through him. Shame, remorse, regret.

'I asked you if she might have gone the other way?'

'*Hell*. I don't know.' His voice broke. A tear ran down his cheek. 'She was... distressed. I don't know.'

David shot him a look of contempt. 'You're a bloody fool, you know that?'

'I know,' Richard said in a low voice.

'We'll get to the edge of town, then go back and try the other way. If she's reached town, she'll be all right,' David said, worried by everything Richard had told him about the evening.

Richard sat slumped in misery. He hadn't given her a chance. He'd done exactly as he'd promised not to do—give credence... again... to the reports. He'd judged her immediately on the flimsiest of evidence. How could he have been so stupid? So blind?

Where *was* she? He only wanted to know she was safe. If he knew that, everything else could wait.

Everything else... and that was what? The pain of knowing she was gone, and it was his own behaviour and stupidity which had caused her to go.

The pain of that would last a lifetime.

'Damn it.' David pulled up and turned to look at Richard. 'We could try her house, but just for now I'd rather run out along the other road and check she's not wandering about somewhere. Then we'll try the house.' There was anxiety in his voice.

He turned the car and sped back the way they'd come, faster now, reaching the Hall in under fifteen minutes. They passed it and continued along the twisting lane which meandered past the farm and through the small village before meeting a B road. There, they could turn left, which led to the wilder hills, or right, which would take them back to town by another, longer route.

David turned right. There was no sign of Jude anywhere.

At last, they drew up outside her house. Her car was there. No lights showed.

'Would she have gone to bed?' David asked.

'I...' Richard swallowed. 'I doubt it. I doubt... she might sit there in the dark.' He pressed his hand over his eyes, trying to check the tears that every now and again threatened to spill out.

'She might.' David swung out of the car and strode up to the front door. He placed his finger on the bell and left it there for a long time, then withdrew it and pressed again.

'My mobile's in the dashboard,' he called to Richard. 'Dial her landline, will you? It's under Jude.'

Richard fumbled to reach the phone and switched on the courtesy light. Seconds later David could hear the ringing of the phone in the hallway of the house. It rang and rang.

'Try her mobile, just in case.' David's voice was sharp with both anger and fear as he stepped back and looked up at the upstairs windows. All was in darkness, but next door, lights showed both upstairs and down. He moved next door and rang the bell.

Somewhat cautiously, the door opened a crack.

'Look, sorry to bother you at this time of night,' David said with a disarming smile. 'My friend...' he gestured to the car, 'has... um... well, to put it bluntly, he's quarrelled with his girlfriend, Jude. Jude Drayton, who lives next to you?'

'Oh, yes? And?'

'She ran off... he's worried about her and we haven't seen her on the road into town... we wondered if you'd seen her or heard her come back?'

'Silly bugger, your friend, wasn't he then? Jude's a nice lass, she is. And no, I haven't heard her come in, but then, these houses have thick walls so maybe I wouldn't.'

'You don't have a key to the place, do you?'

''Ere, what's all this, then?' The door was flung open and the burly man came out onto the top step, peering through the darkness at the car parked by the kerb. 'You expect me to let you into her house? Think I'm mad, do you? You just be getting along, or I'll call the police.'

'Please...' David's voice showed his desperation. 'Please... we're anxious about her. If she's not home, we'll be contacting the police ourselves. No, I don't expect you to let us into her house, but you could check yourself?'

'Eh? And what if she's in? Her car's there. She won't think too much of me, going in like this when she could be asleep, or whatever.'

'She left the car here earlier,' David said. 'Are you married? Could your wife go in? Look, I know this is a strange thing to ask, but... she was very distressed and I'm worried about her,' he finished flatly.

The man stared at him for a long time, his head swinging to take in their car. 'Give me your registration,' he said. 'I'll ask my wife if she'll go in. If anything happens at the house later, it'll be your car the police will look for, understand me?'

'I understand... and thank you. Thanks.' David's voice cracked with relief. He returned to the car, explained to Richard what was happening and asked if he'd had any response from Jude's mobile, not at all surprised when Richard shook his head in mute despair.

The man's wife let herself into the house as her husband ostentatiously tapped the number of David's car into his phone. David leaned against the bonnet, biting on his lip. Please, please let her be there... let her be in bed asleep.

The neighbour came to Jude's front door and shook her head.

David heard Richard's sharp intake of breath as his own body slumped in dismay. He straightened up. A call at the local police station next.

'Thanks,' he murmured to the couple as they stood outside their own house. 'Look, here's my card... could you give me a ring if you hear her or see her, tomorrow? I... I think maybe we'll go round to the police station now. Thanks for what you did.'

David saw them watching as he drove off, having agreed to phone if Jude turned up, by now themselves anxious about their neighbour.

The police would have nothing to do with it.

'Sorry, but she's an adult. Nothing we can do about it at the moment. But we'll let you know if we receive a report about an accident involving your friend. Leave her description and your number, okay?'

In the car outside, David sat in silence. He couldn't think of anything else to do, now.

'Helen!' Richard exclaimed.

'Helen?'

'Could she have gone to Helen's?'

'She might,' David admitted, although he didn't think it likely.

At Richard's insistence, they found themselves, some fifteen minutes later, outside Alec and Helen Gresham's house. He glanced at his watch. Twelve-forty. Damn it. Still, nothing else for it. He rang the bell.

After a delay of several minutes, Alec opened the door, wrapped in a dressing gown.

'David,' he exclaimed in amazement. 'What on earth are you doing here at this time of night?' He peered out past David and saw his car parked at the bottom of the short drive. 'What's wrong?' For something had to be wrong, Alec realised.

'It's Jude,' David said.

'Jude? What...? Has there been an accident? For God's sake, David, what's happened?' Helen, arriving at the door some seconds after Alec, was just in time to have heard David.

'Then she's not here?' David was disappointed. He'd hoped Richard was right, that she might have turned to Helen for help.

'No, she's not here,' Helen replied. 'Look, you better come in and explain.'

'Richard's in the car.'

'Richard? Richard Blake? What on earth is going on?'

As quickly as he could, David explained what had happened, from the moment he'd been approached by Julian Langley, to their visit to the police.

As he spoke, Helen paled, her hand going to her throat. 'Oh, *no*,' she exclaimed. 'This is all my fault.'

'*Your* fault?' What on earth did she mean? Had Helen sent the email? No chance. But what did she mean?

'Look,' she said, her hands clasped together and held under her chin, 'you'd better come in. You and Mr Blake… Richard… you better come in. I'll explain. I'll explain. Oh, poor Jude. My God. I'll make some tea…' she turned and made her way to the kitchen as Alec waited for David to collect Richard.

Within minutes they were all sitting down in the comfortable sitting room, the gas fire flames flickering, steaming cups of tea to hand, as Helen twisted her hands together, a big brown envelope on the floor by her feet.

'I knew… Jude told me… that *you*,' she nodded her head at Richard, 'had been receiving reports about the company which had said things about Jude which weren't true… and which had made you think she was a passenger in the firm. I knew the reports also said she was your father's mistress, and that was the only reason she'd got the job. But it wasn't true. You *know* it wasn't true, because you could see… Jude did a good job. Always has done.'

Richard nodded in a dazed manner. He drank some hot tea, but it did little to counteract the sickness and chill deep inside him, as the enormity of his stupidity continued to overwhelm him.

'This week... I wanted to have a look. I've always wondered about someone... I always wondered it might be Ian who'd sent you those reports.'

Richard's hand jerked, splashing tea onto his jeans as he looked up at Helen, eyes wide. Jude had suggested Ian might have leaked the software to discredit her, but he'd just laughed. Oh, damn it, he'd just *laughed* at her. 'Why?' he breathed. 'What made you suspect Ian?'

'Because I was there before Jude came. I saw the way he threw his weight around. I knew he loved it, being temporarily in charge, which he was, in the first days after your father had his stroke. I knew he had no doubt at all that he would get the job. He saw the ad as nothing but window dressing. It came as a terrific shock to him when Jude was appointed, and even more of a shock when he found out she was a woman. He let his hair down, saw me just as wallpaper, I suppose, and made it clear what his opinion was.' She looked sad as she took a slow sip of her tea before putting the mug down on the small table with a sigh. 'Then when Jude came, he tried to undermine her. Oh, he was very careful, and Jude never noticed how much he hated her, but I did. Maybe I knew him better, I don't know. I know Jude tried and tried to take to him, but she never could and it became a bit of a joke, trying to avoid him.'

Richard gave a faint smile. Ian was always trying to insinuate himself and in a remarkably short time, Richard had found he, too, tried to avoid him. He remembered them dancing at the firm's party, and how he and Jude had moved across the floor to get away from the man.

Helen sighed. 'Anyway, when she told me about these reports, I wondered about Ian, but until this week, I didn't have a chance of checking up on him. When he went off to the Midlands on Thursday, I looked at all the files on his computer. It took a fair while... but on Friday, I found them.' She nudged the envelope on the floor with her toe.

Everyone looked startled. Richard half rose from his chair. 'What? You found the reports? On *Ian's* computer?'

Helen nodded emphatically. '*All* of them, yes. On his computer. I kept a note of the file names and locations and printed the documents. I was going to tell you,' she said, looking distressed as she recalled why they were all gathered there at this strange hour of the morning. 'I was going to tell you on Friday, but you'd already gone. If only I'd come by your house, or rung you, none of this would have happened because you would have realised it had to be Ian again.' She paused and looked horrified. 'Oh my goodness... now I remember... he was hanging round the office on Wednesday, after lunch. I came back earlier than usual and he was *there*. He said he needed some papers for the exhibition and that you,' again she indicated Richard with a nod of her head, 'had said they were on your desk. He... was acting strangely, and I was uncomfortable about it, but I could see nothing wrong. Oh, *no*! If only I'd told you about seeing him there... or mentioned my suspicions about the reports.'

'Was Jude's computer on?' David asked. He was digging in his pocket as he spoke. He pulled out a folded piece of paper and opened it out.

'No. It might have been asleep. She rarely logs off. None of us do, though perhaps we should,' Helen said, looking tired.

David looked at the paper he was holding. 'Sent from Jude's computer,' he said, 'which is what threw me when Langley first told me. The date is for last Wednesday, yes. Time sent...' he paused, '... twelve twenty-three. Was Jude in the office over lunchtime?'

Helen stared at him in surprise. 'Why no, of course not,' she said. 'She had a lunch appointment with Farslane Hill and left the office at about eleven to drive to Leeds for a meeting and lunch. I'd booked the table for her.'

'There you are then,' David threw the email at Richard, a touch of contempt in his voice. 'Our little friend has made a rather drastic mistake there. Helen found him in the office at the time this was sent, he was acting oddly, and Helen has also found, on his computer, copies of these reports you said you'd been getting. Show them to him, Helen. Let's be sure, this time, that Jude is innocent. Beyond any shadow of a doubt, so we can finally convince Richard.'

No mistaking the contempt now. Richard felt it curdle into the morass of misery already churning away inside him.

Looking from one to the other, Helen felt uneasy as she detected the acrimony in David's voice. 'David... they're very convincing, the reports,' she said. 'I'm sorry, but I think Richard maybe had some cause to think as he did when he first arrived over here.'

Richard stared at her, relieved and grateful that someone else seemed to know the insidious power of the messages he'd received about Jude.

'Thank you, Helen,' he mumbled. 'One thing said in them was to suggest Aurora Technology was always lagging, because ideas put forward within the firm often seemed to find their way to other firms, and it was suggested Jude was responsible. When David rang me and told me what had happened, when he mentioned the email, I panicked. I knew Julian Langley and Jude had gone around together, and,' he turned to face David, a glint of anger sparking in his face as he spoke, 'here's one thing maybe even you didn't know, David, but a few weeks ago she had a printout of an advert for a job at TechDrive and she as good as told me she intended to apply for it. This whole damn mess...

yes, no doubt I should have thought about it more, before reacting as I did, but those reports... and then when you said the email was from Jude...'

A silence fell.

Helen stirred. 'Even you said, David, the fact the email was supposedly from Jude threw you. So it threw Richard as well. Add to that he hasn't known her for very long, then I think Richard had some reason to be suspicious and to question Jude. But,' she turned to her boss, looking stern, 'you must have said some stupid things to make her run off?'

'I asked her if she'd been in touch with Langley,' Richard said softly. 'I'm sorry, but she looked guilty and admitted she had. I assumed it was about this and it all blew up from there. I was so shocked, so upset... and it tied in so neatly with everything I'd been told.'

'Well, it would, wouldn't it, seeing as how Ian planned it all?' Helen looked at him sadly. 'As to her being in contact with Langley, I can explain that. She rang to enquire about the job at TechDrive, and there was no-one available to speak to her. Julian Langley called back the next day. I took the call and put him through. She was pretty annoyed with him and mentioned to me he was only trying to upset her. Jude's very honest, Richard. If you asked her if she'd been in touch with him, then yes, she would have admitted to it. But not for the reason you thought.'

David shook his head, a muscle twitching in his jaw. 'Okay. Maybe I'm being unfair. Show these reports to us anyway. I'd like to see them for myself.'

They all looked through the print-outs, except Richard, who, after a cursory glance and a nod to acknowledge they were the ones he'd been receiving, sat staring into space, running the email David had thrown at him repeatedly through his finger.

'Now what?' David threw down the last report. 'Okay, I'll admit the bastard made this look good. But now what?'

'If only I'd told you last night,' Helen said again, looking miserable.

'Helen, we wouldn't have answered the phone and we wouldn't have answered the doorbell,' Richard said. 'You'd have given up and waited until Monday.'

'I might have put them through your letterbox.'

'And I doubt I would've looked... at least until tomorrow morning, which would have been too late again. Stop blaming yourself. The only person at fault here is me.'

Helen recoiled from the raw agony she saw in his eyes, not knowing what to say.

'I'll ring the hospital,' David said, his voice sharp. He left the room, pulling his mobile from his pocket as he went.

They sat in silence until David returned. Every pair of eyes looked at him as he came back into the room. He shook his head. 'No. No-one has been admitted because of an accident or anything else, answering to her description. I don't know where she is. I don't know where to look. I don't know what to do next.'

25

By Monday morning, no-one had seen Jude. Every time Richard had gone to her house to check, Scrap slinking along at his heels knowing something was very wrong, the neighbours had said no-one, as far as they knew, had been back. Every time his mobile or landline rang, he leapt to answer it in case it was her. He dialled her landline repeatedly, letting it ring and ring until he was cut off and the impersonal voice of the recorded message advised him to replace his phone and try again. He knew her mobile was at his house, in her handbag, so he knew she had no money, no cards, no means of communication.

He hardly slept, and grew white-faced, with dark shadows under eyes that looked wild and despairing.

Alec, Helen and David kept in close touch with each other, and with Richard. David had got over his anger and was now simply worried. He'd rung the police again, but they'd nothing to report. The hospital had taken no one in who matched Jude's description, which they knew already. Apart from checking her house, there was nothing more any of them could do. It was a wearing weekend for them all.

Richard and Helen went into work early on Monday morning in the vain hope she might somehow materialise in front of them. Slumped at his desk in jeans and sweater, his hair ruffled, head supported by his hands, Richard stared at the wooden surface, his work lying unheeded around him, despite the close-down and the new build about to take place.

Helen came and stood hesitantly by the door. 'Ian Grey's arrived,' she murmured. 'Reception rang through to let me know. I asked them to,' she explained. 'I'm getting you some coffee,' she added firmly. 'Some coffee and something to eat, before you do anything. I'm not even sure you should see Ian at all.'

'What?' Richard lifted his head. Helen turned to face him, stepping back in shock at the despair in his eyes.

'I said...' she began. 'Look, did you hear anything?'

'Something about coffee,' Richard said.

'Ian Grey has come in.'

Richard reared up onto his feet, his chair crashing to the floor behind him. 'The bastard. Where is he? I'll *kill* him.'

'Richard.' Helen spoke as sharply as she would to one of her children and hoped it would pierce through the glazed hatred she saw on Richard's face. 'It will do you no good at all to lose your temper with Ian. You'd only end up being charged with assault. Okay, yes, maybe it *would* be worth it to you... maybe you *would* like to beat him into a pulp, but it wouldn't be worth it to Jude if she comes back, hear me?'

'Jude won't come back. It's my belief she's left the area and one day, when none of us are looking, she'll come back and remove all her possessions and we'll never see her again or know where she's gone. What do I care if I spend the rest of my life in prison somewhere?'

'Don't be silly.' Helen retorted. 'Maybe Jude's gone away for a while to think things over, but I'm sure she'll be back.'

'Maybe to see you...' Richard's voice tailed off. He thrust his shaking hands into his pockets, crossing to the windows to stare out over the grounds, to the hills rising beyond. 'Do you know what I'm afraid of?' he asked, his voice hushed.

'Richard?'

'That we all got it wrong, and she went off up into the hills and had an accident. I walked out behind the house on Sunday, up to High Foss and beyond, looking for her. I took Scrap... silly, but I wondered if she might smell her if she was up there. We went all along the base of the limestone cliffs, and found nothing, but it's vast out there... she could have got anywhere.'

Helen crossed over to stand next to him. 'I don't think she would have done that. If you upset her, I think she would have gone along the road. She probably got home long before you and David arrived there to check. Her neighbours didn't notice, and she collected some clothes and money, and went off for a while.'

'Then why not take her car?'

'Perhaps she thought it would be unwise to try driving? She could have called a taxi, gone to the station, the airport at Leeds... we just don't know.'

'But if something happened to her?' His voice was fearful. 'I don't know... I feel—'

The phone rang in the outer office.

'Helen—' Richard said, but she had already turned on her heel and left.

Richard hovered by the door.

'Aurora Technology, Helen Gresham speaking... dear God, *Jude*. Where have you been? We've all been worried sick.'

Richard flung the door open and strode towards Helen. She waved a frantic hand at him and he stood still, halted by something in her face.

'Yes, even him... especially him. There have been some developments... Yes, I know what happened on Friday night and I blame myself that things got out of hand... *Why*? Because I knew... well, I had a pretty good idea... who might be behind those reports and I found them all on Friday and... what do you mean, it doesn't matter anymore? Yes, but Jude... I know. I know what he said to you... he told us, he told us everything. Yes, I know... yes, but *listen*, will you? He realised he was wrong, that someone had set you up... It's too late? Oh, Jude... at least listen to him... Wha-a-at? Oh my God. Oh, Jude, no.' Helen sank down onto her chair, her face whitening in shock. 'Yes... yes, all right. Yes, I see. I understand, really I do. I'll tell him, I will. Yes, I'll make it plain. I'll come round after work... yes, I will. I will tell Richard but there are things I think maybe you should know... okay, okay, yes, I know you said it was too late... okay then. Look after yourself, Jude. I'll see you later.' Helen replaced the received and tugged her jersey straight, looking abstracted and shaken. Her fingers found and played with a pen lying next to her keyboard and for a few seconds she looked at her fingers, rolling it round and round before raising pain-filled eyes to meet those of Richard's, full of agonised questions.

'Jude said... Jude said to tell you she's all right but you're not, under *any* circumstances, to see her. She said it's too late. She doesn't care who wrote the reports. She doesn't care if you've now realised she was set up. She said she warned you that if you doubted her again, it would be the end. She said...' Helen put her face in her hands and cried.

Richard took some tissues from the box on her desk and handed them to her, abstractedly patting her shoulder. 'There's something else. You wouldn't be so shocked and upset if that was all she'd told you, for heaven's sake. You knew... I knew... she'd say things like that after what I did. There's something else. What is it?'

'She said I wasn't to tell you and I pro-promised.'

'Then I'm going round there.'

Helen raised red eyes. 'She said no.'

'*Damn* what she said! I must face her, to tell her I'm sorry, even if I know I've lost her. I know it's all over, but I have to at least apologise and ask her to forgive me.' Richard turned and stormed to the door.

Helen rose to her feet and held out the envelope containing the reports and email. 'Take these. Ask her to at least read them... it might help her see... to understand.'

Richard stared at her for a moment before reaching out his hand and taking them from her. 'Thanks,' he muttered.

'And, Richard... I made a promise to her, but you might get a shock when you see her, okay?' Helen gulped and wiped her eyes on the handful of tissues she held as Richard stared at her, a question in his eyes.

Seeing he was to receive no further information, he turned once more for the door. 'Tell Grey I shall want to see him when I come back,' he threw over his shoulder, 'but don't, whatever you do, tell him *why*.'

26

Some ten minutes later Richard was driving like a lunatic towards the far side of town where Jude lived. He took a gulping breath and slowed down. It wouldn't serve his purpose to crash, or to be booked for speeding. He glanced at the envelope on the seat beside him. Not only were the reports inside but also the email and print-outs of his software idea, which David had slipped in there on Friday night.

Thank God she was all right. The relief which had poured through him when he realised it was Jude on the phone had been heartfelt. He'd known she wouldn't want to see him. Frankly, he didn't blame her. He'd done to her what he thought she'd done to him... betrayed her trust and let her down... and he knew how badly that had hurt him on Friday night. The fact she didn't want to see him he accepted... once he'd faced her to apologise, to beg her forgiveness, to release her from her contract, to promise her a reference, to let her go...

To beg her forgiveness.

Richard was almost breathless with pain.

Maybe he could just about bear to live without her if she could only forgive him for his blind, blind stupidity.

Drawing up outside her house, he stared up at the front door. Would she answer the bell?

There was only one way to find out.

Richard was not a coward, but it took him a lot of courage to get out of the car, the envelope in his hand, and climb the steps. He stood for a long moment before raising a trembling hand and pressing the bell. Deep in the house, he heard its peal.

Footsteps approached the door.

It opened.

'*You*!' She made a move to close the door.

His hand flung out to prevent her as he stared at her in horror. 'Oh, no. Jude, my God, no!'

Her face was a mass of bruises, black, purple, yellow, and one eye was half-shut and swollen. A cut, recently stitched, ran from the corner of her mouth. One arm was in a sling and he could see, at the neck of the loose shirt she wore, more bruising.

'Oh, *no*!' he repeated, his hand coming up to cover his mouth and pain filling his eyes. All weekend he hadn't accepted the glib explanations the others had given for her continued absence. He'd known something was wrong. His eyes filled with tears and his mouth twisted in distress. 'This was all my fault,' he murmured in exhaustion, a wealth of sadness in his voice, defeat causing his shoulders to drop, tears escaping his eyes despite his intention to hold them back.

'Why have you come?' she asked through stiff, swollen lips. 'I asked Helen to tell you not to. I don't... I really *don't*... want to see you again.'

'I know and I'm sorry. So, so sorry. She told me but I... I had to come... I needed to see you... to tell you something, but I'd no idea... I didn't know about this and I can't... I can't...' He swallowed and Jude could see he was fighting hard against his distress. Another tear escaped his eyes and trickled part way down his cheek. With a soft obscenity, he wiped at it with his finger and turned away. 'I'm sorry. There's nothing I can say... nothing... I'm sorry. Sorry.'

He stumbled down the steps and leaned for a moment against the side of his car, trying to get his key out of his pocket.

Jude stared at him. She should hate him, but his distress was tearing at her heart. 'Richard?'

He turned his head, his face drawn and aged, hands trembling.

'What did you want to tell me?' Her voice was impersonal.

He shook his head helplessly. The envelope fell from his nerveless fingers onto the pavement.

Jude came down the steps and picked it up. 'Was this for me?'

He looked at the envelope in her hands and raised his eyes to her ravaged face, looking bewildered.

Alarmed now, recognising that he was deeply shocked by what had happened to her, Jude laid her hand on his arm. 'You'd better come in,' she said slowly. 'You better come in and have a cup of tea or something. I didn't understand...'

Despite Helen telling her that Richard had realised he'd been wrong... again... about her, Jude hadn't expected him to react like this. She'd never intended him to *see* her like this. Not vindictive by nature, it had never been her intention to lay this at his door. Yes, yes, she knew it had been his actions that had caused her to leave the house, but no-one could have foreseen that a maniac had been on the loose that night. Her mind whirled. His reaction was that of someone who cared deeply, not of someone who distrusted her.

He was here... and in no state to drive off.

Taking his hand, she led him up the steps, Richard numbly following. His whole body was shaking, even his teeth were chattering. She shot him a concerned look and pushed him down onto a chair at the kitchen table before turning to put the kettle on.

His head dropped onto his arms and Jude sucked in a quiet breath as she saw his shoulders shaking. Quietly she set out making some very hot, very strong and, even though she knew he didn't take sugar, very sweet, tea.

When it was ready, she placed the mug on the table and sat down opposite, watching. She gave him a few more moments in which to compose himself, then murmured. 'Richard? I made some tea. Drink it while it's still hot, okay?'

Slowly, he sat up and with his thumb and forefinger, rubbed at his eyes. He pulled out a handkerchief and blew his nose. He pulled the mug towards him and with an unsteady hand lifted it and sipped. 'Sorry,' he muttered. It seemed all he could say. There was nothing left he *could* say.

If he had not shown such shock, he wouldn't now be sitting there. Jude tried to detach herself from the feelings whirling round inside her, feelings which, at the moment, she didn't want to examine. He was only here because he was ill.

'How...' Richard's voice choked, and he stopped, took a deep breath and tried again. 'How did it happen?'

'Someone attacked me after I...' Her fist came up to her mouth. The horror of the attack came back in full force and washed over her. She shuddered and knew Richard had seen her reaction.

'How come... we rang the hospital, but they said...'

Jude fought down the remembered terror of the night, distanced herself from it, spoke of it as if it had happened to someone else. 'An elderly couple found me. They were late returning from visiting their daughter and didn't know the area. They live only a few streets away from the hospital in Leeds so they took me there,' Jude explained in a flat voice.

'Your arm...' Richard gestured at the sling.

'He dislocated my shoulder.'

'*Hell*, Jude.' Distress crossed his features again. 'Did... oh, hell, Jude, were you raped?'

'No. The police think he was after money... probably for drugs. He took my watch, but he kept asking for money. They think he was withdrawing and got angry because I hadn't got any.' Her voice was still devoid of emotion.

'He could have killed you.'

'Yes. I remember... I heard a car coming. I think-I think maybe that's what saved me. Then when I came round, I crawled out onto the layby. A few minutes later another car stopped. I was terrified, but it was this couple. They were so kind. I was in no state to direct them anywhere so they helped me into the car and took me to A and E in Leeds. I-I said there was no-one I wanted informing...' Now emotion was creeping in and her façade was cracking. Her hands clenched and unclenched on the table.

Richard wondered if the car which had sent her attacker fleeing had been David's. It was possible. He'd maybe done that much for her. *He* had? Oh, no. *David* had. Left to himself, he would have sat there all night in a miserable and self-pitying stupor. He couldn't even comfort himself with stopping the attack.

Tentatively, he reached out and closed his own hand over hers, aching for the pain and terror she had experienced.

She pulled her hand away.

He flinched.

'Anyway, I... he...' Her voice broke, and she turned her head to the side, sobbing, unable any more to keep it all buried within her. They had warned her this might happen, and it was the touch of Richard's hand which had undone her.

Risking rejection again, but unable to ignore her distress, Richard stood up, his chair falling backwards to the floor behind him, and in two quick strides knelt beside her, his arms coming round her, murmuring words of comfort and, although he knew they would be unwelcome, words of love.

A long, long time passed. At last, the storm subsided. Jude sniffed, and he held out his handkerchief, this time for her to use. She scrubbed at her eyes and blew her nose.

'Let me go,' she whispered.

A muscle flicking in his jaw, Richard stood up and went to pick up his chair, sitting down opposite her again. He had no rights anymore.

Jude picked up her mug and drank. Replacing the mug on the table, she sighed. 'I'm sorry. I didn't mean to let go like that, but maybe it was a good thing.'

Richard said nothing.

'Anyway,' Jude said with a faint smile, 'you said you'd come here to say something. Perhaps better get it said and then go, okay? And this...' she touched the envelope lying in the centre of the table. 'Perhaps you could explain what you need me to do with it?'

'David came over after he'd phoned,' Richard began haltingly, not proud of what he'd said, what he'd done, how he'd behaved to Jude on Friday evening. 'He was angry with me for cutting him off on my mobile. He said he'd been going to suggest there was something too pat about what had happened.'

With many pauses, he related what had happened after Jude had fled his house, keeping his voice monotonous, trying to hide from her his devastation as he related the aftermath of his stupidity. He finished with the revelation that Helen had discovered copies of the reports on Ian Grey's machine.

'Ian Grey?' Jude said wonderingly. 'I'd wondered, but... he hated me *that* much? And the email?'

'It was sent last Wednesday when you were out at a business lunch,' Richard admitted. 'We think he... he printed off the notes from your computer and sent the email on Wednesday, to make it seem as if you'd sent them as an attachment, and to incriminate you. There are other little things... Helen found him in the office on Wednesday and said he was acting strangely. David noticed the email and the documents, both supposed to be print-outs on Langley's computer, weren't on the same paper. The document paper matches our printer paper. I think we'll find Ian was in touch with Langley before he went to the exhibition, and organised it all, including the approach to David. It was a deliberate set-up to wreck your career.'

Each admission hurt him and was a nail in his own coffin.

'You should have shown some trust in me.'

'I know. I know I should. I know I've lost you, thrown it all away. I haven't come to ask you to come back to me. Although... ' his voice broke in anguish and Jude's heart wrenched in pity as she saw the genuine remorse in his face.

'I know I've lost you,' Richard said again, dully, 'but I wanted to tell you—I *needed* to tell you—I was wrong. Terribly wrong. I wanted to beg you for your forgiveness. For an insane half hour, I believed the reports had the right of it and you'd used me and betrayed me. I know it was wrong and everything I said was unforgivable. I should have given you a chance and investigated it more carefully. I let you down when I... ah, what the hell,' he burst out, coming to his feet and turning his back to her, 'I'm only bloody human. Those reports taught me to hate you and distrust you, all cleverly done. I fought back against that, but then this came so unexpectedly. No excuse, though...

no excuse...' His outburst faded, his voice tailed off and silence fell in the kitchen.

Jude watched Richard's broad back as he fought for composure again, and her mind raced. He was right. It was all cleverly done. Not just the reports but this latest attempt to discredit her, using Julian Langley, who was no friend of hers, and David Eller to carry the message to Richard, automatically giving the whole thing authority and the impression it was all true. Would she—*could* she—have done any better herself if she had been in Richard's position?

'Sit down, Richard,' Jude said quietly.

'No. No, I'm going now. I only have one more thing to say to you. You never have to come back to Aurora Technology. I'll prepare your severance pay and references. You've left... there are a couple of things at the Hall. I'll pass them on to Helen and she can bring them round here, or you can collect them yourself. It doesn't matter. I won't be there. I'll be at the factory. I have to be at the factory,' he added under his breath, so low she almost couldn't hear him, 'because I've left myself with nothing else.'

He moved to the door. 'I only wanted to tell you I was wrong and that you're free. I-I still love you. I made an appalling error of judgement, and for that, I'll serve a life sentence because I've lost you and I'll have to learn to live without you.'

Jude rose from her seat as he pushed through the door and within seconds, she heard the slam of the front door as he left. She sank back down, her eyes fixed on the door through which he'd just gone.

Her eyes fell on the envelope, still lying on the table.

What *was* this? He never had got round to telling her.

She pulled the envelope towards her and opened it.

The email from her. Very convincing.

The notes about the software. A gold-mine for anyone. Would TechDrive use it when it was so obvious this had come from another company? Definitely not. So it had all been intended to destroy her.

These... computer print-outs. *Hell*! These must be the reports Helen had found on Ian's machine. Jude bent her head and started to read.

Some three-quarters of an hour later she raised her head, staring out of the window. Subtle hints. Subtle comments. Incidents which had happened to Ian but attributed to her, giving them a ring of truth, enabling someone to ask, did this happen, did that happen, and to be told, yes, it did. All of it carefully worded.

Relentlessly, for several months, Richard had been on the receiving end of garbage which painted her in the blackest colours imaginable. The reports started running her down, implying she was only a passenger, dead wood. Then came the suggestion, often repeated, that she'd only been appointed because she'd been old Mr Blake's mistress. The later reports were rather more manic than the first ones, but perhaps over time Richard hadn't noticed the change of tone, or perhaps they'd matched his growing feelings of dislike and unease.

She stared into the distance. Was it any wonder, after reading these and then faced with a call from his closest friend saying it appeared she'd leaked such important information, he'd reacted as he did?

There were so many factors to think about. If David had waited until the cold light of Monday morning in the office and not rung up when he did, as they both lay entwined together after an evening of love-making so deep and intense... If Helen had reached Richard with the news of Ian's traitorous behaviour... If she'd waited a few moments more so she'd been there when David had arrived...

He would suffer a life sentence?

So would she.

How silly. He still loved her and she, God help her after all that had happened, still loved him.

What was the point of them parting and spending the rest of their lives in misery, regretting it, and wondering what might have been?

What was the point of letting Ian Grey win?

Jude was sure what they had between them was too precious to lose, something that few people found. Richard was so remorseful, so full of regret. He would never come back to her again of his own accord. If she wanted to salvage anything from this mess, it would be up to her to make the next move. Could she do it? Could she give him another chance? Well, now Ian Grey had been exposed, it was unlikely Richard's loyalties would be challenged ever again, that was sure. But could she *forgive* him?

Jude stood up. *Yes.* She could allow that it had been very hard for Richard, brought up as he was, faced with the email, Julian Langley, and his leaked software all in one neat parcel, on top of this rubbish. She stirred the reports with her finger in disgust. She had to see him. She had to see Richard. Ian Grey couldn't be allowed to win. If she and Richard allowed this to separate them forever, he would have won.

27

Within half an hour, Jude was pushing open the doors to Reception.

'Jude. What on earth happened?'

'Mugged,' Jude replied. 'Is Richard in, Annabel?'

'He is *now*,' she said. 'Don't know what's going on this morning. He and Helen were in way before me, then Mr Blake rushed out about two hours ago. He came back half an hour ago. Looked ill to me. I wondered if he'd had some bad news or something? Jude, if you could have *seen* him...'

She had and knew why Annabel was so shocked.

'But he wanted to know where Ian Grey was. Well, Ian was out for lunch and he came back ten minutes ago. Mr Blake had said Ian was to see him the minute he came back, and no way was he to be interrupted. *No way*, he repeated, so if you want to see him, I think you'll have to wait.'

'Thanks, Annabel. I'll go up to see Helen and wait there.' She had no intention of waiting.

The lift came and took her up to the office. She opened the door to find Helen standing in the centre of the room, an anxious look on her face. Hearing the door, she whirled round, an expression of extreme surprise crossing her face.

'Jude. I never expected to see you here... Oh, my God, you look awful. Oh, sorry, but really, you do look rough.' Helen was distressed. 'What is it? Why have you come?'

Jude sighed. 'Wow, thanks, Helen. How to make a girl feel good about herself, eh? What with you and Annabel, I think maybe I better go around with a paper bag on my head. Would that improve the scenery?'

Helen smiled tentatively. 'Yes, maybe. But why are you here? You must know Richard's here?'

'Yes, I know. I want to see him. I expect you know he came to the house?'

Helen nodded.

'He had a lot to say. He was very upset...' Jude recalled the heaving shoulders, the few tears which she'd seen before he'd tried to hide them.

Helen shook her head. 'I've never in my life seen anyone so sorry for what he's done as Richard,' she said. 'I doubt he's even eaten since you disappeared. He's been constantly on the go, ringing up all over the place, haunting your house.'

'I know. The neighbours told me,' Jude said.

'Jude,' Helen said, 'could you forgive him?'

'Maybe. That's why I'm here. I read those reports. I could see how they'd poisoned him against me. And I was taken aback, I suppose, by how upset he was when he saw me. I think maybe it would be silly to lose what we have.'

A look of relief crossed Helen's face, soon to be replaced by the anxiety Jude had seen when she first opened the door.

'Helen? What is it?'

'I forgot. Ian's in there, and I'm worried Richard will do something serious to him, and end up in trouble for assault. Ian isn't worth it, but earlier today Richard said he would kill him and he sounded as if he meant it. He said he had nothing left to care about, and prison was as good a place as any to spend the rest of his life.'

'I'll go in,' Jude said with calm determination. 'I have something to say to Mr Ian Grey anyway. I won't let him win.'

Helen watched in silence as Jude approached the inner door, the sound of angry voices reaching her even as she put her hand on the knob and turned it.

'You've lost your job,' Richard was saying with quiet anger, standing with his back to Ian, to the room, as he stared out of the windows. His hands were thrust into the pockets of his jeans as if he didn't trust himself not to hit Ian. 'The damage you've done is incalculable. Don't push me too far by trying to deny it. We have proof. You don't seem to realise that. There's no way you can threaten us with lawsuits. You're damned lucky we aren't laying charges against *you*, but you sicken me too much to bother. You'll get out of here today, with no severance pay, no references and a bag search before you leave.'

'You think I care?' Ian Grey sneered. 'I'll go straight to TechDrive. Langley owes me.'

'I wouldn't bother,' Richard said without turning round. 'I spoke to their CEO before you came in here. He won't be using the ideas you emailed to them, because he knows I can prove they were pirated. He said they would blacklist you. And Langley was sacked. He was happy enough to do your dirty business because he has a grudge against Jude, but it didn't do him much good. The CEO was already doubtful about him because their marketing department isn't doing too well. Apparently, he regrets not appointing Jude. And I'll make sure word gets around about what you've been doing here, so no-one will ever employ you again. With your ambitions and aspirations, I think that would be a better punishment than a court case.'

Ian swore, then spoke again, a note of triumph in his voice. 'At least I did what I set out to do,' he said. 'I got rid of Jude Drayton. I gather she's walked out and has said she's never coming back.'

'You've no *idea* of the damage you've done,' Richard said, his voice bitter. 'Now just get out.' There was menace in the last few words.

A silence fell as Ian regarded the defeated slump of Richard's shoulders. 'I got rid of her,' he repeated slowly, 'but I did better than that, didn't I? I've destroyed the relationship you and she had started, haven't I? Oh, *yes*.' His fist punched the air. 'Both of you. I hadn't intended that, but what a bonus. What a bonus. I've destroyed *both* of you. I'm glad. Do you hear me?' he shouted. 'I'm glad.'

'Well, I'm sorry to disappoint you,' Jude's cool voice broke into the sour echoes left by Ian's spite, 'but you haven't broken us up at all. The damage you've done is only to yourself. Not to me...' Jude crossed the room to where an amazed Richard stood, his face a conflict of emotions, a blaze of hope lightening the despairing set of his features, and slipped her free arm through his. '... and not to Richard. I admit,' Jude smiled up at Richard, 'you were momentarily successful in that you caused us to have a minor disagreement, but that's all over now. How can we let someone so warped, so petty, so *pathetic*, spoil something so great? Richard and I... Richard and I...' she faltered, unable to go on as she saw the love and relief flame in Richard's eyes.

Oblivious to Ian, Richard turned to face her and pulled her into his arms. He shut his eyes and lowered his forehead to rest against hers as he rocked her against his body. 'Jude. My darling... my love...' he murmured in a broken voice, swallowing hard, his throat thick with emotion.

A noise of fury came from behind them, followed by the abrupt opening and deafening slam of the door as Ian stormed from the room.

Richard blinked several times and kissed her bruised face, the cut, her soft mouth. 'Jude,' he breathed at last, 'I was sure I'd lost you and—'

'I read the reports. I could see how it had all happened. I decided perhaps I shouldn't judge you so quickly. And how silly it would be... how *unbelievably* silly.... to let Ian win, as he would have done if I didn't forgive you. How silly if we let him destroy something so precious.'

'You're very generous,' he said huskily. 'Very generous, very loving and very forgiving.'

'Shush. David picked an emotional moment to face you with what appeared to be clear-cut evidence of my treachery. If we'd both been calmer, we might have talked things over more. You really were subverted, weren't you? Hell. I think if I'd been you, I'd have just come over from America and thrown me out.'

'I intended to,' he laughed shakily, 'but when you walked into the office that Monday and I realised you were Anna, the dryad of my waterfall, I couldn't. To be honest, I didn't know what to do. I'd been so attracted to you that day when neither of us realised who the other was, but I hated myself for taking on, as I saw it, my father's left-overs. Do you realise it was Ian who made me understand you could never have been my father's mistress by telling me about Julian Langley? And it was knowing about Julian Langley that made it so much easier to believe you'd leaked information to him. Oh, Jude,' he half-laughed, half-sobbed, 'what a bloody, *bloody* weekend this has been.'

He held her close, making her wince as he put pressure on the multitude of bruises.

'I was going to sell up and go back to America,' he said into her hair.

She pulled back and looked up at him, a question in her eyes.

'I couldn't bear to stay here without you,' he explained.

They stood for some time locked together in thankful silence. The phone rang in the outer office, but whoever it was, Helen stalled them. No-one disturbed them as they slowly came to the realisation it was all over and they had survived.

'Jude—' Richard began once more.

'Hush, Richard,' Jude said, laying her finger on his beloved mouth. 'Hush. There's nothing else to say. It will do no good to go over and over what you should have done, or I should have done. Better if we can to let it go. Let it go,' she repeated wonderingly.

'I'll try, but-'

'No buts.'

She was right. There was no need, now, for any more talking.

'Jude...' he breathed, kissing her with a growing passion. 'Jude. Oh, Jude... we're going home.'

Printed in Great Britain
by Amazon